The Sabre and the Heart

*A Tale of Love and Friendship
in Times of War*

Glen Natalier

Published in Australia by Natalier
Laidley, Australia

First published in Australia 2024
This edition published 2024
Copyright © Glen Natalier 2024

Cover design, typesetting: WorkingType (www.workingtype.com.au)

The right of Glen Natalier to be identified as the
Author of the Work has been asserted in accordance with the
Copyright, Designs and Patents Act 1988.

This book is a work of fiction. Any similarities to that of
people living or dead are purely coincidental.

A catalogue record for this
book is available from the
National Library of Australia

ISBN: 978-0-6486480-7-9

ABOUT THE AUTHOR

Glen Natalier was born into a closely knit rural community in the Lockyer Valley in Queensland, Australia. He chose not to stay on the family farm but completed the necessary studies to become a high school teacher of geography and German language. During these teaching years he wrote a  number of geography text books directed towards the syllabus requirements at that time. This allowed him to travel widely collecting, first hand, material and photographs to be used in the books. Years of teaching have left him with a love of learning and he finds that writing helps detract from the cares and worries which always seem to arise.

The tennis and footballs of previous years have morphed into golf balls which bring great pleasure when seen against the green of the centre of a fairway.

Now retired, he lives with his wife, Jill. They live in a town just over a few hills from where he was born. Their four children and their families are scattered around Australia.

These were troubled times.
Danger was ever near.
Wars raged.
Cities burnt.
Europe bled.
People died.

Humanity endured.
Life did continue.
Many smiled again.
Friendships developed.
People fell in love.

CONTENTS

Detail of
Battle of Austerlitz, 2 December, 1805
François Gérard
Versailles, Musée National du Château

The French Revolution at the end of the eighteenth century ushered in two decades and more of war throughout Europe. At first, the other major powers in Europe — Britain, Russia, Austria, Prussia — reacted unfavourably to the excesses carried out against King Louis XVI and other members of the ruling aristocracy in France. Later, when Napoleon claimed sole power as the Emperor of France and commenced expanding his control further and further into countries to the east, warfare inevitably followed.

Napoleon's ambition was to become ruler of Europe. With his tactical skills on the battlefields, and with the majority support of the French population fired up by nationalism, he almost succeeded. He was also helped by the fact that the leading countries opposing him had their own disagreements and were often unable to present a united front.

These turbulent two and a half decades saw the armies of various countries marching backwards and forwards throughout Europe. This situation was disastrous not only for the soldiers, hundreds of thousands of whom were slaughtered on fields of battle, but also for the citizens of the cities, towns and villages so often set upon by armies wanting provisions and shelter. The countryside was devastated. Countries were destroyed.

After Napoleon was proclaimed Emperor in May 1804, the other main European powers attempted to unite and compel him to keep his armies at home in France. England and Russia formed an alliance and were later joined by Austria. Prussia, however, at this stage refused to commit herself. War ensued. A major battle at Austerlitz (100 kilometres north of Vienna) saw the French defeat the combined armies of Austria and Russia. The Russian army retreated to reorganize and continue the campaign against Napoleon, while the Austrians asked for peace.

Victory gave Napoleon unchallenged power to reorganize much of Europe to his benefit. In one of the many rearrangements of political boundaries, he set up the Confederation of the Rhine — the combining of many independent German states situated to the east of the Rhine River — which became a tributary area for France and a bone of contention for his opponents.

This action, which was anathema to Prussia, finally forced their king, Frederick William III, into action and he declared war in the autumn of 1806. The armies of France and Prussia met in two battles fought in nearby locations — Jena and Auerstedt in what is now southern Germany. The Prussians were routed on both fronts and a demoralised, defeated Prussian army was scattered and the French forces occupied their country.

In June of the next year, 1807, Napoleon caught up with the Russian army, which had been joined by remnants of the Prussian forces, at Friedland in East Prussia. Again, this was a decisive victory for Napoleon's formidable army. A few weeks later at the small city of Tilsit on the Memel River treaties were concluded which subjected Prussia to humbling consequences but imposed much less severe conditions on Russia.

Except for some ongoing campaigns in Spain and Portugal, Napoleon was now the absolute ruler of Europe. This situation prevailed until June 1812, when he decided to invade Russia with his *Grande Armée*. This proved a disaster and when the last of this defeated army departed Russia six months later, his rule over Europe was nearing its end. The Napoleonic era finally came to an end on 18th June 1815, when the French army under Napoleon was decisively defeated at the Battle of Waterloo by a united British and Prussian force. He was exiled to the Island of St Helena where he died in 1821.

Timeline of the major battles and historical events encountered in the following pages.

1804, 2nd December.

Battle of Austerlitz. Austerlitz (now Slavok u Brna in Czechia) was a small town approximately 100 kilometres north of Vienna, and at that time part of the Austro-Hungarian Empire. Here the French army under Napoleon defeated the combined Austrian/Russian forces. The Austrians (Emperor Francis II) agreed to a truce, but the Russians (Tsar Alexander I) retreated to reorganize and continue their opposition to Napoleon. This was known as the Battle of the Three Emperors.

1806, 14th October.

Battles of Jena and Auerstedt on the Saale River in what is now southern Germany. Napoleon's French army defeated the Prussian forces under King Frederick William III. The Prussian army was scattered, and the King retreated to the small town of Memel in the far east of his country. The French occupied his kingdom.

1807, 6th & 7th February.

Battle of Eylau in East Prussia. In blizzard conditions, the French and Russian armies fought a bloody, indecisive battle at this small town. Both then retreated into winter quarters to rebuild and prepare for their summer campaigns.

1807, 14th June.

Battle of Friedland in East Prussia. The French defeated the Russians. This finally forced the Russian Tsar, Alexander I and his ally, Frederick William III of Prussia, to negotiate peace.

1807, 7th & 9th July.

Here, on a raft in the middle of the Memel River, at the town of Tilsit in East Prussia, Napoleon signed treaties — known as the Treaties of Tilsit — with both the Russian and Prussian rulers. This effectively placed continental Europe under French control. Napoleon was at the height of his power.

CHAPTER 1

Bernard and Michelle

The front of Crémieu's town hall was ablaze with light. A continual buzz of conversation and bursts of laughter with a background of stringed music floated through the open doors onto the street below. The antics of the four young men standing around the bottom step of the building showed that they had little concern about what was happening inside. They were engaged in their own lively discussions which were causing raucous laughter, often accompanied by a friendly push or slap on the shoulder.

Their attitude changed with the arrival of a man on horseback.

'Good evening, Captain. I will take care of your horse, Sir,' Luc, one of the young men, welcomed the regimentally dressed arrival.

'I am a major, young fellow. What do they teach you around here? Wait till you're in the army. You'll be taught some discipline there. And some good manners as well, I would hope. Here you are and take good care of my mount.'

'Right you are, Captain. He'll be fine with me.'

'Cheeky young beggar. Can't even tell that she's a mare,' he said to another officer who had just arrived.

The boys waited until the two cavalrymen had entered the hall and then a couple of them swung up into the saddles.

'Charge!' they yelled as they galloped off down the street.

A little while later they returned on foot after having secured the horses and joined their mates.

'Those were a couple of fine horses. You fellows would have loved riding that black one. He was a powerful brute. I wish I owned one like that,' Luc said. 'And Bernard, Michelle is outside the back kitchen wanting to know where you are.'

Twenty-year old Bernard Natalier and three of his friends had accepted the mayor's request to attend to the horses and vehicles of guests arriving for a celebratory ball which he had organised. Although not being allowed to set foot inside the hall, they were nevertheless enjoying the night's activities, being really excited by the horses and the array of vehicles which they had to attend to. They were genuinely interested in them all. Bernard and his helpers had never ridden such fine horses or been in carriages as luxurious as some which were arriving. The temptation to sample their comfort was hard to resist. Seldom was a carriage taken directly to the parking area as per the mayor's original instructions but arrived there by a very circuitous route usually with one of the boys riding inside as a passenger.

One of the official ushers, as they proudly named themselves, would welcome the guests and then enthusiastically relieve them of their transport. Most visitors were happy enough to be welcomed in this manner — after all they acknowledged that Crémieu was a rural town — but a number looked back from the entrance doors with some consternation as they watched the young lads ride or drive off so recklessly with their prized possessions. The young ushers looked and acted in stark contrast to the footmen in fine livery to whom these visitors were accustomed. With a shrug of their shoulders they put it down to the new post-revolutionary times.

'What a beauty. Let's take this one over to the tannery and back. See if we can get the old nag into more than just a trot.' Luc was really enjoying the evening much more than if he were mingling with the invited guests inside; not that he ever expected an invitation.

'Be a bit careful.' Bernard advised caution, but he accepted that all in his team were keen to introduce some fun into their work. He also knew that in dealing with horses they, like himself, were well qualified. His sun-tanned body showed he was used to strenuous farm-work in the open air and as a result not a single gram of soft flesh was to be seen on his upright frame. He was reserved, but still enjoyed the boisterous company of his friends, and was ever ready to join in their pranks. He had been elected "head usher" for the evening, knowing that if anything should go wrong, he was to shoulder the blame. This stipulation had been laughingly added by the team members.

He had a love of horses, was a very accomplished horseman and so enjoyed the fine chargers which were being given over to his care. His riding ability and patient but commanding way with horses was the main reason his friends had voted him head usher.

After dealing with several horses ridden by officers of various ranks — they called everyone Captain regardless of their rank — there was a short lapse in activity. Soon, however, they were eagerly awaiting the arrival of an impressive-looking carriage that came into view.

'Let's see what's behind these two horses coming up the street. I wonder who that could be?'

When it arrived, the boys could see that the man was a high-ranking officer of the emperor's army, and they assumed the woman to be his wife.

'Evening, Captain. Hope you and your wife enjoy yourselves at the party.' Guy, another one of the boys, was quick to open the door and bid the guests welcome.

'Bah!' grunted the officer as he jumped out and strode off ahead of his partner.

'Clearly his wife, hey Bernard?' said Guy once they had entered the hall.

'Well, it was clear that they were arguing on the way here. He probably didn't want to come to a small place like this. They say that some of these officers are real snobs, even worse than the counts and marquises we used to have around the district.' Then he looked up and addressed the driver of the carriage, 'Say, who was that?'

'That was Colonel Gauthrin and his wife. And you were right. They were arguing all the way. I think it was she who didn't want to come here. Where shall I take the carriage?'

'Leave it here. You hop down and we will look after it for you. That's why we're here. Nicolas is an experienced driver. Your dad trusts you with his wagon and draft horses, doesn't he, Nic?'

'Yes he does, Guy, b. . .b-ut I think that these horses . . .'

Guy interrupted him. 'They're just horses, Nicolas.' Then looking at the driver who seemed unsure what to do, he continued, 'There's a room in the building next door where you can wait till you are needed again. Something to eat and drink there too.'

Bernard's friend, Nicolas, climbed up and took the reins. After the driver had headed off and was out of earshot Guy said to Bernard, 'Hop in. Nicolas will take you down to Michelle.'

A short while later they stopped beside a young girl waiting at the back of the hall.

'Your carriage, Mademoiselle.'

'Nicolas! What on earth are you up to? What are you doing driving that carriage down here?'

Bernard was opening the door and about to jump out and join Michelle when Nicolas spoke up, 'Just a m . . .m-inute my good Sir. Why don't I take you and Mademoiselle here for a few circuits of the town square? Hop in Michelle and enjoy a little bit of comfort with his honour, the head usher.'

Commenting, 'You boys! You'll get us all into trouble,' but giggling for them both to hear, she got in, closed the door, and sat down close to her friend.

'Now no arguing like those other two who just got out of this carriage back there,' said Nicolas. Then with a click of his tongue and a flick of his whip, off they went.

As happy and excited as she was to be near the person who was often in her thoughts, Michelle's attention turned to the luxury in which they were sitting, She, as well as Bernard, Nicolas and the others with whom she spent most of her leisure hours, did not belong to the rich families of the area. They had observed the extravagant habits of many of these, they had seen their expensive belongings, and some had even worked in their homes but had never really been able to personally experience living in luxury.

The metal fittings of the interior of the carriage gleamed in the light of the ornamental brass lamps, giving Michelle the feeling that she had stepped into the wonderland of her dreams. She reached up and ran her hand over the silk hood lining, hoping that one day she might have a dress half as smooth and enticing.

Then she caressed the satin and lace of the plush seating and touched the highly polished mahogany panels.

Bernard interrupted her dreaming. 'Luc said that you wanted to see me about something. Well, here I am.'

'Oh, Bernard! Isn't this so beautiful?'

'Probably; but do you want to see me or just sit inside of . . .'

'This is so wonderful and I just . . .' and she threw her arms around a baffled Bernard and kissed him on the lips with excitement and feeling.

Michelle's spontaneous show of passion took Bernard by surprise, but he quickly adjusted to the situation and put his arms gently but firmly around her. The spats of these two occasional childhood playmates had grown into teenage friendship and in more recent times had developed into something much more serious.

They embraced more intently, kissed again and were enjoying each other's nearness. Their passionate embrace was interrupted by Nicolas who called down from the driver's seat, 'What are you two up to down there? It's so quiet. I'm h...h-eading back now to drop Michelle off and then we had better park this thing.'

'Can't you just keep driving around?' Michelle replied. Then turning to Bernard, she continued, 'We should do this more often.'

'What? Drive around in the Colonel's carriage? I'm sure he'd be happy for us to do that.'

'No, you silly! Have time together like this where we can enjoy each other's company.'

'You mean have more kissing time?'

Michelle giggled. 'If you want to call it that.' Then she stifled any further conversation with more kisses.

They did not realise that the carriage had stopped and that Nicolas had opened the door.

'End of the line for you two,' he said slightly embarrassed. 'Well, it is for you, Michelle. And we had better be getting this carriage to the parking area or the Colonel will be court-marshalling us or s...s-ending us off to war somewhere.'

One final kiss on Bernard's cheek and Michelle sprang out of the carriage, gave Nicolas a wave and a big smile and skipped off into the kitchen.

Bernard also alighted from the enjoyable few minutes he had spent with Michelle and joined Nicolas in the driver's seat.

'Better than your dad's wagon, hey?'

'It really is, Bernard. I hope you are not annoyed.'

'Annoyed? What on earth about?'

'Opening the door on you and Michelle back there. I didn't know that you and Michelle were so... were so close.'

'Don't worry about it, Nic. And yes, we would like to see more of each other, but I'm not sure that her parents would agree.'

'I hope it all works out for you both.'

'I'm sure it will,' said Bernard and then changed the subject. 'We had better get back to see how Luc and Guy are handling things without us.'

CHAPTER II

Party Time

The party in this small French town was in full swing and everyone was enjoying the celebration. Animated, but cheerful, conversation sounded from all corners of the reception hall. Many crowded around the buffet table amazed at the array of delicacies on offer. The drink waiters, bearing trays of local wine, had no time to relax. A trio of visiting artists provided a nonintrusive musical background, and promised tuneful leadership for the dancing which would commence later in the evening. Life here seemed carefree, overflowing with happiness.

Mayor Maillard's richly embellished regalia drew grasps of

wonder as he moved graciously from one group to another. Never lingering too long at one place, he was ensuring that no one would leave the celebrations without being welcomed and acknowledged. This was to be a memorable evening for his guests. The recent victory of Napoleon's army was an event to swell, even more, the pride of all French citizens. His sole endeavour at this function was to make sure that this would happen.

Stopping briefly in front of a group of four attractive ladies he smiled, inclined his head in a miniature bow and commented on their choice of dress materials, suggesting that cloth of such high standard must surely have come from one of his factories here in town. They smiled their agreement. He welcomed a couple of the town's leading businessmen, wishing a positive future for their endeavours. These gentlemen nodded their approval. He introduced couples who seemed to be overcome and embarrassed in these unfamiliar surroundings. Soon everyone felt comfortable. A genuine smile never left his lips. Crémieu's short — he was known to boast of his 165 centimetres — rather rotund mayor was clearly the complete host.

He was a well-loved town leader as well. The reactions of his guests when he was talking to them indicated his popularity. He would laugh with them, generally not the loudest, but never the quietest. His eyes would sparkle, his double chin quiver and his whole body would shake in merriment at the merest hint of humour. It appeared that no ill will could dwell in so jovial a body.

For the past two days the town council's small staff had been involved in preparing the venue for this occasion, under the watchful eyes of their employer. The brass fittings of the municipal hall now glittered in the candlelight. Recesses and nooks were filled with the colour and scent of bowls of flowers. Rainbow-coloured bunting was affixed to the windows, doors and ceilings creating a pavilion effect. Two large banners dominated, one at each end of the hall: *Vive la France* and *Vive L'Emperor*. These set the theme for this gala ball here in Crémieu in southeast France. The evening was to reinforce what its citizens were well aware of: that Mayor Anton Maillard was an enthusiastic supporter of Emperor Napoleon Bonaparte.

However not all French citizens were ardent followers of Napoleon. These detractors, these Royalists, looked back to the time when France was governed by a monarchy and rued the day when it was overturned and the lives of their king and queen so violently cut short. They despised this usurper who had gained such power and stolen the hearts of so many. These people looked forward to the day when the government of the land would once again be in the hands of much-loved royalty. Many kept this dream alive and worked clandestinely towards this end.

The last decade and a half had seen very troubled times throughout France. Although somewhat remote from the barbarity and excesses of revolution which had been experienced in Paris and other larger centres, the 3000 citizens of Crémieu had not remained untouched. There had been instances of local social upheavals during which innocent people had fallen victim to mob violence and lost their lives. Several stately homes, now somewhat damaged, had remained unoccupied, but no longer were locals surmising what may have become of their long-time occupants. Some things need to be forgotten. Years had passed since revolutionary mobs from nearby Lyon dared show their faces in this quiet village. Those were uneasy times best left in the past. However, all is never forgotten.

Now France was celebrating not only Napoleon's many achievements at home — in areas of law, education and religion — which were becoming more and more noticeable, but also the successes her armies were having further afield. The French nation was spreading her wings. Battles were being fought and won. France ruled much of Europe. Each victory was a reason to celebrate.

Life for most in Crémieu had returned to normal. The farmers were once again tilling their grain fields and tending their vineyards, confident that they would enjoy returns for their hard work. A number were able to increase their production, having taken over some of the estate lands which had remained unoccupied. The products of the tanners, spinners and weavers were in high demand by merchants from the larger cities who were charged with ensuring that the country's armies were adequately equipped. Local hotels and lodging houses were catering for ever-increasing numbers of artists and travellers seeking peace and rural serenity.

Most of the town's leaders — led by Mayor Maillard — who thought about and discussed these matters, pointed to Napoleon Bonaparte as the reason for the present settled and more prosperous times.

Napoleon, although received favourably by most of his subjects, was a name creating unrest throughout the rest of Europe.

Through daring, and organisational brilliance, this ambitious young man had quickly risen through the ranks of the French army during the early years of the revolution which overthrew the monarchy. His fame grew and his popularity blossomed so that when he proclaimed himself Emperor of France in 1804 few of his countrymen showed any dissent.

It was now early in 1805. Word of his latest comprehensive victory in the far eastern Austrian town of Austerlitz had spread quickly. His *Grande Armée*, although vastly outnumbered, had routed the Russian and Austrian forces which had gathered there. The French Empire was all-powerful. Napoleon was at the height of his popularity. The nation was celebrating.

Crémieu was celebrating. Mayor Maillard was ensuring that the citizens of this area did not remain unenlightened about the emperor's achievements.

Putting aside his mayoral obligations for the time being, Anton Maillard was standing at the temporary bar with his life-long acquaintance Henrí Natalier. Henrí lived with his family on a small holding on the edge of the village, growing grain and grapes. He was hard-working but often struggled to provide sufficient for his needs. Nevertheless, he accepted his lot and laid no blame on others. He was a citizen of Crémieu and of France, was interested in the welfare of the local people and held opinions on what might and might not be beneficial. He was very uneasy about Napoleon's apparent ambition to rule Europe and so his view of the future was less optimistic than that of the mayor, even though the village was now prospering.

'The worst is behind us and these are the good times? I

find that hard to believe,' he commented, avoiding being too outspoken about his views on Napoleon. He knew that he was living in a village where there was overwhelming support for the emperor.

'Trust me, my good friend. He has brought peace within our nation and will bring greatness to France,' enthused Anton.

'And to Crémieu? To our village here? Will this greatness reach us? Will our lives be any better here in Crémieu? Better than they are now? Better than they were before?'

'Indeed, they will,' beamed Anton as he drained the last of the wine from his glass, placed it on the bar top and nodded to the attendant. 'Everyone of us — you, me, Julius here, all our citizens — can walk tall, be proud and claim that we are Frenchmen. Thank you, Julius.' He took up his refilled glass and turning to Henrí continued, 'This is very good wine that Julius is serving. It is some of yours, isn't it, Henrí?'

'Yes, it is. This one… Wait a minute…' Then turning to Julius behind the bar he said, 'Julius, could I have a look at that bottle for a second?'

Julius retrieved it and handed it to Henrí. 'Here you are, Sir.'

'Ah, yes. I thought so. This is from my vines on the hillside over near Montouvier. Those fields never fail to produce quality wines. I'm sorry I don't have more land over there, but I suppose I must be content with what I have.'

Henrí Natalier was one of a now growing number of independent farmers in the village. Ever since the time of his grandfather, his family had resisted their land being taken over by one of the wealthy estates and had struggled to retain control.

As the pressure from a number of landed nobility who had lived on the estates no longer existed, the farmers were now free to work in peace. The personal danger of speaking out against the unjust practices of the privileged aristocracy was also a thing of the past but other dangers had taken their place.

Groups still existed throughout the nation which wanted to see the monarchy restored. When detected and caught they were severely punished. Henrí certainly was not an outspoken Royalist, for he knew that an unguarded, anti-Napoleon comment could be wrongly construed by listening ears, and this would lead to trouble. And by nature, he was a quietly spoken, taciturn person, generally contented to avoid controversial topics and never one to dominate a conversation.

'That's what I've been saying,' responded Anton. 'We are all doing very well and there are many who want to expand their business. You are a good example: you can't produce enough wine and I'm sure that you have no trouble getting rid of all your grain.'

'Well, that's true,' Henrí had to admit. 'And from what I hear, your factories are moving along very well too.'

'Yes, I can't get enough wool for my spinners and weavers. I have to search far and wide for supplies. Our sheep farmers here need to increase their herds.'

'Maybe things would be better if so many were not taken out of the country to feed Napoleon's army.'

Anton looked up at his friend recognizing some feeling in his comment. He was about to explain that there was several reasons for the falling numbers of stock in the region, but Henrí did not give him the opportunity and changed the topic.

'What do you know about this latest victory we're celebrating tonight?'

'They are calling it the Battle of the Three Emperors. It was near a place called Austerlitz,' replied the mayor.

'Three emperors? I assume Napoleon was there and one was probably the Austrian. We seem to be fighting the Austrians all the time. But who was the other? And at Austerlitz, you say. Where on earth is Austerlitz?'

'We were confronted by both the Austrian and Russian armies. Tsar Alexander was there as well as Emperor Francis of the Holy Roman Empire leading the Austrians. If you count those two and Napoleon you have three.'

'And our army defeated their combined forces?'

'Yes, we had them running. It was one of our great victories. You probably know that our Gustav is home on leave. He told me that Austerlitz is over in Austria somewhere near Vienna. He was there with his unit. He's been made a captain now, have you heard?'

Henrí looked surprised and shook his head. He was about to comment but Anton did not give him the opportunity. 'What? Well, that's strange, for Marie has been telling everyone. She's such a proud mother. Mind you, I'm quite proud of him myself. We have great plans for him. He'll be coming to the ball later this evening, wearing his new captain's uniform.'

CHAPTER III

Saturday Market

Most of the folk manning their stalls at the Crémieu market square next morning had not received an invitation to attend the event the night before. They were realistic farming, or simple town folk and as they kept telling each other, had not expected to be at their mayor's fancy do. Let him and his friends celebrate Napoleon's victory in some far distant town without us. A posh ball was a long way from picking onions in wind-swept fields or spinning wool in a dark factory. It wasn't them. They were just as happy not to attend.

This did not stop everyone from having an opinion of the

function. They all seemed to know which of the local people had attended and many were able to state categorically which dignitaries were in attendance and which were not. Many of the very lively conversations then, centred on the question of why this person was there whereas so-and-so had been overlooked.

Bernard Natalier, as usual, was in charge of his family's wine stall at the markets. He had arrived early with a cart loaded with crates of wine, had set up his table and organized the wines which he had for sale. That completed, he was now standing dreaming of his short meeting with Michelle in the fancy carriage the night before. He was brought back to the present by the arrival of his friends, Guy and Luc. They also began reliving some of their experiences at the ball — outside the hall they would readily point out — especially those which were causing them to break into loud outbursts of laughter.

Their frivolity was interrupted by the arrival of another young man.

'Well, talk of the Devil,' Luc began.

'Hello, you fellows,' replied Gustav Maillard, the mayor's son. 'It seems as though you had plenty of fun last night even though you weren't really at the ball. Some of my comrades inside had interesting things to say about their welcoming committee.'

'Oh?' queried Luc, looking quite puzzled.

'And I heard them asking my dad where he got those fellows from.'

'Oh,' commented Bernard, 'and what about your dad? How did he feel about it all?'

'He thought the evening was a great success, so I wouldn't worry about him being mad at you. You added some local colour. What did you think of that black stallion?'

Luc showed his pleasure. 'He was a beauty, but I would be wasting my time dreaming about owning something like that. Guy and I raced him and someone's mare down to the fountain. The mare didn't stand a chance.'

'Oh, tell me more.' Gustav's curiosity seemed aroused. 'What did you fellows really get up to?'

'I'll tell you something, Gustav,' Guy came in, 'I reckon we had a better time than most of those who were all dressed up and inside the hall. *Bal costumé* is not for this gentleman.' He stood erect and then bowed graciously, which brought a round of laughter.

'What are you fellows l...l-aughing about?' Nicolas had just arrived with Michelle walking shyly beside him.

'We were discussing last night,' Bernard replied.

'It was good fun with those horses and carriages,' Nicolas agreed, 'and we didn't lose any either.'

Gustav looked sternly at Nicolas. 'Were these scoundrels teaching you bad habits, Nicolas?'

Michelle replied for him. 'I think they were just enjoying the celebrations.'

It was only then that Bernard and his two friends acknowledged Michelle's presence.

'Good morning, young lady,' and Guy bowed once again, 'and how may I be of service?'

She blushed, not knowing what to say.

Nicolas came to her rescue. 'I asked her to come with me to see Bernard.'

'To see me?' queried Bernard. 'What for?'

'Well, you told me last night that you would like to see more of her. I thought that this would be a good o...op-portunity, for you would be here at the markets.'

There was silence. Bernard and Michelle were blushing. They all seemed unsure of where the conversation was heading.

Guy broke the embarrassing silence. 'Yes, it was an interesting night, last night. We were talking about how great everyone looked. You too Gustav. We saw you going in the side door.'

'Yes,' said Luc looking at Gustav, 'I don't know how you army types can enjoy yourselves all dressed up in those uniforms you wear. And what about when you are on a campaign? Can't imagine a group of dandies dressed like that doing very well on the battlefield. You'd be too worried about getting your uniform dirty.'

'Maybe the opponents would just start laughing and not be able to defend themselves,' laughed Guy.

'You looked very elegant, Gustav,' added Bernard. 'Where did you get that outfit which you were wearing? I'm sure Napoleon didn't make it for you. So where did you get it?'

'It was made in one of my dad's factories here. I had to get a new uniform for I am now a captain in a cuirassier regiment. Hadn't you heard?'

'You've got to be joking,' said Bernard. 'You could hardly ride a horse when you joined up last year. And now you are a captain! How high up is that?'

Guy joined in. 'He's now able to get up on the horse's back. That's how high. And he doesn't have to go around picking up horse shit anymore.'

This caused another outburst of laughter from Bernard and his friends. Gustav was less amused and simply smiled in his attempt to brush Guy's comment aside. It was something he had become quite used to doing.

These five young men had grown up together, spending time in and out of each other's homes, roaming the forested hills around Crémieu, making all sorts of suggestions to the local girls, enjoying being together. Gustav, although somewhat older, was always less outgoing. Nicolas also was more reserved, some would say shy. Bernard, Guy and Luc would jump headfirst into all situations, often without thinking. Gustav and Nicolas were also less athletic and not able to keep up with many of the activities.

The differences became more obvious as they advanced through their teen years. The strong bonds that had developed between them were showing signs of fracture but their friendship remained. The other four however were very surprised when their friend, Gustav, had volunteered to join some cavalry unit of Napoleon's army. He would not have been conscripted like other young men in the village. He could have shown that working in his father's factory making uniforms was contributing to the Empire and this would have excused him from serving in the army.

Gustav never admitted it but many thought that his father had persuaded him to join the army. Mayor Anton Maillard had enthusiastically accepted the new thinking of revolutionary France. Each person was now a democratic citizen and not simply a subject of the king as before. The monarchy had been overthrown, King Louis XVI executed, and now France was a community of all the people. With this new way of thinking came responsibilities. Fighting in Napoleon's army was one such way of carrying out one's responsibility to the nation. Gustav had agreed with his father's ideals and willingly, so it seemed, went off to the battlefields.

Other young men of Crémieu had also gone off to war in the previous few years, but not willingly. They had been conscripted, briefly trained and then dispatched to different units throughout Europe. A few returned to continue with their previous life. Some returned only to be marched off again. Many did not return. Their bodies remained at Rivoli or Marengo, at Ulm or Stockach, some even in far-distant Egypt or Palestine. The location of others was unknown. They had quietly slipped away after battles, began a new life in large cities or remote villages and were waiting for peaceful times when they could return to their homeland.

Gustav had survived his first forays into enemy territory and returned home briefly before resuming his role as an officer. Even after a short time it was clear that Captain Gustav Maillard's relationship with his village friends had undergone a change. He seemed less interested in village activities and the anecdotes related to him brought few positive responses. His whole demeanour suggested that their common interests were lessening. His life had taken a different direction. It now revolved around the army, his new officer friends and fighting for Napoleon. Village pranks were too banal.

'What about girls, Gus? How did you get on with them? Prettier than our local girls?' Luc wanted to know as he gave Guy a poke in his ribs and Michelle a big wink.

'What do you mean?'

'Come on, you know exactly what I mean. What about those friendly camp followers and the whorehouses you would visit after a drunken party?' Luc explained.

'And I've heard you cannot become an officer in the cuirassiers unless you bed three sweeties in one evening,' added Guy.

'Not to mention the cognac,' was Bernard's contribution.

At first Gustav seemed a little embarrassed and flustered on hearing these personal questions but he quickly regained his composure, stood erect and answered, 'There are some topics, gentlemen, we officers choose not to discuss. Especially in front of a lady.'

Michelle had turned away and was blushing.

'But seriously, Gustav,' asked Bernard, 'how did everything go out there fighting for your hero?'

'Well, I didn't have to go around picking up horse shit, but at the beginning I did spend a lot of time looking after officers' horses as well as my own. At Austerlitz I was in the thick of it and probably lucky to come through alive. Many didn't. I realized how important it was that I was taught to ride and fight like a true cuirassier.'

'And how is that?' Luc wanted to know.

'Fearless when riding on a galloping horse into the enemy.'

'Tell me, Gus, what made you volunteer to join Napoleon's army? Was it you or your father? And what's the point in going to the other side of the earth to slash the life out of some poor, ignorant muzhik or Austrian peasant?'

'Russia and Austria are Napoleon's enemies, and we need to conquer them to make France great.'

'I don't see the connection,' stated Bernard. 'I'm sure those poor beggars would have been happier at home with their families and a vodka bottle, or beer, or whatever, than risking death for their emperor. I know where I'd rather be.'

Gustav avoided starting an argument and just smiled. He knew how his former good friends thought. He said instead, 'But I have learnt how to ride a horse as well as anybody. And you know what? I'd be happy to race any of you whenever you like. Yes, even without an enemy in front of us. I bet the result would be different from what it was before I left last year.'

'Just say the word, Gus, and we'd be pleased to oblige.' Luc spoke for all of them.

'Oh, and another thing,' added Gustav.

'Yes?'

'A surprise is coming your way in the near future.'

With that, Gustav gave a mock salute and marched off. The four friends stood looking at each other, thoroughly baffled. Michelle was straightening some wine bottles in Bernard's display.

C H A P T E R   I V

Kinischken

The Minge River in far eastern Prussia winds its way south, eventually joining with the distributaries of its bigger brother, the Memel, in its delta lowlands. From here its waters, now combined with those already drifting aimlessly throughout the swamplands make their way into the Kurisches Haff, a large, shallow lagoon separated from the Baltic Sea by a long sand spit. In these lower reaches of the river, with marshlands predominating, waterfowl find an ideal summer habitat. Further south, across the wide Memel, a wall of green indicates the beginning of the Ibenhorst Forest, a wilderness area home to several families of wild elk.

North of the delta region clumps of willow and stands of poplars grow in those areas which are generally above the waterline and birches with their quivering leaves and pale ghostly branches follow the banks of the small streams which meander through the area.

Evidence of human settlement in these wetlands is hard to find; but it does exist. The amount of arable land available was never large and those patches which did exist were separated by swampy tracts. Farmers had sought out the higher areas and on these, generally near streams, they ploughed their fields, grazed their cattle, and built their villages. In this challenging environment the farms were few and villages small. Kinischken was one such village.

Its existence did not significantly detract from the overall natural feel of the environment. Unpainted timber houses, varying little one from another, stretched along both sides of a main thoroughfare which continued down towards the river Minge. They were mainly squat, rectangular structures, each with a stone or brick chimney rising above a timber-tiled roof. Some owners had added a front porch. These additions of differing styles were all variations of the same general design. This set them apart from their neighbours but there were certainly none that could be called palatial.

Each of these farmhouses had a large timber barn, occasionally standing to the side, but mostly to the rear. A few boasted a second barn.

The houses may have seemed cold and unappealing from

the outside, but the rural comfort found inside was very welcoming. Living in these wooden houses of roughly-milled local timber gave the families a feeling of intimacy with their natural surroundings.

Kinischken was not a place which demanded headlines in the history or geography books of Europe. Indeed, researchers would be hard pressed to find a single mention of it in any published chronicle. To those who compose the academic tomes which record the world's history it was insignificant, probably unknown.

The inhabitants of Kinischken, although isolated in the far north-eastern extremities of the Prussian state, were as human as those who lived in the mighty capitals of Europe, in Paris, Vienna or Berlin. When it was cold, they shivered. When food was lacking, they starved. In times of sadness, they cried. In times of joy, they laughed. Like the powerful and wealthy, they were born to live their allotted lives and then to die.

Here, by-passed by history, mostly unaffected — to date — by the turmoil created by the ambitions of the French Emperor Napoleon, seen in so many other regions of Europe, life progressed as it had done for generations. Throughout the centuries nature herself had shown little variation from the normal, with springtime following winter and the summer giving way to autumn. The lot of the villagers, tied so closely to that of their natural overlord, continued to be regulated by the rhythm of these seasons. They were born to follow this pattern of existence.

But the isolation of this small village could not forever

avoid the ripples of change which were moving across Europe. The years around the beginning of the new century had seen Kinischken tottering on the cusp of a new chapter in its history.

Whereas the human character of the people living here had changed little, if at all, throughout its existence, the nature of the village itself had. It had always been a typical Lithuanian farming village with a dozen or more farmsteads and a few cottages occupied by those who did not own any land but worked for the landholders. The farmsteads would stay in the same family for it was understood that they be handed down to the next generation. If this were not possible, there being no children for example, another village member would purchase the vacant farm, enlarging that family's holdings and life would continue. In this simple way the integrity of the village and its long-held tradition would remain intact.

This situation had been changing since Herr Hermann Schulte took up residence there. Hermann, his wife, Wiltrud, and their three teenage children had arrived after the big flood at the end of the previous century.

The memory of that flood had been cemented in the minds of all who lived along the banks of the Minge. It had established itself as a reference point in time. The land was devastated, the village residents traumatized. The river had reached heights rarely experienced in this area well known for its flooding. Houses were inundated and damaged, crops submerged and destroyed, livestock swept away. More tragic was the loss of human life. Valter and Tiesa Mazeika had apparently underestimated the strength of the raging current and were swept away while returning from a friend's place across the road from their own home.

Their death was a sad loss for the closely-knit community and it set in motion a chain of events which resulted in a change of identity for Kinischken. The couple's passing meant that their farmstead was without an owner. According to Lithuanian tradition the children were to inherit the property but their only son had drowned while fishing on the Kurisches Haff two years previously. The farm became available for anyone to buy.

Normally someone within the village would be able to purchase it and so add to his own holding. However, because of the destruction of crops and buildings due to the flood, no one within the village was in a position to buy the vacant farm. Distant relatives of Valter and Tiesa living further to the north of the country had been contacted but they were unable or did not wish to be involved with the property. The Mazeika farmstead remained unoccupied. Its price was then much reduced. Hermann Schulte from Tilsit, a larger town some fifty kilometres to the south, saw an opportunity here and took it.

CHAPTER V

A Prussian in Kinischken

It had come somewhat as a surprise to the whole population of Kinischken to learn that a German timber merchant from Tilsit had purchased the Mazeika farm. For many of the older residents the initial surprise soon turned to anger towards this foreign family which was buying its way into their closely-knit community.

'He'll find no friends here,' predicted Antanas Zukas who lived next door to the slowly deteriorating, vacant property, which was now about to be occupied by an unknown quantity.

Old Grandad Grigas, for years the accepted leader of the

secluded settlement was quick to agree with this and suggested what might happen to their town in the future. 'If we let this Prussian come here and buy up our town we will end up like Pauleiten or even Kalgillen. We all know what happened there.'

'But they just let things happen in those places. They didn't seem to care. I think most of them were only interested in the money and not the future of the place. We're a bit different here, aren't we?'

'Maybe, but that's what I'm saying, Antanas. They sold their farms and thought how rich they were but soon had spent all their money. And what were they left with? Bugger all! Now they have to work harder than ever. And work for the German estate owners. Work for a few marks on land which they once owned themselves. Why have we let this Tilsit man buy Valter's land?'

'I agree with you Grandad. But no one here could buy Valter and Tiesa's place and it was just going to wrack and ruin. This German fellow will probably clean it all up.'

'I'm sure he will. Most of them apparently love to work; and not only the men themselves. They have their wives and children work just as hard. Not like some of us locals. We spend too much time at the schnapps house.'

The ill-feeling directed towards the new family coming into the village, which could be heard in most of the village conversations, was further exacerbated because it was built on an underlying anger present since the death of the much-loved identities. Apart from the sorrow there was a feeling of anger that the heavenly powers had allowed nature to take two innocent lives. Why did this happen? Valter and Tiesa were two who directed so much love towards all of their friends and neighbours, especially since the death of their only son.

There also existed an element of hopelessness and frustration that they themselves were not able to buy the vacant property and now had to live with the uncertainty of what the new owner might do.

Hermann Schulte was a timber merchant in Tilsit, the large town on the left bank of the Memel River. Large quantities of logs, felled in the forests of Russia and Poland would be rafted down the river. At Tilsit they would be milled into usable timber. Hermann owned one such timber yard. He was not a rich person, but most of his fellow businessmen recognized him as a frugal and well-off individual.

He was also regarded as a very good manager. They could see that his timber yard was always running so efficiently. When asked by his friends to share his secret he would simply smile and shake his head. 'It's no secret how I operate.'

'Well, if it's no secret, tell us how you do it.'

'It's really something I learnt from my dad.'

His listeners nodded knowingly and someone noted, 'Yes, I remember that he also operated a very well-run business; and successfully too. So what was his secret?'

'Learn to speak Lithuanian, the local language. It's as simple as that.'

'What, learn to speak Lithuanian? But we are Prussians and most of our business is with people who speak German. And most here in Tilsit do speak German.'

'Yes, I have no doubt that those you socialize with do speak German. The same goes for me. My social friends, my wife's friends, all speak German. Isn't it funny? There have been Prussians and Germans doing business here for the last two hundred years and we still speak German. No wonder the local people regard us as foreigners. They find that hard to take. My dad told me that if I wanted to get on well with the locals I was to learn their language. And I did. I make sure that my children do too. They spend most of the time with local kids learning their ways and language.'

'And you think, that's all there is to it?'

'All? I'm certainly not sure that's all there is; but it's a good start. When I'm at work in the yards, that's all I speak. My workers don't have to try to speak German if they want to ask me something.'

'What about the raftsmen who bring your logs down?'

'They are mostly Jews. I know enough Yiddish to make them happy. They even feel a little above me knowing that they can speak Yiddish better that me. It's a real joke with us.'

This policy of doing business seemed so simple to his business colleagues, even if it did grate somewhat with the feeling of superiority some felt over against their paid workers. They could not argue with Hermann's results seeing his prosperous business and the more than comfortable home in which he and his family resided. Everything seemed to be running so smoothly for him. His circle of acquaintances was surprised when they heard of his future plans.

Herr Schulte had decided, with the somewhat reluctant

agreement of his wife and a "Yes, Papa" from his children, to move from the bustling business world of Tilsit to the previously unknown village of Kinischken. He arrived there as a "foreigner" but had the distinct advantage of being able to speak the language of those there. He was aware that there would be opposition to his, and his family's presence. He knew of similar situations occurring through the adjoining districts. There was a rich Prussian — a long-time friend — who had moved into a village quite close to Tilsit and proceeded to establish a large estate at the expense of the local people. Such an activity would always build tension between the two groups.

Hermann was determined not to put his family in a position where they would be ostracized in their home town. Once settled in he kept a low profile and quietly, with hard work, went about restoring the farm to its previous state. In all this he wanted to be seen as paying respect to the memory of the previous owners. His wife, Wiltrud, often suggested that they demolish the humble, timber home in which they were living and erect something more substantial. Hermann resisted, suggesting that this would probably happen after they had gained the complete confidence of the village; but not before.

He also insisted that his children mix freely with the local children and always speak Lithuanian, at no time giving the impression that they were better for coming from Tilsit or being Prussian. Except when alone as a family in their home, they were always to speak the local language.

This was especially hard for Wiltrud. The humble, timber cottage in Kinischken which demanded much attention was a far cry from the house in the city run by two servants, which allowed her to engage in a very full social life. Unlike her husband or children, she had not had the opportunities of speaking anything but German while living in Tilsit. At first she was excluded from normal village neighbourly gossiping. On many occasions Hermann would come in from labouring in the fields to find his wife crying, saddened by her loneliness and isolation. The occasional visit to the old friends in Tilsit would provide some short-term relief but something more long-term was required. This was provided by Marija, the daughter of their neighbours, Antanas and Edita Zukas. Hermann employed this teenage girl to be a companion for his wife, mainly to teach her the Lithuanian language. The move caused many local eyebrows to be raised and many disparaging comments to be made.

'You are working for those Prussians? How on earth do your parents allow that?'

'No, I'm not really working for them.'

'Aren't you in there sweeping, cleaning, cooking; something which that woman should be doing herself. You shouldn't be her slave.'

'No, I'm not doing that.'

'Well, what are you doing inside her house half the day?'

'Frau Schulte and I just go around doing things together and talking to one another.'

'What sort of a job is that?'

'I am teaching the Frau our language. She is very nice and wants to be able to speak to all of you. Now she is very embarrassed that she cannot talk to you. I am to correct her when she makes mistakes but she doesn't get annoyed when I laugh at some of the things she says. And she is teaching me some German and French words too. She learnt French when she went to a special school in Königsberg.'

'Where?'

'Königsberg.'

'Where on earth is that?'

'I think it's way past Tilsit on the coast where the big ships come.'

'Don't you think you should be helping your parents rather than working for those new-comers?'

And so initially, poor Marija had to put up with a lot of abuse from her friends and people who didn't really understand what she was doing. She thought she was merely helping someone who needed her help. She continued to visit her neighbour and talk to her in Lithuanian and was very thrilled to see how quickly Frau Schulte learnt. Soon her student felt comfortable holding conversations with other women in the village and they could see the result of Marija's efforts.

The relationship between the Schulte family and others in Kinischken underwent a change with the newcomers gradually earning the respect of the local people. Hermann increased the yield from his crops by introducing techniques learnt from successful farmers in the Tilsit area. He willingly explained these to others who wanted to try them. He drained some of the marshland increasing the amount of his arable land. The neighbours could see his success and they benefitted from it as well.

Few had anything bad to say when he acquired another farm in the village.

A few years into the nineteenth century and the Prussian newcomers had been accepted. Peace and harmony reigned on the banks of the Minge River. Life in the town moved slowly forward like the waters of the river. The same could not be said of Europe as a whole. Armies — French, Austrian, Russian and Prussian — were crisscrossing the continent spreading fear and destruction. The continent was in turmoil.

Napoleon's armies had been creating disruption and fear wherever they went. They were unstoppable.

To date, no armies had disturbed the peace found in Kinischken. Neither enemy nor friendly force had appeared and demanded food and shelter for the men and fodder for the horses. The village, however, was not completely insulated from what was happening outside its small community. News of the conquests of the French Emperor, and how he was treating the citizens of Prussia, had reached the banks of the Minge.

It was brought by Vadimas Zukas.

CHAPTER VI

Levée en masse

Less than a week had passed since the mayor's celebratory ball in Crémieu and activities in the town hall had reverted to normal. The music could no longer be heard. The flowers and decorations having served their once only purpose had been removed. The happy, partying assembly had dispersed, now back once again in the rhythm of everyday life. Remaining for all to read — and this by strict orders of the mayor himself — was the reason for that distinguished event. The two banners decorating each end of the hall still displayed their messages: *Vive la France* and *Vive L'Emperor*.

It was mid-morning on a Friday and once again a steady stream of people was entering the town's public hall. The mood of the people gathered on this occasion contrasted vastly with that of those who attended last week's extravaganza. On this occasion they had not been invited, but summoned. Most were expressing their displeasure, for they were aware of the significance of the meeting. Those present were displaying a whole gamut of feelings ranging from anger, through sadness and anxiety to resignation.

A high-ranking military officer flanked by a number of lower ranks sat around a table on one side of the hall shuffling a few piles of paper. The mayor, two other councillors and the town constable stood near them talking among themselves.

Colonel Gauthrin, who had attended the ball with his wife, was the officer in charge of proceedings. He stood up, and with a rap of his cane on the table quickly gained the attention of all in the hall. He proceeded to outline the reason for the meeting and emphasized the fact that he was at this meeting on Government business and representing the emperor. On saying that he looked up at the banner lauding the emperor and nodded his head slightly. He continued, explaining that according to the regulations of the *levée en masse* which had been made law in 1793 each area in France was responsible for providing a proportional number of men for service in the nation's military forces.

At this point there was a quiet, but distinctly audible, moan from some of those present. Colonel Gauthrin paused, looked up and stared sternly in the direction of the murmurs. Silence reigned. After a quick glance at the banner which proclaimed, *Vive la France,* he continued with his introduction.

Those young men listed and ordered to attend the present meeting constituted this year's quota for Crémieu. He and his officers would be interviewing each of these men to determine whether any of them had any reason not to go into training for the national army.

'So this is the surprise our captain friend, Gustav, promised us,' Luc mentioned to his group of friends who mumbled their agreement. 'Fine friend he is!'

'Yes, he could have come out and told us but I suppose he needed to have his little secret. We shouldn't complain too much for we all knew that this would happen sooner or later. Napoleon may have won that battle at Austerlitz but that doesn't mean the end of fighting. There must be countries that are still fighting against us for he still has most of his army all over Europe. The conscription won't stop until all the wars stop.' Outwardly Bernard seemed a little more resigned to his fate than some of the others.

His friend Michelle was clinging to his arm. 'But what will happen to all of you? We've all seen how some of our men have come back home. Just look at René's Hubert, hopping around on one leg. And there are others. And what about those who haven't come back? What's happened to them? And now they are taking more away! Will you all come back like poor old Hubert when the fighting is finished? Or will you come back at all?'

Everyone could see that Michelle was getting very worked

up and they knew from experience that when she was upset, she couldn't stop talking.

'Will any of you be able to come back home when the fighting is finished? Bernard, I don't want to be like poor Zoé. She has been waiting for her husband to come home for years, but no one can tell her what's happened to him. . .'

Bernard tried to interrupt, 'But, Michelle. . .'

He got no further. 'And what about Pauline and Sophie? They are still waiting too! At least Madame Mariner knows that her man has been killed in Italy somewhere. That's hardly any consolation. And now it's your turn. How many of you will be sent away to heaven knows where? Well, probably all of you unless you think that you are unfit. Will. . .'

'Don't worry,' consoled Luc, 'those Austrians or Russians, or whoever they are, will find us hard to catch. We'll be back in time for Christmas.'

'That's easy for you to say but you really don't know anything about fighting in a battle. All the fighting you have ever done is when you were drunk and you always seemed to be on the losing side. I remember two or three weeks ago when. . .'

'Come on now. . .'

But Michelle cut Luc off before he could say what he wanted to. 'Well, OK but you know as well as I do that some of those from here who were forced to go last time will never return. Don't you remember Simon and Roland?'

'The point is, Michelle,' Guy explained, 'we can do nothing about it. None of us are doing work which would let us be excused. Now if I was making soldiers' uniforms in one of the mayor's factories I would probably get out of it. Or if we were married we would be let off too.'

Luc feigned a worried look. 'Looking around at some of the married couples here and the way they are always squabbling, it might be better if the husbands were away fighting in the army.' Then he smiled.

They all laughed. Someone suggested they all go out each find a girl and get married.

'Oh, Bernard,' said Michelle, 'instead of running around the village making fools of yourselves why don't we get married?'

Everyone looked at the two of them and laughed. But they stopped when they realised that she was serious and had blushed a bright red. They stood quietly waiting for something to happen.

Bernard took her gently by both arms, pushed her slightly away, looked lovingly at her and said, 'What a wonderful thing to say, Michelle. And do you know something? I would really love you to be my wife, but that's just not possible.'

'But why?'

'Well for a start, it's way too late to be thinking something like that. I have been summoned and will have to go. For all I know there could be someone else wanting to marry you. And another thing. You all know as well as I that your parents would not hear of it. You are too young. But I'll tell you what. Ask me again when I get back from chasing Napoleon's enemies around Europe.'

'Maybe we will be able to convince those army chaps up there that we are needed here too much. Let's tell them that we would break too many hearts if we had to join the army,' Guy suggested half-heartedly.

'Oh, hell!' exclaimed Luc.

'What now?'

'That big fellow up there. I've just remembered. He's the chap who came in that fancy carriage and was arguing with his wife. I can see why he's in the army. It's safer there than at home. You remember the one, don't you, Bernard?' and he gave Michelle a big wink. 'I hope he doesn't recognize us. His driver probably told him that we went driving around in his carriage.'

The Colonel had finished his address but then they were interrupted by a call from one of the army captains. 'Attention, please. Would Luc Arnaud report to station 1 and Nicolas Bacot to station 2. Thank you.'

'Well, this is it,' said Bernard. 'Looks like you're first up, Luc. Then poor, shy Nicolas. At least they seem to know their alphabet.'

Across the room they saw Nicolas who worked in one of the mayor's factories, leaving his parents who were quietly talking to another couple.

The boys' parents were probably more concerned about their sons going away to fight than the conscripts themselves. They were well aware of the casualties suffered by both sides when infantry companies shot into a wall of advancing flesh or charged forward with their bayonets fixed at the end of long rifles. They could picture the slaughter of man and beast when trained cavalry units met. Some veterans in the village, discharged because of wounds, had been part of such battles.

They had also witnessed the carnage when gun batteries had found the correct range.

The bravado shown by many of the young men called up to enlist would not stand against the reality of battle. Many of the parents were well aware of this. But for some of them that was not the main issue. Proud Frenchmen and women that they were, they questioned the necessity of continuing warfare in which France — and more importantly, their sons — was engaged. They were not convinced that Napoleon was leading their country in the right direction. Many looked back to more peaceful times and wondered whether they would come again if the monarchy was reintroduced.

'I just do not understand. Why all this fighting? It's been going on for years.' Luc's father was clearly opposed to his son being called up to fight. 'And where are our armies fighting? They are either in Italy or in Central Europe somewhere.'

'Norbert and Clara's boy had to go to Egypt with Napoleon's army.'

'But that was before he was emperor, wasn't it?'

'It probably was. It was a long time ago. But it makes no difference. Why on earth should we have to go and fight in Egypt?'

'Has there ever been any fighting here in France? With Napoleon, that is,' Henrí Natalier asked. 'You know, I was talking to Mayor Anton about that at the ball last week, but all he could say was that it's great to be a Frenchman these days. He said that wherever armies might be they are fighting for the glory of France. I know I shouldn't be saying this, but I often ask myself whether all this fighting is mainly for the glory of Napoleon himself.'

'I wonder whether the general there, whoever he is, could give us an honest answer to that?'

'That's if we could even get him to talk to us,' another disgruntled father commented. 'Perrin, you know the mayor quite well. Call him over and see whether we can get to talk to that officer.'

'I can at least try. You will need to remember that he is one of the emperor's professional soldiers and even if he does agree to talk to us he will only tell us how great Napoleon is and how that France is the ruler of Europe.'

Later in the afternoon everyone was surprised to see the colonel and his assistant officers mixing with the parents of the boys called up for duty. He was telling them how proud they should be, knowing that their sons are honouring the call of their emperor and helping to make France great.

C H A P T E R   V I I

Royalists

A pall of concern and despair blanketed the market square of Crémieu the day after Colonel Gauthrin's fateful visit. What normally was a loud, vibrant gathering of local and nearby people had become a sea of gloom. Word had spread quickly about the colonel's visit and it would have been difficult to find a single person who was unaware of what his visit meant for the town. Many, indeed, could name each single individual who had been conscripted.

Bernard was particularly despondent as he went about his regular tasks of running the family's wine stall. He had come away from the meeting feeling down and apprehensive and during the night his mind did nothing but dwell on what might be lying ahead for him. All the young men, and Bernard was not an exception, had been aware of the possibility that they would be conscripted. This was always something in the future. Reality had struck when his name was called and it was then emphatically confirmed by the attendant officer that he would be required to fulfill his obligation to the nation. During the night that reality played over and over in his mind, reoccurring in countless different forms.

There was sunshine on the cobblestones in front of Bernard's stall but not in his heart and mind.

'A few more weeks and we'll be off,' was Luc's greeting which brought Bernard's mind back.

'Don't remind me. And good morning to you too, my friend.'

'At least we now know for sure,' Luc tried to sound reassuring but no change appeared in Bernard's vacant countenance.

After a moment's silence Bernard asked, 'Did he tell you where we might be sent to do our training?'

'I asked him but he either didn't know or was not willing to tell me. "You go where the army sends you", was all he said. We'll just have to make the best of it.' Luc seemed quite resigned.

'But tell me, Luc, do you really want to go and risk your life for the emperor?'

'You know me, Bernie. I don't really think about things like that. I leave the politics to others. What about you?'

Bernard looked at his friend. 'You probably have a good idea what I think. I don't like what Napoleon is doing. His wars with those other countries are costing us so many lives; and for what? No, Luc, I don't like the idea of fighting for Emperor Napoleon, but I am a Frenchman and would be happy to fight for France.'

'Happy?' asked Luc.

'Well, probably not happy, but willing enough to do what was asked of me. Doing my duty to our country, I suppose.'

'What about poor Nicolas Bacot? How's he going to get on? I do feel sorry for him. He has always been so shy and I can't see that he will ever change. Perhaps he should get his hand caught in one of Mayor Maillard's machines.'

That same afternoon Henrí Natalier travelled out to one of his vineyards situated on the road to nearby Montouvier. He was now sitting in one of the storage barns next to a large cask sampling one of his new wines with a couple of like-minded citizens of Crémieu whom he had invited. Any consensus concerning the quality, or not, of the new light red liquid was secondary to their main concern. They were discussing political matters which, in this case, was better done behind closed doors. They were three of a small number of men in their town who disagreed with the foreign policy being pursued by Emperor Napoleon, indeed with his whole government, and were hoping to see the return of the monarchy.

The recent conscription meeting was one of the items on the agenda. All three men who were there had a very personal interest in this for each of them had a son who in a few weeks would have to leave for army training camps.

'There were some very sombre faces in the market square this morning,' said Eugene Bacot. I had to help Beatrice on our stall for Nicolas was just too upset to show his face for most of the time.'

'Yes,' consoled Henrí, 'it will be hard for him. New recruits who are shy or a little different can really be targeted by the bullies and old instructors who should know better.'

'I also spent time at the markets today,' the third man in the room, Martin Arnaud, remarked, 'and yes, there were a lot of sad people when I arrived. Strangely enough, as the day went on, the mood seemed to lift.'

'Really,' said Eugene. 'Beatrice and I were so depressed the whole morning that we hardly knew what was happening.'

'It probably changed when people arrived who are avid supporters of Napoleon and what he is doing,' suggested Henrí. 'There are some, friends of the mayor mainly, who do not seem to dread the levy as much as in previous years. Are people in Crémieu warming towards Napoleon? It would seem so.'

'Yes,' took up Martin Arnaud, 'I was speaking to Guy L'Espenard, you know, a good friend of your Bernard, Henrí, and my son, Luc. Well, he said to me that he was a little disappointed not to have been called up to serve. Now, I'm not so sure why; whether he will miss Bernard and Luc or whether he really wants to fight for Napoleon. He seemed quite enthusiastic about it. He said that he would like to send the Russians running. From where he got such thinking, I have no idea. He wouldn't even know where the armies are.'

'He's merely quoting someone else, I would think,' suggested Henrí. 'Gustav Maillard, probably.'

Eugene Bacot also seemed surprised at this. 'It makes one think. What have the Russians done to us that would make Guy, a simple labourer here, so eager to make them, or anyone else for that matter, go running. He needs to stop and think for a minute what that involves, instead of wanting to be a hero.'

'It seems that there has been a change in thinking for many here,' Henrí shook his head showing some disappointment. 'These young men are not thinking things through. Take young Guy for instance. He would be putting his own life in danger and this I cannot understand. And from the other point of view, he would need to kill the opponent with a bullet or his bayonet; a poor, frightened conscript whom someone had labelled the enemy. I've no doubt he also would rather be back in his own country harvesting wheat or drinking vodka.'

'Changing the subject,' Martin interrupted, 'I have been keeping my ears open listening for any comments that might lead to others who would join our cause. I have not heard anything.'

'I agree,' said Eugene, 'and from what you are saying it appears that things here are becoming more and more in favour of Napoleon. Don't get me wrong but I wonder whether we should continue in our attempt to build up a strong Royalist group here.'

'Are you serious, Eugene?' Henrí seemed taken aback.

'I believe,' said Martin, 'that the longer things go on the less support there is for the monarchy. Remember too, that we are a small group here far away from the larger cities. Maybe there, people are showing more enthusiasm in bringing a king back.'

'Don't misunderstand me, please,' Eugene could see that his comments were not well received. 'I will continue to support you. I am trying to look at things in perspective. Remember back to that terrible war in the Vendée when so many died for the king. We don't want something like that inflicted on the country again. It is also a fact that the present forces are well in favour of the present Republic and definitely support Emperor Napoleon. They far outnumber the scattered groups of Royalists. I also think that it is becoming more and more dangerous for us to be approaching people.'

'No, these times are not easy for us,' conceded Henrí. 'We can only do what we feel we must.'

Their discussions continued but ended with the three men being disappointed with the way things seemed to be heading. Henrí did mention to Eugene Bacot that he might be able to offer some advice to his shy son, Nicolas.

The Swiss Option

Those last-minute errands being run at twilight had been completed and except for a weary farmer or two coming home late from a long day in the neighbouring fields, the streets of Crémieu appeared to be deserted. Night had closed in but an almost full moon shed its radiance over the peaceful scene. A dull light seen through the window of most of the homes allowed family members living there to conclude their duties for the day and prepare for the night. Most citizens were behind the closed doors of their homes.

But the streets were not completely devoid of life. From time to time a shadowy figure could be seen moving through the moon-lit night. Some of these could be husbands returning home from one of the wine bars in the town. Others, moving in the opposite direction, might be headed towards those more brightly-lit establishments which provided a variant of entertainment. They were being encouraged by the happy sounds spilling out onto the street. Not all in Crémieu wanted to sleep at this early hour.

There was a smaller number who were concerned that their evening outing is not noticed. Small villages as well could have much to conceal. The majority of those involved in such affairs moved mostly in the night. One such pair, a father and his son, grown already to be a man, stood at the front door of Henrí and Vivienne Natalier's modest home on the outskirts of the town. The door opened and Eugene Bacot and his son, Nicolas, moved inside.

A glass of wine to welcome the visitors was quickly poured and enjoyed, accompanied by general comments on town and district affairs. Once finished, their minds turned to the purpose of this evening visit; to more serious matters.

'Yes, almost everyone in the town knows how shy Nicolas is. Nearly everyone I now meet makes a comment. "How will he cope?" they want to know. It will be the death of him.' Eugene's father was a worried person.

'Nicolas, how do you feel about all this?' Madame Natalier wanted to know.

Nicolas was so upset, worrying about his being conscripted that he was on the verge of tears. Only with difficulty was he able to give a reply, 'I do not know how I will s...s-urvive without the support of my family here. If I am treated as badly as everyone says

I don't know . . . I would probably end up . . .' and he broke down in tears.

'And,' continued Eugene, his father, 'Nicolas has always treated everything — I mean people, animals, tools and belongings — so gently. As for killing . . . It is against everything he believes.'

'Did you explain all this to the captain when he was talking to you at the meeting?' Henrí wanted to know.

'Yes, I tried to but he only l...l-aughed and said that they would soon toughen me up.'

'I feel so sorry for you boys who are forced to do something you really do not want to do,' said Vivienne Natalier. 'It's the same with Bernard. I do not want him to go off to fight in a war we do not agree with. I know that he is in two minds about it as well.'

Everyone looked at Bernard who had sat quietly to this point. 'Yes, Mother, I know how you and my father think. It's not just me having to train to be a soldier and the dangers that will bring. It's really because of Napoleon. I know how you feel about him and what he is doing with France. I agree with you in a lot of what you say but I have been called to do my duty to France. I do not see what I have been ordered to do as serving Napoleon but serving France.'

'I admire that attitude, Bernard,' praised Eugene Bacot. 'From what I have heard, you would certainly be able to come through the training and be a very good soldier. Nicolas, however, is a completely different person but not a coward. He also is a proud Frenchman. Knowing him as he is, I am convinced that his life would be destroyed before he even came near a battlefield.'

'Is there somewhere else I could be where I didn't have to be part of the army, like serving in a hospital, or somewhere like that?' Nicolas wanted to know.

'Officially, no,' Henrí replied. 'It is unfortunate but once you are called up you must go to the army. There are no exceptions. At least I am not aware of any. But there is a way out. Not everyone agrees with it, and I don't know how you will see it. That is to leave town and go into hiding somewhere.'

'Who would want to do that? The person would be branded a coward for the rest of his life.' Eugene seemed surprised that Henrí would suggest such a thing to him.

'As I understand, many have chosen to do exactly that. It is occurring more and more frequently. Previously there was a large degree of stigma attached to it and many suffered accordingly. Things have changed and it is being viewed less and less negatively today. More people are disagreeing with where Napoleon is taking his armies. That's the main reason.'

'Aren't they pursued by the authorities?' Nicolas asked.

'Definitely,' Bernard was quick to answer. He had thought about this before. He pictured a squad of soldiers running through the town demanding answers to their questions. He could especially see them confronting his parents, threatening, being violent to them. It would not remain a secret forever that his father was less than enthusiastic about the emperor and soldiers would soon find this out. Outspoken critics would be severely dealt with. He feared for his parents and would hate to do anything that might result in them being punished.

'If Nicolas decided he wanted to avoid the army, where could he go? Do you have any suggestions?' Eugene looked from one of his hosts to the other.

Vivienne Natalier nodded and began answering, 'Yes, I feel that I can make a suggestion to you. I have a cousin who lives just over the border in Switzerland, near Geneva. She resides in a farming village called Chellex. I know how she feels about what is happening here in her homeland. She would not refuse to help boys who have fled from France, take them in and give them work. They would have to earn their keep.'

'But Mother, we have talked about this. One dare not take the risk. The frontier there would be very well guarded. What would happen if we were discovered? It's too dangerous.'

'It might be well worth the effort,' said Nicolas.

'Sure, if we get to mother's cousin safely,' agreed Bernard, 'but if caught? Have you any idea how they deal with those who try to avoid the call-up? And with their families too. I'm sure they would suffer as well.'

The others were looking at Bernard.

'I'll tell you. They are thrown into a fortress prison and left there living on bread and water. They say no one ever comes out alive.'

'If I feel that's my only h...h-ope then I suppose I shall have to risk it. What must I do?' asked Nicolas.

'I will write to my cousin and tell her to expect you,' said Vivienne.

'Write a letter? What if the letter were intercepted? The post is very unsafe in these times,' Eugene seemed somewhat concerned.

'Don't worry. I shall write the letter with no specifics. It will be written so that only she will be able to understand its true meaning. We must do all we can to hinder this Corsican tyrant. We should thank, and try to help, those who refuse to fight for him, enslaving even more of the continent.'

'Mother, Mother, stop or you will soon be on the streets taking up arms against our emperor!'

'I shall write the letter,' stated Vivienne firmly. 'What happens then is up to you and your family, Nicolas. I may be able to convince Bernard to go with you.'

Later that evening Eugene and his son moved back to their home a little less desperate but still very concerned.

CHAPTER IX

Loving Farewell

Michelle made her way hurriedly along the town's old wall as she went to meet Bernard. The stones had been laid in position when the wall was built 350 years ago. The structure had been long and strong with towers and gates designed to protect the town from enemies in those unsettled times. It had served the town well, but time and long periods of peace had hastened its decay. The stones that remained served mainly as a reminder of Crémieu's medieval history. Others had been carried off and used on other projects.

Suddenly she saw him standing at their favorite meeting

spot, under the old beech tree — the trysting place, as they laughingly and lovingly called it. She paused a moment to look at him, admiring him as he stood here. This was her golden man with his long, fair hair, the touch of a moustache and skinned tanned from the hours spent working in the summer sun. She felt that she could search the world without finding someone better than he.

He was leaving tomorrow to join Napoleon's great army and feed the rapacity of the emperor's ambition. Privately she, like her parents, hated Napoleon for his vision of a great France. The best of French manhood was being shovelled into the furnace of his personal desires. Those left were the ones who would end up rebuilding France and they were the leftovers or those crippled by war. How could that be a good thing?

However, Michelle was not going to spoil their meeting by mentioning any of this tonight. Tonight was theirs to say their sad and fond farewells. She stopped and then quietly and slowly crept around the back of the tree to take him by surprise.

'Boo!' she said softly as she poked her head around the great bole.

'What!' yelped Bernard and flung his head around to see what was happening. His face broke into a broad smile as he saw his lovely Michelle. Michelle, whom he would have to leave tomorrow as he marched north towards the capital and the next episode of his life.

He grabbed her in his arms and held her tightly as the realization of all he was about to lose came to him. How could he leave this dearest person in the world? How could he march bravely and nonchalantly off tomorrow when his heart was breaking?

'Don't you be a cheeky hussy with me,' he laughed as his hands felt her beautiful, dark hair and ran lightly down her back. He kissed her face, her neck, her shoulders.

They laughed as they walked past the small woodland, a favourite spot for the lovers from the town. They talked together as they ambled along, stopping occasionally, and then more frequently to kiss and hug as they went. They came to a well-preserved remnant of the old town wall rising from a patch of green grass.

Here they sat on one of the larger stones looking out over the village where they had spent all their lives. The sun was slowly sinking over the distant horizon leaving behind a rosy-orange glow. A squadron of ibis was silhouetted in the fading light as the birds made their way to the safety of their nesting grounds.

Michelle snuggled closer to Bernard.

They stopped talking and, in the silence enjoyed nature spread out before them. It seemed a shame that such beauty should be spoilt by thoughts of tomorrow. But the sun would rise again in the morning ushering in the inevitable. Michelle shivered slightly for the setting sun had brought a slight chill. But for them both the chill went deeper. Tomorrow Bernard was to leave to take his place in the *Grande Armée.*

He lent to the side and grasped the bottle of wine which he had left there when he first arrived. It was one of his father's better wines, especially selected for this private farewell which he had planned with Michelle. He picked up one of the glasses which had been standing beside the bottle, filled it and handed it to Michelle who placed it on a convenient stone beside her without tasting it. He then filled his own and slowly replaced the bottle on the stone.

Holding the glass in front of him he contemplated the light of the setting sun which was dimly reflected through the pale liquid.

'I wonder where I'll be this time tomorrow,' Bernard broke the silence.

'Well, I hope you won't be sitting somewhere with a pretty girl drinking wine.'

'No such luck. That would only happen if I stayed here with you.'

'Oh, Bernie, why do you have to go? So many young men who go off to war, do not come back. So many of them are killed. You could be killed. I can't bear thinking about it. Do you know what you should do now?'

'No. There are a few things I would like to do now; but what do you have in mind?'

Michelle blushed at what she thought he meant but went on, 'Why don't you pack a few things in a haversack and set out for the mountains in Switzerland? You could stay in a village there until all the fighting is over.'

'You know I couldn't do that.'

'Yes, you could. They say the village people there hate Napoleon for what he did when he marched through their country with his army some years ago. They would look after you. And I have heard something about Nicolas Bacot. You know, poor, shy Nicolas.'

'No, what about him? Has he chopped his hand off in one of the mayor's factories?'

'He hasn't been there for the last week. He is not at home. No one seems to know where he is.'

'Oh?'

'Yes, some people say that he has run off to hide somewhere because he couldn't bear going away and training to become a soldier.'

A whole raft of thoughts was running through Bernard's mind. He was sure he knew what had happened to his friend, but should he tell her? No, even though Michelle was a special person and he would trust her with his life, Nicolas' business was something best kept from her. So he simply replied, 'Poor Nicolas, I hope he's OK. I don't want to be a soldier either. Sometimes I think my mother would like me to run off as well but even she couldn't convince me.'

'You have definitely made up your mind?'

'How could you think that I haven't, Michelle? There is more to it than just what I would like to do. It's my dad, my family. When it's all boiled down it is also you and me. None of us want me to go off to the army, but no one wants to see me as a coward either. I don't want to bring shame to my family.'

Michelle who had been tasting the wine put her glass down and threw her arms around her friend of many years.

'Oh, Bernard!' and she kissed him once more passionately on the lips.

Her actions were so unexpected that the glass in Bernard's hand went flying and smashed against the stone wall. Completely oblivious to the fate of his glass and his father's quality wine which it contained, Bernard embraced Michelle and pulled her ever closer. In the beauty and solitude surrounding them, these two young people in love quickly ignored any thought of army training, ignored the future and thought no further than the now and each other. The love they felt for each other and the pleasure they were experiencing in their fervent embrace indicated something much deeper than lifelong friendship.

For a moment their lips released and they looked at each other. Bernard began, 'Michelle, I . . .' but before he could continue Michelle's lips made speaking impossible.

Their mutual feelings became ever more passionate as they both realised the horror of their separation in the morning. They were now lying on the forest floor together on a bed of soft grass and sweet leaves from the trees. Their kisses and embraces became more and more intense until Bernard pulled away.

'I can't do this Michelle. I love you too much to risk leaving you with a child to raise alone if something should happen to me. It would be too much for you and your parents to bear. You would lose your friends. The people in the village would shun you. We must stop.'

'No. No, Bernard. Please do not stop. They are not friends if they laugh at me. I don't care about the people here in Crémieu. My parents would help me. I would be happy to have part of you with me for the rest of my life.'

They lay there intertwined, looking up at the darkening foliage of the trees and the coloured sky above. Suddenly the reality of tomorrow and their love and passion for each other took hold of them again.

With their bodies pressed close together, their hands began a frantic search to show and to personally experience the emotion each was feeling.

Her hands pinched the back of his neck as she pulled his head down closer to her. They moved frantically down his back. The cloth of his shirt impeded closer contact but they soon found access through the buttoned front. They caressed his bare skin. They dug into his chest.

His hands soon found the inviting flesh of her breasts. He began stroking them tenderly as she relaxed and moaned. Her erect nipples encouraged his touch.

Her hand brushed against his arousal. It stayed there. Their restless moving and searching stopped. They were breathing as one; relaxed, but not really. They knew instinctively that they were on the road to greater intimacy.

His right arm extended to pull her buttocks closer to him and then the hand soon found its way under her skirt to the warmth of her thighs.

'Here?' asked Bernard. 'Should we make love here?'

'Here. Anywhere,' she panted as she struggled out of his embrace and jumped up. She stepped out of her skirt and stood unabashed before him. Then Michelle started unbuckling Bernard's belt and trousers. They fell from his hips to the ground revealing his feelings. The two of them stood there, eyes lowered. As one they embraced and with their lips pressed tightly together they lowered themselves into the long green grass behind the wall.

Their first taste of sexual love for one another was breathtaking but brief. It had exploded in a torrent of ecstasy they could never have imagined. They remained lying united physically and emotionally. They were savouring the experience of joining with each other, of sharing their bodies. Slowly they came back to a sense of where they were and the depth of their recent experience. They looked lovingly at each other and then rolled apart.

'Michelle, I love you so much; so much. Why do I now have to go? But you will wait for me? You will wait until I return?'

Michelle lay there and smiled. 'I will wait, dreaming of this moment. I shall not forget our time here together. Please come home soon. Don't keep me waiting.'

'Wild Prussians and barbarian Russians had better not try to stop me!'

CHAPTER X

. . . .

A Visit to Tilsit

Marija Zukas was becoming more and more excited for they were coming closer and closer to Tilsit. She did not know just how far they were from the town but assumed that their journey must soon end because for the last few hours Herr Schulte had kept assuring her that they would soon be there.

'How far is it now, Herr Schulte?'

'Wait till we get to the top of this slight rise. Just a few more minutes.'

Then after two days of travel, there it was.

'Wow!' cried Marija. 'Look at the size of that river. Is that the Memel you are always talking about? It's certainly bigger than our little river. But how are we going to get across? The town is on the other side.'

Hermann Schulte reined his horses to the side of the road and suggested they all step out of the carriage for a while. Antanas Zukas, his wife Edita, and daughter Marija were soon standing around their neighbour from Kinischken listening carefully as he pointed out features of the city to them.

The Zukas family had come to Tilsit to see their son, Vadimas. For the last year he had been training with a Prussian dragoon regiment that was stationed there. This had come to an end and there was to be an important parade to recognize the completion of his, and the other recruits', initial training. Hermann Schulte knew, mainly through his wife who employed Marija as help in her house, how desperately the Zukas family wished to attend this passing-out parade. He also knew that it would be difficult, very difficult, for this to happen.

He came to the rescue. He still had business connections in his hometown and on this occasion had organized one of his regular visits to correspond with the dragoon parade. He convinced Antanas Zukas to accept his offer for them to travel with him in his personal carriage. After travelling for two days they had reached Tilsit, surprised at its appearance and size.

'And we shall have to cross the river on that pontoon bridge you see there.'

'Where?'

'The bridge is that dark line crossing the river in front of that tall church tower standing out above everything else.'

'That? Is that really a bridge? We won't fall off into the water, will we? Maybe the horses will become scared and jump over the side.'

'Don't worry,' Hermann assured Marija, 'they are well trained not to do that.'

Their journey continued and they soon crossed the floating bridge without any incidents and Herr Schulte headed towards his Tilsit residence with the Zukas family, especially Marija, staring in wonder at the buildings which lined the streets. They drove past the German Church with the high spire which they had seen from the other side of the river. They looked down an open square towards the city hall with a tower almost as inspiring as that on the church.

'We are soon at my home. I trust Manfred and Martha will have everything ready for us.'

Ponia Zukas looked towards her husband on hearing Hermann Schulte mentioning how Manfred and Martha would have everything ready for them.

'Antanas,' she asked, 'are we staying in Herr Schulte's house while we are here? You did not tell me that.'

'No, dearest, you would have argued and become very upset and spoilt the trip. Herr Schulte said that it would be much easier for everyone if we stayed with him. He said his housekeeper and her husband would enjoy looking after us. The house has had few visitors since he moved to our village.'

'But why didn't . . .'

Hermann butted in. 'Please, Ponia Zukas, I would never be comfortable leaving you by yourselves in my hometown. Besides, my wife gave me strict instructions.'

They had entered *die hohe Straße* (High Street) with the Zukas family still looking with amazement at the houses on both sides of the street. A short distance and they stopped in front of a three-storied residence. Their carriage had barely come to a halt when the front door of the building opened and a man and a woman, dressed in dark uniforms with white trimmings came out and stood to attention on the front landing. Then the man hurried down and opened the carriage door for the travellers to alight.

'Welcome home, Herr Schulte.'

'Thank you, Manfred, it's good to be here once again. I'm pleased to see that you and Martha are looking so well. These are my guests who will be staying with us as I notified you. See that they are made comfortable and have some light refreshments made ready for them. We have had a long day.'

Manfred stood to attention and shook hands with each member of the Zukas family as they moved away from the step of the carriage, giving a "welcome Sir" or "welcome Madam" as appropriate.

The party moved up the front steps where they met Martha who curtsied slightly by way of greeting her newly-arrived guests. These could only look at one another in amazement as they found themselves transported to a different world; a world so different from their humble rural existence which they had known all their lives. That this had been made possible by their neighbour made everything even more unforeseen. That this friendly, everyday neighbour, who, with his wife and family was living in a very modest farmer's wooden home in remote Kinischken could be "home" in Tilsit with its servants and comforts, was hard for them to comprehend.

Martha showed them to their rooms on the second floor overlooking the street. Marija continued gazing around at the beauty of the house as she was led through the entrance hall, up the staircase and along the hallway. In her bedroom she could now admire the delicate ceramic water jug and basin on a multicoloured washstand in one corner of the room. The soft velvet curtains, of a pastel golden colour, matched tastefully with the bed setting standing slightly off centre in the room. She threw herself down on the bed giving out a sigh of pleasure as the mattress enfolded her.

She was so tired from the travel and the bed was so inviting that she could have remained there and fallen fast asleep, but her excitement soon had her standing up and opening the adjoining door to her parent's room. Its grandeur, too, took her breath away.

'Mama! Papa! This is paradise.'

'Yes, daughter,' replied her father, 'it seems that we really don't know our neighbour. I wonder what other surprises he has waiting for us?'

'Ponia Zukas had hardly said a word since their arrival in Tilsit. Like her daughter she too was overwhelmed by what she was experiencing. She now spoke. 'Refreshments. I would enjoy something now. I wonder where the dining room or reception room or wherever we have to go is.'

'Come on,' enthused Marija, 'let's go and find out. But remember Mumija we are only having refreshments. You will probably need a good appetite for dinner tonight.'

Herr Schulte was waiting for them in the reception room which contained a central table supplied with a variety of drinks and delicacies. He made them feel comfortable in these surroundings which they had never experienced before.

'And don't feel embarrassed to be just standing here eating and drinking and doing nothing to help. Believe me, Manfred and Martha would be very offended if you offered to help them. They would feel that they were not doing a good enough job. Sit back and let them fuss over you.'

'That will be very hard to do,' said Ponia Zukas, who was usually not happy unless she was helping someone.

'Oh, and I must apologise that I am unable to join you at dinner this evening. I am not staying in Tilsit for very long this time and there are several people I need to talk to. Something has come up and it can't wait.'

'I'm sorry that our being here has made things difficult for you. If I had known. . .'

'Hermann interrupted Antanas before he could finish what he wanted to say. 'No. No. It is not your fault, and I do want to be with you at the parade tomorrow. All I ask is that you be down here for dinner at eight o'clock. Martha likes people to be punctual for her meals. Be here and they will look after you.'

'I can't wait,' said Marija.

Her parents looked at her, her father with a slight frown,

probably thinking that her enthusiastic statement was a little frivolous, and her mother shaking her head.

Then Herr Schulte wished them a good evening and left them to enjoy what the decked-out table had to offer. If this was a light refreshment, they could only wonder what dinner would be like.

They heard the front door close.

'I said you would have trouble sleeping after all that you ate and drank at dinner.' Ponia Zukas was lying in bed speaking to her husband who was standing in the dark room looking out onto the street.

'That's strange,' said Antanas as he moved closer to the window to get a better look.

'What's strange?'

'A few moments ago a person, a man I think it was, came to our front door. And now two more walking towards here.'

'Why on earth should there be men visiting at this time of night? Did you hear Herr Schulte come home?' asked his wife.

'No. I didn't hear him. Wait a minute. I think that's him walking across the road now. Manfred must have let the others in.'

'You're right. It is strange. What's going on here?'

C H A P T E R   X I

Dragoon Parade

Next morning Hermann Schulte's carriage, with three very excited occupants, joined the steady flow of people and vehicles moving along *die deutsche Straße* towards the dragoon barracks. The Zukas family felt special as they looked out at the others who were no doubt also hastening to see the parade. There were proud parents, as they themselves, father walking tall in a frock coat, colourful cravat, hat and walking cane with his wife clinging to his arm. They saw old veterans in full military dress with shining medals, some marching purposefully, most however, moving more slowly, who added colour to the streetscape. Groups of young ladies were also hurrying to see their beaux or their casual military friends displaying their military splendour. This was a special day for the garrison town of Tilsit.

'You are so kind doing all of this for us,' said Ponia Zukas who in her excitement had hardly stopped thanking Herr Schulte.

'I am happy to be doing this,' he replied. 'Your son has chosen to become a soldier to defend our country, to defend Prussia, and this is how I am showing my gratitude.'

'It will be great to see him all dressed up in his uniform and on his horse. He has told us what a great horse it is. It is as though the beast was a member of our family, but we haven't seen it in reality,' said Marija. 'Have you seen it, Father?'

'No, Marija. You all know how I like horses and so I am also very excited to see all the war horses and their riders on parade. No doubt they will be so different from my two old work horses at home and the old hack I ride about.'

'Yes,' said Hermann, 'you will be seeing them at their best, all polished and shining. And I know that a dragoon does grow to love his horse and that is a good thing for when they are on a campaign, they depend on each other.'

'That's my real worry,' commented Antanas.

'What is?' asked his wife.

'When Vadimas and his company are called off to war and have to set off on a campaign to some foreign place and all the hardship they have to put up with there. They have to live in all sorts of uncomfortable conditions and the food supplies are often scarce. It's OK for the officers. They find good accommodation and are well looked after, but not the lowly soldier. And it's best not thinking about battling the enemy.'

'Oh, dear,' uttered the two women.

'I admit,' continued Antanas, 'that I am quite proud of the young man for what he has chosen to do. And it wasn't just because of his love of horses. He does want to help defend Prussia from the French.'

'An admirable thing to do,' agreed Hermann. 'Our king and queen are relying on soldiers like Vadimas to keep Prussia great and retain our independence.'

Marija was looking worried throughout the conversation. 'Will there be a war against Napoleon?' she wanted to know. 'I don't want Vadi having to go into battle to be wounded and possibly killed.'

'It will have to come I'm afraid,' said Hermann. 'Our King Frederick William is trying to stay at peace with Napoleon, but the queen and many other leaders and advisors are saying that Prussia must make a stand and stop Napoleon from controlling all of Europe.'

'We poor peasants won't have much to say in it. We will have to accept what they decide.' Antanas seemed resigned to the fact that he, and most others as well, had no say in how their country was governed. They could only hope that their rulers had some kind considerations towards the common people.

'Yes, that's how it works,' agreed Hermann. 'The men in power make decisions. The orders are issued. The soldiers are told to fight. Let's not think about what might happen but enjoy the military spectacular today. There might even be some important generals there and we will get to see some of those who make the decision.'

Already on walking through the entrance gates they could hear a brass band playing stirring music. A uniformed soldier escorted them to an area reserved for parents and close friends of those who were celebrating the conclusion of their initial training. The number of spectators swelled as the official starting time approached. The band music had ceased.

There was an air of expectation and excitement as the visitors waited for proceedings to commence.

'What's happening, Papa?' Marija asked her father who was a tall man.

Antanas swayed to the right and then to the left to see past those standing in front of him. He looked one way and then the other.

'Nothing that I can see.'

'It's time to start, isn't it?'

'The Prussian army should start on time. Ask Herr Schulte for he would know.'

Then a drumbeat was heard, sounding out a marching time.

'The band is coming through a passage between those two buildings there.'

'Where?' Marija was standing on her tiptoes and jumping up and down, trying to catch a glimpse of them.

In a short while the band had taken up a position just to the right of the temporary dais which had been erected at the head of the parade ground. Vacant chairs were lined up on the dais.

There was a loud shout from the bandmaster which brought the musicians to attention. A downward wave of his baton and the music which followed was something that stirred the souls of not only the military men in attendance but of all who were present. The drums rolled, the trumpets sounded, the strong four/four beat of well-known tunes had everyone's spirit marching.

After what for many was too short a time the music stopped. The audience was looking around to see what would happen next. They did not have long to wait. Three open carriages, each accompanied by four foot-soldiers entered the arena. One by one they stopped allowing the two passengers who were seated in each to alight and make their way to the official chairs.

'Who are they?' Ponia Zukas wanted to know.

'Important military officers, no doubt, judging by their uniforms and all their medals,' replied her husband. 'I have no idea who they are. Do you know, Hermann?'

'Not all of them, no. The general in the centre I think is the Duke of Brunswick. He's one of our most senior generals.'

'Looks a bit old to me,' commented Marija. 'I couldn't see him doing too much fighting. He looks old enough to be my grandfather.'

No sooner had the official group taken their allotted seats and their carriages withdrawn when a section of spectators to the rear of the parade ground began to cheer. The cheering moved quickly along the crowd, increasing in volume, so that the whole arena was filled with the sound.

'What's happening now, Papa?' Marija wanted to know, again standing on her toes and swaying from side to side to obtain a view through the crowd.

'The dragoons are entering through a gate at the back,' her father replied.

'Can you see Vadi?'

'They all look the same to me.'

'Can't you pick out his red beard?'

'Most of them have beards and under those tall, black shakos with their visors it's hard to tell one from another. We will have to wait till they ride past us.'

Eventually four ranks of horsemen had formed up at the rear of the ground, four rows of chestnut horsepower, guided by the blue-uniformed masters sitting erect on their backs. The cheering had now died down. What would happen now?

A loud shouted order, incomprehensible to most in the arena, was faintly heard. Three trumpeters riding identical white horses trotted forward. In unison, they lifted their instruments to their lips and a series of notes rang out speaking to the mounted dragoons.

The band began playing and led by their squadron commander followed by two lieutenants, three columns of dragoons moved down the side of the ground. Each trio of riders, stirrup to stirrup, moved as one, keeping an exact two horse's length behind the trio in front. Ten metres before the band's position, the captain wheeled to the left to lead his soldiers in front of the reviewing officer and his official party.

He saluted, sabre in hand, as he passed the official party,

being followed by his two lieutenants who did the same. Each trio of dragoons passed with eyes fixed straight ahead. The procession then turned to head back along the other side of the parade ground.

'There's Vadi!' yelled Marija excitedly. She was just one of the many calling out the names of their sons, brothers, husbands or lovers. The well-trained dragoons showed no indication that they had heard or recognized their names being shouted. Their formation did not alter, their rhythm was unchanged, their eyes remained fixed ahead.

After the mass salute and the inspection of the troops by the Duke of Brunswick, mounted on a shiny black Trakehner, the spectators were able to look more closely at a section of Prussia's pride lined up listening to the official speeches.

'. . . and like your grandfathers before you who rode with our much-loved King Frederick the Great, making our country great, a country to be feared in Europe, you brave dragoons have the privilege of being ready to fight for our king and his beloved wife, our Queen Louisa. We are ready, are we not, not only to fight when needed, but also to die for our nation? There is no greater honour for a soldier than to pay the ultimate price...'

Marija was half listening to one of the generals giving his speech but her eyes and thoughts were really on her brother, stationed now where she could clearly see him. And what a proud picture he made there with his horse. There he sat, head held high with the black, square-topped shako making him even taller. His light-blue jacket with its bright yellow buttons and red trimming fitted over him with no creasing or ruffling. The white bandolier and belt with its black scabbard gave the impression of holding everything in its correct place.

How proud she felt. Here was a soldier to behold!

He sat erect and his horse stood to attention, rigidly still, with the black leather bridle and saddle shining in the sunshine. The blue saddle cloth with the sabre scabbard dangling across it combined with the rider to create a dashing image for young Marija. It was an image of her brother who would soon be riding off to fight for his king and queen and country.

The speeches concluded and the soldiers cheered, obeying a trumpet call. Then they retreated, being dismissed from their parade. But no, not all retreated. Two rows of recruits lined up at the far end of the parade ground. Another blast of trumpets and forty sabres were unsheathed and held high. Another brass blast and with deafening shouts, the dragoons, on their snorting steeds with pounding hooves, charged down the parade ground. Metres from the dais they halted and with their standard bearer leading the way they left the area in three columns.

'Wow! That was something, wasn't it, Herr Schulte?' Marija turned as she asked the question. She looked around but he was nowhere to be seen.

'Papa, where is Herr Schulte?'

'He left a little while ago. He told me he had some important business to deal with at his timber yard,' her father replied. 'He said also that Manfred would take us back to his house when we are finished here.'

CHAPTER XII

Business in Tilsit

Hermann Schulte had left the military parade as it was nearing its climax. He felt the excitement, almost anxiety, of the crowd as he made his way towards the exit area. The galloping charge, here presented as a friendly display, was so real and frightening one could only imagine the terror it would evoke if approaching in anger on a battlefield. He himself, was very impressed by what he had seen. *Yes,* he thought, *we certainly have the manpower. Let's hope we have the leadership that will make full and good use of enthusiasm like I have just witnessed.*

He left the arena, but as he was walking along his mind

dwelt on that mock charge. So well executed he had to agree, however he was experienced enough to realise that what was enacted pictured only half of reality. In battle the brave dragoons would be galloping towards a line of enemy equally trained and equally intent on victory and protecting their own lives at the expense of the enemy. Or they would be charging into a barrage of deadly bullets with luck their only defence. War is not a game, not a parade.

His thoughts changed when he reached the river, the Memel, as it was slowly flowing along. The green fields across the brown water spoke of peace and tranquility, not of disruption and turmoil. He could see a farmer ploughing his field; a dairy maid driving her two cows home from their pastures; a farm wagon being pulled by its two plodding horses; scenes that could be witnessed most days in the village he now called home. He stood and briefly enjoyed this rural landscape but his mind could not stay on that other side of the river.

He realised that he had to move on, for other matters, different matters, awaited his attention. The river traffic of boats and rafts, the financial stresses of business and trade, represented another side of his life beside the Memel and Schulte was very much involved with this. He turned and walked briskly towards his arranged meeting.

Tilsit's river wharves were located just downstream from the city centre. Here a jumble of factories and warehouses benefitted from the transport available on the river. For generations the Schulte family had been an integral part of the industrial scene here. Hermann was now owner of a large timber mill next to the river. The main source of his logs was many kilometres upstream in Polish and Russian areas. Here the trees were felled and trimmed, the logs joined together to form rafts and then floated downstream. Teams of Jewish men lived on the rafts as they controlled their progress to the mill.

Hermann arrived to see noisy activity on the riverbank. The logs from raft, which had recently arrived, were being dragged into storage areas on dry land. The team who had arrived with the raft was easily recognized. These men were sitting under a tree in their long black shirts and unkempt beards, lustily singing Yiddish songs. In between verses, their throats having been lubricated by the contents of a dark green bottle, they shouted unneeded but friendly instructions to the mill workers.

Hermann waved and walked up to them.

'Hello, Boss,' they greeted him cheerfully.

'Gooday to all of you, you bearded rogues. What's new on the river?'

'A lot of Russian soldiers moving backwards and forwards. They're an unruly mob, they are. Must be still fighting in Poland somewhere. They'll never beat the French.'

'No trouble going back last time?' asked Hermann, not wanting to get involved in criticizing Russian soldiers.

'No, none at all. Everything went as planned. Anything to take back this time?'

'I'll let you know as soon as possible. And not too much slivovitz and vodka in the meantime,' said Herr Schulte with a smile which was greeted with loud laughter.

'Don't you worry, Boss. You know us.'

'There is something,' another rafter said.

'Yes?' and Hermann frowned.

'We got a few extra logs for you this time. We saw them floating along so we rescued them for you. Good ones too.'

'I'll have a look at them and see if they are worth anything. And check if they have already been branded.'

'We had a good look at them, Herr Schulte, and reckon you would be happy to give us, say, one half of what the others cost.'

'Or even more,' another one of the rafters suggested.

'Did you now? You will be wanting a job buying logs for me soon. I'll see you later tonight and we will work something out. I have a meeting now so I will have to go.'

'Good day, Herr Schulte,' they all replied and each shook hands with him as he left.

The atmosphere in the meeting room overlooking the timber yard was not as jovial as that outside with the workers and rafters. The topic being discussed had the full attention of the three men present and it was of a very serious nature.

'Spies, you say,' exclaimed Hermann looking very concerned.

'We cannot be sure, that's true; but we, and you especially, cannot allow anyone to know what is happening.'

'You're right, Reinhardt. We will have to assume that they are spies working for the French authorities searching out where smuggling is happening. The question is, do they know specifically what I have been doing or are they only looking generally in this area?'

'That's hard to say, Hermann,' observed the third man. 'We can assume that they are not stupid. It is easy to see that if goods are coming to Königsberg from England, one route to Russia would be through here and then up the Memel. They probably don't know that you are involved, but simply that someone here is. They seem to be interested in what is happening along the river front and not watching only your yard.'

'It's a worry, August, and sooner or later they will find out if I am not very careful. Someone could say something by mistake.'

'Yes, that has me very concerned for you. Can you trust those of your workers who are aware of the smuggled goods coming into the warehouse? And what about that group of Yiddish fellows who take the stuff up the river for you? Can they be trusted?' asked a concerned August, a lifelong friend of Hermann's.

'My workers who know anything about what is happening are all Prussians, very patriotic, and I would trust them with my life. That Jewish group? I pay them very well and they would probably do the right thing by me; but who knows? If more money was involved, any one of them could give me away.'

'So, what is to be done?' Reinhardt wanted to know.

'This is what I think,' suggested August. 'From now, stop all the goods coming through Tilsit. If you have anything in your warehouses, Hermann, leave it there and make sure that it is well hidden. I will arrange that nothing more comes to us from Königsberg.'

'I think we can be agreed on that. Also, we do nothing about those two who you are worried about. If we were to have a couple of our Russian friends take care of them, it would only arouse suspicion, and there would soon be others here asking questions even harder to answer. The French would realise that something is going on here.'

'Another thing, Hermann,' began Reinhardt, 'are you having any success in finding another route for our smuggled goods up where you are? Any ideas yet?'

'Yes,' continued August, 'it's pretty isolated where you live and I'm sure the farmers there would be no friends of Napoleon.'

'I've been treading slowly,' replied Hermann. 'It took me quite a while to be accepted in the village, for they don't like outsiders. However, I do have a route worked out and I'm now regarded as one of the locals. Perhaps not as one of the real locals but certainly more accepted than before. One of the boys from the village has just become a trained dragoon in the regiment here in Tilsit. I actually brought the family down to see the ceremony. I've just come from it myself.'

'They see themselves as part of Prussia, then?'

'Yes, indeed. Then there's an old fellow up there who used to be in Frederick the Great's army. He's a patriotic Prussian, if ever there was one, and he can hardly speak any German. I will start putting out some feelers and am sure that I will soon have something operating there.'

'Bring the stuff down from the port of Memel. Is that your plan?' asked August.

'No, that would be too obvious. I was thinking of bringing it in through a small fishing village called Nidden, on the Haff, and then across the lagoon to our village. From there across the border to Russia. The local farmers are struggling throughout the whole region and would welcome some extra money.'

'That sounds good' said August, 'and Reinhardt and I will watch those two spy suspects and find out who they really are.'

'I shall be taking the Zukas family back to Kinischken tomorrow. They are the ones I brought down to see their son's parade. When the occasion arises I will speak to Antanas, that's the husband, about the possibility of a smuggling route up there. Without giving too much away, that is.'

'Only if you think it's safe.'

'Don't worry. If something important comes up here in town you can let Manfred know at my house. He and his wife are certainly to be trusted, as you know. Now I will go and speak to my Jewish friends. They can still pick up the horses at Mt Romulus but will probably be a little disappointed not to be taking a few loads of goods back. They have come to depend on that extra money. But I will give them a good price for some logs they had with them this time which they said they found. Probably stole them if the truth be known. That should help to keep them happy.'

'Good-bye, my friend. Keep safe,' said both Reinhardt and August as they shook hands with Hermann.

C H A P T E R   X I I I

Terror

Peace had returned to the villages around Austerlitz. No longer were canon booming from the Pratzen Heights as they did on that cold, foggy December morning last year. Trampled fields were now the only reminder of charging cavalry. The luckless bodies of the dead — French, Austrian, Russian — had been buried. The armies had moved on. The farmers had returned to assess the damage and to piece together their livelihood. Their normal boisterous Christmas celebrations had been very subdued in that year of 1804, but they were very resilient. They must look to the future, hoping that their turn of suffering the presence of fighting armies was completed.

The Battle of Austerlitz had been fought and won; won by Napoleon. He had achieved a major step in his plan to have the French empire dominate Europe. Not only in Crémieu, but throughout all of France, the news of this victory over the Russians and Austrians, had resulted in rejoicing and celebration.

The Battle of Austerlitz had been fought and lost, lost by the opponents of French domination. The loss had validated what had been of concern to the European leaders for the previous eighteen months. Ever since the popular (for most of the French people) proclamation of Napoleon as Emperor of France other nations became concerned. When the new, powerful emperor made it clear that his intention was to dominate Europe the concern turned to alarm and panic.

Diplomats and envoys, ministers and ambassadors, high functionaries and plenipotentiaries were constantly crisscrossing Europe working to avoid calamities and seeking solutions. Coalitions were established to combat Napoleon's intentions. But he was not to be restrained. Alliances collapsed, wars were declared, campaigns mounted and battles fought — won, lost, drawn — but Napoleon moved on. By defeating the immediate opposition at Austerlitz he could dictate the terms of all discussions. He was the Grand Master presiding over the checkerboard of Europe. Detachments of his army were scattered across the continent like pieces on a chess board.

Europe was no longer strong enough to punish any bloody deed instigated by Napoleon and carried out by his loyal army.

No matter which individual ruler might cry out against the injustices carried out by the French in their lands, little could be done. The defeated simmered and plotted, but few voices were raised.

Were a rebellious voice to gain attention and as a hero, raise a nationalistic group which denounced the injustices taking place, and were he in a mini uprising to gain some success against a small French outpost, a larger, more powerful, French detachment would soon arrive and the dissenters put to the sword. Rulers of smaller principalities as well as kings of larger countries, soon learnt that Napoleon would trample on those who did not join him.

It was with impunity that he caused the breakup of the Holy Roman Empire, an institution which had brought some unity to Europe for a thousand years. Many of the previous members of that organisation were forced to join the Federation of the Rhine — a group of vassal states set up under the control of France — a right bank, German speaking, extension of the French Empire. Previous independent principalities such as Bavaria, Baden and Wurttemberg came under his control. To further his grip over regions, in a flurry of grand scale nepotism, he made family members, his generals and ministers, kings and dukes of strategic regions. His brothers became kings. He created duchies for his friends to wear ducal crowns.

Most in France gloated and celebrated. Most outside of France simmered.

French armies continued to be stationed in lands east of the French border ensuring that the authorities there were well aware of their responsibilities to the emperor and were carrying them out as demanded. A constant stream of new recruits required to bring the various sections of the army back to its desired strength kept arriving from the homeland. Most of these were young men conscripted under the terms of the *levée en masse*. Bernard Natalier was one of these new recruits and was attached to a cuirassier company in the Kingdom of Wurttemberg near the Swiss border. Here he was sent to carry out his training.

'Do we really receive training here?' he asked another recruit who had arrived at the company headquarters a week before he did.

His friend smiled. 'Training? Training here is trying to keep up with what the other company members are doing.'

'Is that all?'

'Is that all! My friend, surviving is the first thing you need worry about.'

'It can't be so bad. Don't the other soldiers help?'

His friend, Pierre, smiled again and shook his head. 'They are the main trouble. Before they came down to fight at Austerlitz they were in a camp at Boulogne, up on the English Channel. They were preparing to invade England but the English navy defeated us in a naval battle and so we were not able to cross the channel to England. Most of those soldiers came down here to fight the Austrians and Russians. They are tough, professional soldiers who regard us recruits as weaklings. They make life hard for us.'

Bernard seemed a little shocked. 'But what about the officers? What do they do?' he asked.

'They let things work out by themselves. They do show up from time to time but spend most of their time drinking and gambling. They have their own living quarters and we only see them when something important is happening.'

'So what will happen to me?'

'Yes, you, the newcomer. Be prepared for some tough initiations and a lot of dirty work at the beginning. I have been here in the camp for a little over a week and there have probably been ten times when I was going to run away.'

'But you haven't?'

'No, where would I go? They would probably track me down and I would end up in prison. Oh! And how well do you ride a horse?' Pierre wanted to know.

'How well? I have been around horses all my life, so I think I ride fairly well.'

'Can I give you a word of advice?'

'Yes, sure,' Bernard replied.

'Don't make it known that you can do something well, whatever it might be. That gives the old soldiers ammunition to make things hard for you.'

'Thank you, Pierre. I think I understand what you are trying to tell me. I hope I will be able to repay you sometime.'

And so began for Bernard a very tiring and difficult time. As with the other recruits, he was given the dirty jobs to do. He was punished for not knowing things he was never told about. He was abused for not being competent at doing tasks which had taken experienced soldiers years to perfect. He was forced to perform pointless tasks. He dared not offer an opinion. Many times in the weeks that followed he thought of absconding and making his way to Switzerland.

His thoughts often turned to Nicolas Bacot whom his mother had helped to flee to Switzerland. Did he ever arrive at that Swiss village safely? He had no idea. He would probably never know until he was given leave to travel back home to see his family and friends in Crémieu. But even then, he imagined that those who might know were not likely to betray his whereabouts.

It was the horse that convinced him not to become a deserter.

Pierre had warned him that he would be issued with a horse which had a reputation for being uncontrollable, wild and dangerous. It was even suggested that this horse, as well as some others, was kept solely to show newcomers to the company that they had much to learn about horses. This powerful black gelding with a white flash on its forehead would be issued to a newly-arrived soldier by officers who knew that he would have little hope of ever riding, let alone ever taming it.

They would pay special attention to those who indicated that they had good experience with horses. Bernard, when asked, played down his experience saying that he had ridden a tired old hack on his father's farm where he worked. He made no mention of the fact that he was known throughout the Crémieu region for his ability to tame and ride difficult horses.

When the day arrived for him to be issued with his horse, and it was the black gelding, he approached it knowing its reputation, but also having a good idea of how he would approach it. From what Pierre had told him it seemed clear that the horse had been badly treated, had resisted previous, inept attempts to control it, and had a dislike, even fear, of people. It had been conditioned to be a challenge to anyone who attempted to ride it.

Bernard was not surprised then to see many on-lookers when he was first introduced to the black terror. Officers who very seldom made appearance, hardened soldiers who enjoyed tormenting new recruits, they were all there. He could see immediately by the tension in the horse's stance, by its blazing eyes and its snorting nostrils and by the tossing of its head, that he would need to approach carefully.

'Come on soldier, you're a cuirassier now. Show us how you can ride.'

The horse was tied to a post on the edge of the training ground. Bernard slowly approached it. The Terror, as it was generally called, was angrily tossing its head up straining on the bridle reins tied to the post, probably anticipating some sort of human assault.

He stopped four metres in front of the horse and remained perfectly still, looking, hoping to catch the other's eye. Eventually their eyes met and for a few moments were locked. Then with a snort the black head was jerked aloft and contact lost.

Bernard turned and took a couple of steps away from the horse, then turned and walked back, stopping before it, a little closer than before. Again their eyes locked, for slightly longer this time, but again the trembling gelding broke contact with a fling of its head and even stamped the ground with its forelegs. Bernard turned again and retreated temporarily before repeating his approach.

He made a couple more approaches but the audience was becoming restless. This was not what they had come to see. They began shouting abuse at Bernard who could see that the noise was further upsetting the horse.

'Ride the thing instead of making bloody eyes at it!'

'You want to be a cuirassier, then show some guts and get on the beast!'

'Show the bugger who's boss!'

'We only want men in this company!'

Bernard turned and walked up to the company commander who had taken time to be present. He saluted.

'Yes, Cuirassier?'

'Sir, all the noise and shouting is upsetting the horse.'

'The battlefield is a noisy place, lad.'

'Yes, Sir, I could imagine that; but this is a training ground and not a battlefield.'

'Don't be insolent, soldier!'

'I do not mean to be, Sir. The horse is nervous and untrusting. And he is scared to look me in the eye. He is reacting to previous mistreatment. He is a very strong beast and I would have no hope of controlling him by force. I need time to gain his trust. When we trust one another, he will allow me to ride on him and I will need no cruel measures to have him accept me as his master. But this will take some time.'

'You speak with confidence, soldier. What is your name?'

'Bernard Natalier, Sir.'

'Well, Cuirassier Natalier, let's see what you can do with our black terror.'

'Thank you, Sir.' Bernard saluted and moved away making his way back to the horse.

In the meantime, the captain had called up one of the sergeants, the one who was leading the abusive chorus, told him to clear the area of spectators. Bernard was left alone with the horse.

Within a week he felt comfortable riding his new "Terror" as he now called his companion. He would speak the name quietly and with affection so that the horse, unaware of the literal meaning of the word, would react with pleasure when hearing it from Bernard.

Bernard received some begrudging respect from many, but not all, of the company when they saw the relationship which had developed between the new recruit and the untamed terror. Terror, on his part, when approached by unwelcome persons, would make it known that his affection belonged to Bernard alone.

However, he was still recruit who was constantly being reminded of his position in the troop.

CHAPTER XIV

Ready for War

The worst days of the Baltic winter were over for another year and the people of Kinischken were starting to spend more hours out of doors. The nights were still cold — often below zero — but the returning sun, clouds permitting, was able to supply some warmth. Although not enough to unfreeze the ponds and completely clear the landscape of snow drifts, its welcome warmth could be felt on the faces and arms of those who ventured outside. It was approaching that time of year when people would make a special effort to spend time out with nature simply for the pleasure it provided.

The farmers of the village had jobs outside of the house which entailed confronting the coldest of winter days but once these necessary tasks were completed they would choose to return to the warmth of the inside fire. They could see no purpose in staying out in the freezing temperatures longer than necessary. They were aware that cold can kill. It forced them to take refuge inside the wooden walls of their houses. These were hardy folk but the weather regulated many of their activities.

On this April day in 1806, Hermann Schulte, neighbour Antanas Zukas and his son, Vadimas, chose to stay talking in the sun in front of Hermann's house. Hermann and Antanas had become firm friends after the Schulte family had demonstrated its commitment to the village and had not been aloof and distant as many suspected it would be. They would often be seen together.

Since becoming a fully trained member of the dragoon company stationed in Tilsit, Vadimas spent little time in his home village. He lived in the cavalry barracks in the town. In winter, the members of the units stationed there were allowed more leave than during the warm summer months and Vadimas took advantage of these opportunities to return home. He was a dedicated dragoon and enjoyed military life but was always glad to be back home with his family and living a less regimented life.

Everyone was interested in his new life as a soldier and was always eager to include him in their conversations. Being a dragoon, dressed in an attractive uniform and riding a well-groomed horse with shining brass and polished leather added a touch of glamour to his presence. All wanted to share in this.

The talk among the three men on this day revolved around village concerns, but with Vadimas present it unsurprisingly turned to military matters. Once Vadimas had satisfied their curiosity and interest about how he filled his day and how he personally was enjoying the discipline of army life, the topics broadened to more general military and political questions.

Napoleon's success against the Austrians and Russians at Austerlitz in December a few years before still dominated most discussions and had people shaking their heads in disbelief.

Hermann was shaking his head. 'It appears that no one can defeat that Frenchman,' he commented.

'That seems to be the case, Herr Schulte,' replied Vadimas, 'and you must realise too that not only the Austrian army was there at Austerlitz, but the Russians as well.'

'Yes, I realise that. Napoleon scattered all the opposition and now he can do as he pleases,' commented Hermann.

'Well, yes,' said Vadimas, 'the Austrians signed a peace agreement so they are unable to do anything. They've lost their power and are completely humiliated. But the Russians have not given in. Their army escaped capture and moved to the east and is still holding the French off, waiting for reinforcements to arrive from their homeland. And don't forget us Prussians.'

'Us Prussians?'

'Yes, us Prussians. Don't forget that we have a strong army

just waiting to fight against the French. They might be in for a surprise.'

'Oh,' remarked Ponas Zukas, 'and what makes you say that? If we have such a strong army why haven't we taught that French fellow a thing or two already?'

'That's the big question being asked at the moment,' said Herr Schulte. 'When I was down in Tilsit last week, that's all everyone was talking about. Why don't we go to war against France? He's doing what he likes here in Europe, well away from France itself, and no one is doing anything about it. He's taking over so many German-speaking areas and setting them against us. He's even demanding that they provide soldiers to help fight his wars.'

'Well, if that is the case, why don't we declare war,' asked Antanas Zukas. 'I might be a Lithuanian, but I am a Prussian citizen and I care about my country.'

Before anyone could make further comment, they were interrupted by old Grandad Grigas accompanied by one of his grandchildren, Orlin. It was known by everyone in the village, and happily accepted, that the old fellow was always walking around hoping to meet someone who had the time to talk to him. He homed in on the trio in Hermann Schulte's front yard. On this occasion they were quite happy to have him join in their discussions, knowing that he would have an opinion, or two, on any topic relating to Prussia's military prowess.

After a round of greetings Grandad Grigas looked questioningly at each of the three and then asked, 'Well, what problems haven't you solved yet? Nothing private, I hope.'

The three looked at each other, knowing what the other was thinking. They smiled at this character, much loved by the whole village. They each saw before them not the slightly-stooping, eighty-something year old grandad, but a ramrod erect Grenadier Vladislava Grigas, proud soldier in Frederick the Great's Prussian army of the mid-1750s. The neatly trimmed brown moustache and beard of half a century ago had snowed over and their appearance suffered from a lack of attention. His hair also had thinned and turned white, but his military posture had remained — especially when speaking to friends.

His grey-blue eyes, ever alert, could sparkle with light-hearted frivolity but also turn dark and piercing when his feelings were aroused. Today they were clear and laughing no doubt from entertaining his grandson with humorous reminiscences. This could change, and probably would, when the topic of conversation was about Napoleon.

Antanas Zukas responded to the newcomer's question. 'You should know that nothing is private in Kinischken, Vlad. We were talking about Emperor Napoleon and wondering when someone is going to chase him and his armies back to France where they belong.'

'Napoleon!' and the old grenadier spat on the snow. 'He's lucky he wasn't born 50 years earlier or we would have already chased him back to that island where he came from.'

'Unfortunately, we are not able to turn back time Grandad,' replied Vadimas. 'What do you think we should be doing today? Most of us in the barracks feel that we should go to war.'

'Yeah, you young fellows are always a bit hot blooded. What do your officers think?'

'Most of them are keen to show Napoleon what we are made of. They say we have good generals who know something about war for they have been serving since their youth. Others, I fear, share the king's apprehension.'

'Our king is in a very difficult position,' began Hermann. 'He knows that there are many who want to go to war, but he really wants peace. Peace is a very precious thing and the country needs it for its prosperity. Wars only bring debt, suffering and death.'

'That's the trouble,' said Grandad Grigas, 'for we don't have a good leader. We don't have someone to whip up the enthusiasm like we did back in the 50s. Not like our king back then. Old Fritz, we used to call him. Now, that was a man who could stir you up. I still remember when we were having a hard time of it down at a place called Meissen. . . No, it wasn't there for we were fighting mainly French soldiers. There were Austrians at Meissen. It was probably at Rossbach. . . Yes, that's right. . . Rossbach. We had just fought off an attack and were resting and recovering, sort of licking our wounds, when Old Fritz rode up and shouted, "Come on you, bastards, let's get after them. Do you want to live forever?" So, tired as we were we got to our feet, loaded our muskets and chased them.'

Young Orlin was listening spellbound. 'Did you really, Grandad?' he asked with his eyes wide open.

'Sure did. We had a great victory that day. It ended up like shooting pigeons off a fence post.'

'But you're not really a good shot, are you, Grandad?'

'Not a good shot! What do you mean, my boy?'

'Don't you remember when we went to shoot some rabbits last year? You missed the rabbits and hit a stork instead.'

'Some things are best not remembered, Orlin,' replied the old grenadier as the others smiled, 'and they certainly should not be talked about.'

Hermann Schulte wanted to change the subject to avoid Orlin making any more embarrassing remarks, so he asked, 'What about Brunswick and Mollendorf? They're in charge of our army today. Do you remember them?'

'Yes, they were there in Frederick's army. Good soldiers, great leaders they were back then. But heavens above, they are as old as I am. They are too old to lead a campaign against Napoleon. Too old for any army work, I would think. At this stage they should be enjoying the comforts of life rather than putting up with life on the march. There's a story going around about poor old Mollendorf. One of his officers helped him on to the left-hand side of his horse, but he fell down the other side. Many see him as a bit of a joke.'

Vadimas tried to defend the reputation of his army. 'But we soldiers are young and strong. We've had a lot of training. And you should see us on parade. Everything is done exactly right.'

'Yes, Vadimas,' replied old Grigas, 'I'm sure you are a good dragoon and I know you ride a horse very well. But that's on the parade ground, showing off to your girlfriends and family. What would happen on the battlefield when you have a company of crazy French cuirassiers charging at you waving their swords and yelling their lungs out? Most of you would shit your pants, frightened as hell.'

'Were you ever frightened, Grandad? Did you ever shit your pants?' asked Orlin, smiling a little.

His grandad looked at him. 'There are things you shouldn't worry about at your age, boy. And don't let your mother hear you talking like that. But we had better keep moving or we'll get cold standing around doing nothing. And I don't want young Orlin here listening and picking up things he needn't know about from you fellows. Come on, young trooper, let's advance. Gooday to you, gentlemen.' And he took Orlin's hand and moved off down the road.

'That's Old Grigas for you,' said Antanas Zukas. 'He might exaggerate somewhat, but from reports he was a very good soldier. And he has a shrewd idea of how things stand at the present time. We might be a long way from Berlin but he does meet with some of his old comrades over in Heydekrug every now and then. They seem to know what is happening.'

'So right now,' concluded Hermann, 'it seems we must live in uncertainty. I know we, I mean Prussia, must do something about Napoleon and what he is doing to Europe, but who knows what we could do for the best. For your sake, Vadimas, I hope we don't go to war.'

CHAPTER XV

Battle of Auerstedt

The Saale River rises in a spring in the picturesque Fichtel Mountains of northern Bavaria and makes its way north until it combines its accumulated waters with the larger Elbe River. These then find their way to the North Sea passing the large port city of Hamburg on their way. In the middle reaches the lively, bubbly Saale winds its way through the undulating farmlands of Thuringia in southern Germany. No large cities here, but many smaller urban centres have grown upon its bank — Rudolstadt, Halle, Naumburg, Saarfeld and Jena.

Jena, with a population of around four thousand, was the

largest of these. It was one of the most important university towns of the late middle-ages, a town of learning, of philosophy and culture. Napoleon's presence here in the early nineteenth century added another chapter to its history — an uninvited one.

Some 25 kilometres downstream from Jena was the smaller town of Bad Kösen. Here a tributary stream joined the Saale from the left. Ten kilometres up the valley of this stream could be found the small village of Auerstedt. This area was a quiet farming region, with the farmers going about their every-day business without worrying too much about what might be happening in the outside world, in the larger cities which they seldom, if ever, visited.

The outside world, however, visited them. Around this short section of the river in the autumn of 1806, over two hundred thousand trained fighting men met in a bloody conflict. Prussia had declared war on France. Now in this area, 113,000 soldiers of the Kingdom of Prussia had assembled, determined to stop the advance of the 125,000 strong *Grand Armée* of Napoleon.

It was 4 am on Tuesday, 14th October 1806, and the predawn silence east of Bad Kösen was shattered by the shouting, moaning and complaining of members of the French Marshal Davout's III Corps. They were preparing, many unhappily, to march west to Apolda, and then further to Erfurt where it was thought the Prussian forces were gathering. The route chosen would take them up a small valley and through the village of Auerstedt. Preparations for breaking camp were somewhat impeded by a dense fog which blanketed the whole region. In spite of the inconvenience, 25,000 troops were soon heading west on the Bad Kösen-Auerstedt road with a cavalry screen leading the way.

Bernard Natalier's Cuirassier Company was part of the advanced guard. He and Pierre had become firm friends during the first week of his arrival at the training camp. Now they were riding side by side moving camp once again. So far on this, their first campaign they had spent many tired, anxious days but had never sighted the enemy. Would they, this time, when they arrived in Erfurt? Privately they told each other that they hoped not to have to draw blood with their swords, but as trained French cuirassiers they would do what they had to do.

Meanwhile the Duke of Brunswick's main Prussian force was encamped around Auerstedt and not at Erfurt. He also had received incorrect information. It suggested that Napoleon was in his vicinity with his main force. As Brunswick had not been able to join up with the balance of his Prussian troops camped somewhere to the south, he decided to play safe and not endanger his men who, he knew, were eager to confront Napoleon. He would move his forces away from immediate danger, first crossing the Saale River at Bad Kösen — the nearest bridge crossing — and then march north, thus avoiding a battle for which he was not ready.

And so it was that at 6 am on the very foggy morning of Tuesday, 14th October 1806, his columns, 60,000 fighting men, began moving east along the Auerstedt-Bad Kösen road. A company of Prussian dragoons, selected from Vadimas Zukas' proud Tilsit Regiment, was leading the way.

The Prussian dragoons rode slowly along in the fog, chatting quietly among themselves.

'I hope the captain knows where he is going.'

'Probably not, but at this pace we will become lost very slowly.'

'So who's the comedian? I have no idea where we are going.'

'And why did we have to start so early to get there?'

'I heard back up north.'

'Back north! Are the French somewhere up there?'

'Don't think so.'

'So why are we going north?'

'Brunswick doesn't want us to meet the French without the whole Prussian army. They would outnumber us without the others.'

'Does anyone know where the rest of our forces are?'

'Not that I know. Probably lost somewhere. Who needs them anyway? Aren't we ready to fight?'

'Someone heard that there were a few skirmishes to the south near Jena. We didn't fare so well. We had to withdraw.'

'What! Prussians withdrawing? Can't believe that. I can't wait to get a bit of French blood on my sword. If you are fighting for our queen, you do not withdraw.'

The soldiers kept on talking. Brunswick's Prussian troops continued to move east along the road.

At the same time a company of French cuirassiers was crossing the bridge over the Saale at Bad Kösen and following the road up a slight rise. Most riders were still unhappy.

'They are all mad. Why so early?'

'Did you see any lights burning in that town?'

'Lights? No. Why?'

'Because everyone was still wrapped up fast asleep. Like we should be. The peasants here have more sense than our brass.'

'Goethe lived here once.'

'Who's Goethe?'

'Why so early. And all this fog.'

'Maybe it will be clear at the top of this hill.'

'It probably was the captain's wife. I've seen her before.'

'No, I think it was someone filling in for her.'

'The captain was the one filling in, if you ask me.'

'Ha, ha, ha. . .'

'Keep the noise down up there, or it will be silent riding!'

'Are we waking the birds?'

'Are the others following?'

'Who would know? I assume the whole corps has moved out.'

Bernard and Pierre contributed little to the general conversation. At quiet times like this Bernard's thoughts would turn to Michelle and what she might be doing back home in Crémieu. He slouched in the saddle with the reins hanging loosely to the side. His horse, Terror, followed the others along in the fog.

The column of French cuirassiers kept moving west along the road.

The morning continued to be foggy and dark, and the Prussian dragoons were allowing their mounts to pick their own way along the road. The horses' senses were probably more acute than their riders'.

'I'll tell you who must be lost.'

'Yeah, who?'

'The food wagons. There was nothing this morning. I'll be eating my horse if this keeps up.'

'You know what some of the old regulars say?'

'No, tell me.'

'They say it's a soldier's own fault if he wants for anything in enemy territory.'

'That's great, but we are not in enemy territory. These are Prussian lands. We can't force these poor beggars to hand over all they've got.'

'Let's wait until we are in France and see then if that works. But why weren't the food wagons there?'

'Too early.'

'Too early to be hungry? You are joking, yes? I've nothing left in my bag.'

'Freddy shared the last of his with us. Now we can all go hungry together.'

'Maybe that's why we are going home. Get some home cooking.'

'Going home. Who told you that?'

'Where is your home, Vadimas? Tilsit?'

'No, a little village just north of Tilsit. Kinischken.'

'Kin. . .Kin what? You Litts have strange names for places.'

'Is that some light I can see starting there in the east. When is the sun to come up? I'm sure it's a little brighter there.'

'You're dreaming. Probably thinking of that Fräulein you had yesterday. Opened your eyes, did she?'

'Probably not the only thing she opened.'

'Ha, ha, ha, . . .'

'Keep it down! You will wake Napoleon's army up.'

The Prussians kept riding east along the road.

The French cuirassier company had settled into the boredom of riding to the next destination. The fog further dulled their awareness. The horses kept them moving. Bernard and Pierre continued riding with their own private thoughts. They realised that their first encounter with the enemy could happen in the next few days. They were riding towards the engagement somewhere near Erfurt if rumours were to be believed. They were quiet. Others kept up a continuous chatter.

'That has to be a building. Are we coming to somewhere?'

'Probably, but where? This can't be Apolda.'

'Can't be where?'

'Apolda.'

'Never heard of it. What's at Apolda? Anyone else ever heard of Apolda?'

'No, I don't know what it is. A town probably. I thought I heard the captain say that we were headed there. Say, there's more buildings.'

'Is the fog lifting?'

'Wooh! Steady on, you silly bugger. What's wrong with you? Bloody horse!'

'Mine woke up too. Can they see something we can't?'

'Probably sense some other horses in their stalls here in the village.'

'It seems to be getting a bit brighter. Hey, is that a light there?

Someone here can't sleep.'

'What about your Terror, Bernard? Did he smell anything? You are always saying how great he is. How's his nose?'

On hearing his name, Bernard awoke from his daydreaming. He immediately noticed a change in his horse's relaxed movements. 'He is tense. I can feel it. He doesn't like the fog, but I'm sure there is something else too.'

They passed by the village, barely discernible, still heading towards Auerstedt.

The Prussians had also settled into the tedium of long marches, with the fog adding an element of nescience.

'When will this God-cursed fog lift so that we can see where we're going? Is that a brightening there in the east?'

'Is that really the east?'

'Who knows? What the. . .? What's got into you, you silly beast?'

'What are you on about?'

'It's my horse. Something's gotten into him.'

'That's funny now that you mention it. Mine's acting strange too. Restless. Jerking his head up. Settle down you crazy animal. Go back to sleep.'

'Oh! Look! Look!'

'Look where?'

'There ahead. Can't you see? There are horses and riders up ahead! Sergeant, see up there ahead? Is that the enemy?'

'Enemy! Who? Good God, they're French cuirassiers. Bugle Boy! Where the hell is he? Bugle Boy!'

'What's going on? Why the bugle? Attack?'

'Yes, attack. The French cavalry is ahead coming towards us.'

The bugle sounded "Charge". The company quickly awoke from its daydreaming. With swords drawn and held high, a wave of blue dragoons galloped through the fog towards their sudden enemies. Months of training would now be put to the test. This was no display on the parade ground. For the first time, Vadimas Zukas and his charger would be tested against a real enemy.

Alarm swept through the unsuspecting French ranks as they heard the muted notes of the bugle and saw waves of Prussian dragoons emerging from the fog in front of them. The noise of the oncoming shouting, amplified by the fog, added another element of terror as they realised that some, or many of them would soon be slashed, bleeding or dying. Individual soldiers thought — many correctly — that this would be the end.

Should they flee? Unthinkable.

Although taken unawares, the French quickly organized their defence to combat the attacking cavalry; but they were unable to overcome that initial disadvantage. They suffered heavy casualties and were forced to withdraw, but not before leaving many blue-coated dragoons lying dead or wounded.

The battle had begun.

General Gudin's 3rd Infantry Division was following the French advance cavalry and when he realised what was happening, he immediately ordered his troops to form square in case the enemy could not be stopped by the cuirassiers and overrun his lines. His assumption proved correct. Elated by their initial success with the French horsemen scattered and bleeding, the Prussians continued to advance eastwards but were met by Gudin's troops in a tight defensive position. They rained accurate rifle fire on the attacking dragoons who were unable to break through. After their first success they were forced to retreat.

Not knowing the strength of the Prussian force they had run into, Marshal Davout nevertheless ordered Gudin to advance.

At this time the fog began to lift and each army saw the opposition aligned before it: the massed colours of the uniforms, the shining canon, the sparkling brasses, all lit by the emerging autumn sun. Two huge armies faced one another. This was a spectacle to behold but one that caused the opposing generals to wonder in amazement. How could this be? Neither should be there. The Duke of Brunswick's Prussian forces were to head north after crossing the Saale River avoiding enemy contact. Marshal Davout's troops were moving to join up with Napoleon's main force and were not anticipating meeting the enemy.

But they had met; met on the Auerstedt-Bad Kösen road. One was marching east and the other moving west.

The battle, unexpected as it was, could not now be avoided. The first shots had been fired. The first blood had been drawn. Victory awaited one and defeat the other.

Death awaited many.

Redbeard

They heard the bugle. "Stand by horse!" had been sounded. The tired members of the French cuirassier company responded. Not as quickly as their captain would have liked, judging by his angry comments, but they did respond. Members of Napoleon's army were given no option but to respond. Were they preparing for their third charge since the battle commenced? This was a question in many cuirassiers' mind.

'Oh, not again!' one cavalryman said to his comrade Bernard Natalier. 'How many of us are to be slaughtered? How many

Prussians must die? Do they know what they are doing up there?'

Bernard offered no reply. He stood there lost in his own thoughts. He was too tired to speak. It was far easier to think than to speak. His mind was locked in the immediate past.

In battle, man to man, my sword would strike. It did. It struck in defence rather than in anger, for I feel no anger towards those who ride against me. They have been made my enemies by those in power. They have charged at me, voices shouting, swords flashing, hooves thundering, intent on my destruction. By the grace of God, I have survived and am able to continue in the fight, but for how long?

The swords merely grazed me. The bullets whined past; unlike poor Pierre struck down while riding by my side by a bullet which could have met me rather than him. So, this is battle. I really had no idea. So, this is the glory of France. Why should the glory of my homeland lie only in the defeat of neighbouring countries? Can glory only be obtained at the expense of others, by slashing the life out of others? Must there be battlefields that run red with blood?

And what is this glory? What is the glory of France to me? I am but a poor peasant from a vineyard. The soil is important. The sunshine and rain are important. I can produce bottles of fine wine with hard work and God's blessing. What do I owe to Napoleon for these? To Emperor Napoleon? He may cause empires to fall, but not the rain.

How will the defeat of the Prussian army here so far from my homeland, here in foreign lands, add to the enjoyment of my life back in Crémieu? Will it help my friends and neighbours there? Michelle?

Will the death of one opponent make any difference? Ten maybe? Even a hundred?

But I am in the French army and orders are orders. I am now to gallop into the forest and sweep it clear of the enemy; chase them away, slash them adrift from this life. I am to do this knowing that at any time the lead from a pistol or musket could be waiting for me to cross its path. Then I too, like my dear friend, Pierre, like many of my other comrades, like uncounted foes, will fall bleeding from Terror.'

But the waiting was over. The bugle sounded once again. "Mount. Forward at a trot". Forward into these foreign forests.

The depleted company of French cuirassiers advanced not knowing what deadly surprises awaited them there among the oaks, beeches and elms already dripping with blood.

Among the scattered trees ahead a wounded Prussian dragoon was pinned beneath his dying horse. His cornflower-blue tunic was stained with the dirt and blood of battle. His shako no longer covered the long ginger-red hair. It lay there in the forest, battered beneath the thorns of a briar bush, no longer fixed on a proud dragoon, no longer strapped tightly around the ragged beard.

The drooped head lifted at the approach of the enemy's horse. The dragoon saw a French cavalryman whose dark brown eyes, like those of an approaching storm, peered into the deep blue of his own. Were they flashing anger? Were they seeking a victim on whom to quench a desire for revenge? Revenge for a comrade recently taken by a cannonball? His own held no anger, no sign of defeat, no plea for mercy, certainly no joy, but sadness and resignation. He merely was a wounded soldier, a dragoon indeed, but accepting the fate that had fallen on so many of his companions who had charged into the face of the enemy that morning.

Now his time was approaching. A fleeting glimpse of his wooden home in Kinischken, of his father, mother and sister laughing around a table flashed before his eyes.

As Bernard approached, sword held high in his right hand, the fallen soldier lifted his head higher. But the sword did not fall on its victim. Rather, it was slowly lowered as the Frenchman reined his horse to stop a few metres in front of the blue dragoon.

Was this the enemy?

This red-bearded warrior was sitting with his horse's head resting on his lap. The horse was stretched out to his left, half hidden by the spindly branches of the forest's undergrowth. It also had raised its head at the approach of another warhorse and had made a feeble attempt to get to its feet; but in vain. It struggled. Two legs waved weakly, pawing at the ground, while the other two lay pinned beneath the wounded body. The blood oozing from its chest could not hide the shining black coat of this fighting thoroughbred. No resignation was seen in his eyes. They were ablaze with anger and frustration, determined to fight on despite its weakening body.

Bernard looked down at the wounded soldier comforting his dying charger.

So, this is the enemy!

With a flick of his wrist, he raised his sword to a near vertical position. It flashed in a ray of sunshine that had penetrated the green canopy. He raised his arm and then slowly lowered the weapon towards the earth as a salute to this man and his horse.

Then he turned and rode away. 'They have trained me to be a soldier,' he muttered to himself, 'but I am not a murderer.'

He had not gone five metres when behind him he heard the click of a weapon being made ready to shoot. 'Dear Lord!' flashed through his mind. Then the loud crack of the pistol being fired.

But he felt no pain; no bullet striking him. He waited a second before turning around. The pistol was pointing to a bloody hole in the horse's head, now motionless beside its fallen master.

He did not understand the words spoken by the man. He did not see the tears in his eyes. He could not feel the sorrow in his heart. He looked and murmured, 'God protect you, Redbeard!'

Then there was silence but for a moment. The silence was broken by shouting and shooting in the distance. He turned his horse and rode on.

The bleary, tortured eyes of the defeated dragoon looked at the body of his beloved horse quivering in its death throes. He looked up and away and saw the form of the retreating Frenchman. Pain swept up his left side and he slumped over the horse's head and lay still.

CHAPTER XVII

The Taste of Victory

The bugle call of victory for the French sounded throughout the battlefield near Auerstedt. The armies of Napoleon had once again emerged victorious at the end of a bloody day. His generals had won the day.

On that early morning with the sun barely penetrating the autumn fog, the stage was set for the two opposing commanders and their generals to assess the situation and quickly develop a plan of action. What followed was eight hours of carnage in which the battle tactics of the French high command proved superior to that of their, sometimes hesitant, opponents. The startling result was that Davout's French force, some 26,000 strong, routed Brunswick's 60,000 Prussians.

The Duke of Brunswick was mortally wounded early in the clash and King Frederick William himself took control after the commander's demise. But he was not up to the task required of him in this dire situation and was soon fleeing the battlefield with his defeated, disorganized army.

To add further to Prussia's humiliation, while the battle near Auerstedt was raging, the second main Prussian force had encountered Napoleon, 20 kilometres to the south at Jena. Here also the French won an overwhelming victory. Confusion reigned as remnants of the once proud and powerful Prussian army fled their victors.

The fragmented force became scattered throughout the area with individual units seeking safety and fleeing the area to evade the pursuing French.

At the end of the day Bernard's cuirassier company had assembled on a hill overlooking the town of Auerstedt. They were to bivouac overnight and be ready to advance through the village where a few days ago the Duke of Brunswick had established his headquarters. Now French campfires flickered, each surrounded by a small group of very weary men.

The lucky ones were finishing the rations that they had saved from the day before. Others were complaining that food supplies had not arrived. Spirits were varied. There were those who were highly elated because of their victory in battle. Others were lamenting the loss of a dear comrade.

'Who guides the bullets?' asked Bernard of his small group

whose faces were dully lit by flames. 'The bullets were flying towards us and we kept charging. Was each of us wondering, like I was: Is there a bullet meant for me?'

'Be thankful that today one did not hit you, Bernard.'

'I am thankful for me, but sad for all those who were not so lucky.'

'Your mate, Pierre, was wounded, wasn't he? Do you know how he is?'

'I have no idea. He was alive when the medical team took him away to the field hospital. I don't even know where that is. We were charging side by side. He was hit and I wasn't.'

'Yes, it's a complete lottery. We've now had the experience of charging into the enemy lines with bullets, swords, lances, cannonballs waiting for us. What can you really do to avoid being hit?' asked another novice soldier.

Bernard shook his head. 'What can you do indeed? Nothing. You can't dodge a bullet or cannonball which has you name on it. A sword or a lance? Yes, you can weave and dodge and use you own weapon to fend off an attack. Here training is very important. And I see now, more clearly than before, that in battle you must fight or be killed.'

'And did you get blood on your sword today, Bernard? Did you strike one of those Prussian pigs?'

'Blood? Yes, my sword had blood on it. Was it the enemy's? Yes, it was. I slashed at Prussian uniforms. I defended myself from Prussian swords and lances. Luckily, I survived, but I did not enjoy it.'

'You are a recruit, aren't you? This must have been your first real battle?' someone asked.

'Yes, it was. And all the training we had did not prepare me for it. Oh, my God, I shall never forget it; the noise, the guns firing and cannons booming, the shouting and screaming, the clashing of swords, neighing of horses, the praying and cursing, the whole field of broken, bloody flesh. It was all too much for me. I hope to God that I shall never have to experience something like that again.'

'We all hope that, Comrade, but believe me we shall experience more battles. We are Frenchmen, French soldiers, far from home in another country. We are here in Prussia and the Prussians do not love us. They will fight again.'

A couple of veterans, professional soldiers for a number of years nodded in agreement. They also had a fair idea what the future would bring. The battle here at Auerstedt had been won. They would learn on the morrow that Napoleon's forces a little to the south, at Jena, had also tasted victory. These battles had been won but the war would continue.

Sleep that evening did not come easily to Bernard. Having to use the saddle cloth as a mattress and his saddle as a pillow did nothing to help him fall asleep. These however were not the only disturbing factors. The camp became quiet it is true, but the fires kept burning and these created shadows dancing on the nearby trees. He could see charging horses, raised muskets, headless bodies and a bodiless head hovering above him. He sat up and screamed. 'Oh, why? Why? Why am I here and not back home with my vineyards, with family and with Michelle? Why must this be happening?'

Then he remembered the red-headed dragoon sitting nursing the head of his wounded horse in his arms and lap. Would he survive? His act of mercy towards this helpless soldier did lessen somewhat the remorse he was feeling for the hurt and injury he had inflicted on others. He murmured once again, 'God protect you, Redbeard.'

The faint moonlight pushing down through the branches created silhouettes, not of vineyards and carefree teenagers, but of cannon and infantrymen. Visions of the actual battlefield returned and these overwhelmed Bernard's attempt at picturing more pleasant occasions. Weariness finally prevailed. His body, exhausted from the day's exertions, drifted into a fitful sleep.

Time spent with his horse next morning helped Bernard recover somewhat from the horrors of the previous day. The months spent with the same horse had cemented a relationship between Bernard and the mount. Over that time both horse and rider had created a bond of trust, reliance and friendship.

The relationship had not always been harmonious. It had started off on very shaky ground. After months of concerted effort by the rider and often stubborn resistance by the horse a mutual respect grew and a close friendship developed. Horse and rider had become a unit and others in the company could see the strong bond which existed and openly admired what Bernard had achieved.

Comments abounded: "They can read each other's minds."

"He has that dangerous beast eating out of his hand."

"Stay clear of Bernard's horse if you know what's good for you. It's a one-man horse."

"How did he do it?"

Bernard liked nothing better than spending time with and talking to his horse as he fed him or brushed him down.

'Well, Terror, we can relax now. The excitement of yesterday is all over. Maybe they'll send me home for a while. Yes, you would like it there, away from all these other beasts. But you would have to be gentle with Michelle. She can be scared of horses. But I am sure she would love you. You are such a fine horse.'

As he continued brushing, Terror, turned his head and nuzzled him in the back showing appreciation for being brushed. There had been no time after the battle to clean the horses, many of whom had become coated with the dirt and blood of battle.

'Redbeard had a fine horse too. But you two did not seem very friendly to one another when you met there in the forest. I'm sure he was so sad having to put it out of its misery. But what else could he do? I hope I shall never have to do that to you. But I was lucky yesterday. And so were you. Not even a scratch.'

Bernard stood and talked to his equine companion. Terror would stand, ears erect and a look at his face as though he really understood what his master and friend was saying. If he didn't understand the actual words he was acutely aware of the emotion and feeling behind what was being spoken.

The call to morning parade had been sounded and the cuirassier company assembled ready for the new day. Bernard's section was to scour the countryside to the east looking for isolated fragments of the Prussian army. The aftermath of the battle must continue. Should any be located they should be captured and escorted back to headquarters. Should they, as their captain put it, "be foolish enough to offer any resistance, they were to be dealt with accordingly." These Prussian peasants he continued to explain, need to be taught a good lesson.

The company dispersed to carry out its orders for the day. Were this not war and were the dreadful memories of yesterday's battle not still in his mind, the ride through the autumn countryside would have been very pleasant. They moved through their assigned areas, passed hills covered with pines and elms, skirted fields being worked by the local villagers.

These would stop their work, stare at the approaching groups of horsemen, fully aware of whom they were: Frenchmen searching for Prussian soldiers. These were Napoleon's troops coming to defeat and rape their land. They would silently move to the far end of the paddock. The calm autumn air, the sunny meadows, the fertile fields and forests swaying in the gentle breeze, all belied the animosity of the local population.

Word of the defeat had spread quickly, mainly by fleeing soldiers. The local population, who in normal times were friendly villagers, were now anything but friendly when the foreign visitors demanded to search through their houses and sheds. Their pride and independence were being violated. If they were sheltering anyone — and some were — they made sure that he was well hidden.

Within a few days it was established that the immediate area no longer secreted fleeing soldiers. It was time for the French presence to move out. The order was given that Marshal

Davout's III Division was to head to Berlin and there occupy the Prussian capital. In doing that they were moving further east, further away from the French homeland.

Bernard Natalier was not the only disappointed and unhappy man in that Division.

'I had thought that we would have been given leave to return home to visit family and friends,' he complained.

'Yes,' his pal replied, 'we were forced to join the army at short notice and for the last six months have been moving around the countryside. Surely, it's time for some leave. We won that battle. What else is there for us to do?'

'Get used to it, boys,' replied a battle-scarred veteran. 'You will soon find out that in our emperor's army there are always wars to be fought and battles to be won. You're in his army now and you have no say on where you go. Home is for women, children and old men.'

The Reality of Defeat

Dragoon Vadimas Zukas, wounded in the forest near Auerstedt, awakened from his semi-conscious state with a start. He sat up and blinked, looked around, but could decipher nothing. Complete darkness had settled over the battlefields. After a few moments of bewilderment, he realised his predicament but he was still very confused. *Where am I*, he thought. *No, I was not killed in battle; only wounded along with my fallen horse. Oh, Brutus! I'm sorry but I could not let you suffer. And that French sabre . . . that French sabre. It did not strike me as I expected. It did not strike in anger but was lowered in sympathy.*

Sympathy? No, perhaps respect. Whatever. But I am alive because of that cuirassier's action. Why did he do it? Oh, my arm and leg!

The fallen soldier cried out in pain.

Then there was quiet, but not really quiet. Was it a breeze sighing in the trees? No, it was not a zephyr moving the leaves, but a human sighing, a weeping, a moaning. Reaching him was the last amen of soldiers dying on the battlefield which surrounded him.

Many thousands had fallen in those few intense hours of battle. The lucky cries of many of the wounded during the fighting had received medical attention and these patients had been taken from the battlefield to a field hospital there to face an unknown future. Tragically many more had remained where they had fallen unable to raise their mutilated bodies from the bloodied turf. They would gradually drift into unconsciousness. Their cries for relief, their screams of pain and desperation would gradually diminish, weakened by pain and the loss of blood until death snuffed out the last whimpers.

A restless sleep had saved Vadimas from a whole night of suffering. Although he was encompassed by darkness some inner feeling now indicated that morning was arriving. He struggled to free himself from his dead horse. The struggle caused the pain to return to his ankle. The blood from the cut in his head had congealed and was no longer dripping onto the ground. His left arm lay in an unnatural position.

I must move from here, he thought. *I must not stay here feeling sorry for myself. That will lead to a quick death. I am young. I am strong. Surely my youthful energy will lead me away from this field of Prussian misery. I must save myself from the disappointment of being bettered in battle. I must go home.* 'Oh, God, give me the strength I need,' he cried out to the God whom he did not really know.

He pushed upward on the saddle and clenched his teeth in pain. His left hand dangled useless by his side. He pushed with his one uninjured arm and the one leg he could freely move.

He looked around after finally struggling to his feet. He looked and saw only yesterday's morning with the thick fog of mid-October. Early yesterday, riding out of camp his horse merely had to follow, as it was the responsibility of someone else to lead the way; to make a safe path. He now had no horse. There was no-one to lead; no-one to follow. He alone must plot his path forward.

That enemy cavalryman has given me a chance to grab my life back. I must not allow his kindness to be in vain. I need a plan. Think! What must I do? Oh, the training. I have been through training to do this; training to do that, but never has there been training to help one struggle from a battlefield wounded, defeated. Maybe I could reach one of our Prussian fortress cities. They boast that they are impregnable. There I would be safe to recover.

He looked around. Ghostly spectres of nearby beeches peered at him in the silence, their almost bare branches offering no assistance. A faint brightening in the sky beyond the scattered trees could indicate the beginning of a new day; could indicate the east. Should he try to struggle in that direction?

He must move away from here; from where he had fallen. To remain would be fatal. The enemy may not return but the marauders would arrive to strip the battlefield bare. They would see profit in the weapons, clothing and personal belongings of fallen soldiers. The life of a wounded Prussian dragoon would be worthless compared to the value they would place on his uniform, weapons and belongings.

How did it come to this? he wondered. *How could it be that I and thousands of my countrymen now lie dead or wounded? We were told that victory was there for the taking. What went wrong?*

The Prussian army had been assembling at Weimar confident of defeating Napoleon and beginning the push to send him and his armies back to France. Their aged leaders had looked back half a century to the glory years when Frederick the Great ruled Prussia, was successful in battle and his army was feared throughout all Europe. However, they had underestimated the will of the French soldiers, the destructiveness of their cannon and the tactics of their leaders.

Their attempt to chase the emperor and his armies back to the other side of the Rhine had failed. Napoleon remained to dominate Europe. The Prussian nation was destroyed, now to become a vassal state submitting to his will.

Following these battles beside the Saale River, Napoleon had assembled his armies, the majority of which marched to the town of Jena to rest, treat the wounded and account for those who had fallen in battle. Other detachments were scouring the countryside making it difficult for remnants of the Prussian forces to evade capture.

Many, demoralized by defeat and weakened by hunger,

tiredness and the exertion of fighting, willingly laid down their arms and submitted to their victors. Others, because of personal pride and dedication to their king, queen and country, found the energy to avoid capture. They struggled along unknown roads, through forests and marshlands, often having to avoid hostile communities to reach their headquarters or their home.

Vadimas Zukas was a soldier alone, far from his home. He was determined that his army's defeat would not defeat him. Would he ever again snare fish in the Minge River or harvest grain from the fields around Kinischken? How could he survive the many months travelling the thousand kilometres back to his family? He must try.

CHAPTER XIX

Good-bye to the Battlefield

With a sigh of relief that he was still alive Vadimas stood and concentrated on his physical situation, forgetting for the moment the dire plight in which he found himself. He assessed his injuries. He felt pain in a badly misshapen left arm which seemed to indicate some fracture. It hurt terribly if he allowed it to dangle by his side but when he supported it by placing it across his chest inside his uniform jacket the pain lessened significantly. The slash on his head had ceased bleeding, temporarily closed by congealed blood. A dull throbbing in the side of his head was a constant reminder of this wound. The damage to his ankle, which he knew would be the greatest problem to his mobility, proved to be less severe than he at first thought. A few tentative wriggles convinced him that it was not broken but had only been twisted when caught under his falling horse. It would be an inconvenience but with the aid of some sort of walking stick he would be able to slowly move along.

He was standing with a contented, almost happy, feeling that he could escape from what at first appeared to be a death prison when his dry mouth indicated a thirst and a rumbling in his stomach, a hunger. He looked around. *But it is food I crave and drink and some magic potion to ease my pain. Dear God, give me strength to escape this dreadful place. Lead me to some help and guide me from the enemy, and to some food and drink.*

He knew he had none. The supplies which he had carried in his knapsack were finished more than a day ago. He was aware that this applied to most of his comrades as well. Providing provisions for the army had been a problem. The Prussian soldiers' hunger had certainly helped the French and paved a way for their own defeat.

Move. I must move. Move while I still have the strength or I shall tumble to the ground and gradually die of starvation. But strength. Give me strength. Oh, for a piece of bread and a bite of sausage. Wishing will get me nowhere. I must move out.

He felt for his sabre which was still in its scabbard, drew it out and used it as a prop to move forward. *That glow is in the east,* his mind was alert, *so I will move to the north by keeping it on my right.*

Unfortunately, his sabre afforded him little help as he struggled forward. At times it was more a hindrance for its sharp point would bury in the soft soil causing him to stumble and fall. He made slow progress with the jumble of corpses and dying bodies also hindering his way.

Some fallen soldiers were still moaning pitifully as life was slowly ebbing away. Others cried for help as they recognized an upright person moving slowly amongst them. Their pleading eyes endeavoured to engage him, but Vadimas was unable to help.

'Water! Water!' some begged.

With heavy heart he moved forward as quickly as he was able, wanting desperately to leave this field of blood and dying behind and try to save himself. Amid the destruction he spied a section of a broken lance. He seized upon it and by luck it was the correct size to use as a walking stick. He replaced his sword into its scabbard by his side and now moved along more comfortably as well as a little more quickly.

He was now moving into an area with fewer bodies but which still showed the aftermath of fierce battle — broken wagons and cannons, bloodied cannonballs, scattered knapsacks and muskets. What saddened him even more was the number of dead and dying horses, all still completely harnessed. 'Why should such fine creatures have to suffer and die?' he muttered to himself. But he could do nothing.

He struggled on with the evidence of battle still scattered around him. The number of bodies became less but piles of undamaged Prussian muskets and knapsacks took his attention. Clearly these had been discarded by troops in their effort to avoid capture. *Had they only stayed and fought,* he surmised to himself, *the battle may have been won for Prussia.* And with that he made a decision: *I also shall attempt to avoid capture, but if faced with members of the French army they will find that my sabre and pistol can still cause hurt.*

The fog was lifting and the day was brightening so Vadimas could now see further than just the immediate surroundings. He had come to a major road which he recognized as the one along which his company of dragoons had travelled the day before. On the other side lay a small village surrounded by grain fields. This was the settlement of Poppel which their captain had alerted them to. Vadimas was undecided. Should he cross the road and make for the village hoping that he might find help there or should he try to put as much distance as possible between the battlefield and himself?

It was on his route north so he decided to cross the road and rest in the vegetation beside a drain which skirted the houses. From here he could watch and see if there was any danger, any French soldiers searching there.

He crossed the road as quickly as possible and with a sigh of relief sat down beside a small shrub which afforded some cover from searching eyes. He waited and waited for some length of time becoming more and more restless. His hunger compelled him to move on. He had no sooner struggled to his feet once again, was about to head for the village when he heard in the distance the shouting and laughter of Frenchmen. Soon a group of horsemen came along the road from the west and turned into the village.

Vadimas recognized them as cuirassiers with uniforms like the one worn by the man who had spared his life in the forest. But he dared not expect the same sympathetic attitude from these enemy troops and he quickly returned to the protection of the shrub. He sat and waited.

For how much longer could he wait? Hunger, thirst and pain had to be attended to and he could not address any one of these three while sitting under a bush beside a dry drain. He was about to move on when he heard more laughing and loud garbled conversation. He noticed that a group of horsemen was headed directly towards him. He pushed further under the bush. *Is this how my life will end? Being shot at for sport by a group of drunken Frenchmen.* He closed his eyes and awaited the worst. But they rode past without looking in his direction.

For how much longer will my luck hold? However, he could not stay where he was indefinitely.

Once they had passed out of sight, his dire circumstances forced him to risk moving on, walking along the drain hoping the small trees and shrubs growing there would shield him from the casual glances of any other French troops who might appear.

There was also the possibility of finding a pool of water, no matter how stagnant, so he cautiously moved forward, away from the road and village. At one stage he noticed another small group of cuirassiers riding across the bare, harvested wheat field in the distance. They were heading away from him, and he remained undetected. It was clear to him that he had to remain vigilant if he were to avoid capture.

He hobbled on. His pain increased. Blood was oozing

once more from his slashed head. Noon must surely have passed. The sun, in these areas often such a rare and longed-for guest, was generous with his favours today and beamed down from a cloudless sky. The heat of this early autumn day became intense. It was only his determination and the scanty shade afforded by the trees that kept him moving. The drain remained dry; the summer heat having evaporated all signs of moisture. There was no left-over water pool to quench his thirst. When despair was about to set in he noticed the spire of a church in the far distance to the left. There would surely be a village surrounding the church.

He moved on, hoping the drain would take him closer. Previous sightings of the enemy had shown him that it was essential to stay in the cover of the drain vegetation. Limping slowly across bare fields in his uniform could place him in view of search parties.

Soon it appeared that his wishes had been granted. The drain was joined by a tributary coming from the direction of the spire. He could now clearly see that the church was surrounded by farmsteads and an abundance of shady trees. He had to risk going there.

He branched off onto the smaller, but still tree-lined drain. The possibility of help in the village seemed to lessen his woes and increase his speed. Within a short time he was near the edge of the village, where he stopped to rest and watch to see if there was a French presence there. It would be soul-destroying if after struggling the whole day in pain, he were to walk into the arms of the enemy.

But his aching, sickening body would not have him wait too long. It was crying out for attention. After a short while watching villagers strolling around, but no sign of foreign invaders, he risked proceeding. He headed for the church which was on the edge of the settlement. He arrived at the front door of the building of light-coloured, roughly-hewn stones and collapsed. No one had noticed the wounded soldier who had arisen from the drain and struggled into the village of Spielberg.

He attempted to shout but a mere murmur emerged from his parched lips. He attempted to raise his arm to tap on the door with his broken lance, but it fell from his grasp. He attempted to rise but slumped into unconsciousness.

CHAPTER XX

Help in Spielberg

In the parsonage in Spielberg, across the lane from the village's stone church, Pastor Gottlieb Wehlau was sitting down to supper with his wife and family. They all folded their hands and solemnly bowed their heads:

'*Komm Herr Jesus sei unser Gast*

Und segne, was du uns bescheret hast. Amen.'

Once the blessing had been recited in unison the children were free to begin choosing from the sausage and bread set out in plates on the table. Their choice was limited; grainy brown bread and either one of the two different types of sausages already sliced. To compensate for this lack of choice they were able to soften the bread with a spreading of newly-made butter.

In these times of war, provisions for the villagers were often scarce should some country be carrying out a campaign in the vicinity. Local farmers were compelled to provide the army with food and shelter if required. This meant that they often had to go without while the soldiers commandeered their supplies. Butter was more regularly available for if the farmers were able to retain their cows, daily milk would be available for milk, cream and butter. Pastor Wehlau owned no cow but his family was supplied with dairy produce by members of the several villages which he served.

'Are our guests comfortable, Marta?' the pastor asked his wife after they all had begun eating.

'Yes, I brought them down out of the attic when I was sure the French cavalry had left.'

'What about food? Have you been able to . . .'

At this stage he was interrupted by a banging on the front door of the house. They all jumped, startled by the urgency and loudness of the knocking.

'The French! Have they come back?' The pastor's wife looked alarmed.

'Stay here. I'll go and check.' The pastor left the table and made for the door where there was another round of knocking. He opened the door.

'Herr Pastor! Herr Pastor!' came from one of the three young boys crowded on the doorstep. 'There's another one!'

'What? Are the French soldiers back?'

'No, not the French,' replied the second of the boys. 'We don't think so. We think he's a Prussian.'

'He's not moving.'

'We think he's dead.'

'No one saw him coming and all of a sudden he's there!'

'Boys, boys, steady down. Steady down and tell me what this is all about. Hans, why don't you explain.'

'Yes, Herr Pastor. It was like this. Me, Rudi and Peter had decided to go home and were walking past the church . . .'

'We were really checking the apple tree,' interrupted the smaller boy.

'Be quiet, Rudi. I'm telling the story. Well, we were near the church and saw this fellow lying on the front steps. We called out to him but he didn't answer so we went over to him.'

'We looked at him,' continued freckled-faced Rudi, 'and he looked dead so we touched him. He didn't move. Then Hansi said we should come and tell you.'

'Good boys,' replied the pastor. 'I'll tell Frau Wehlau and then we can go over and have a look. And Peter, you run home and ask your dad to come over. If he's unconscious we may have to carry him into the house and would need your dad's help.'

His supper forgotten the pastor had soon crossed the street to the village church. With the two boys eagerly looking on, he was examining Vadimas. He was attempting to straighten him into a more comfortable position when the soldier opened his eyes, groaned and muttered, '*padėk man. Esu troškulį.*'

'What? That's not German. What's he saying? Is he French?'

'I don't think that's French,' suggested the pastor. Then he addressed the soldier, 'Can you speak German?'

'Yes, German I can speak also,' whispered Vadimas. 'I am a dragoon from Tilsit. Please help me.'

'Good. Now relax and we will look after you.'

At that moment Peter arrived with a couple of burly farmers. In a very short time Vadimas Zukas was lying on a couch in the parsonage at Spielberg. Frau Wehlau and another woman from the village were fussing over him, assessing his wounds and deciding how best to help him.

Vadimas was in a very bad way, drifting in and out of consciousness. The women were worried that their skills may not be enough to save him.

'What else can we do, Frau Pastor?' the concerned farmer's wife asked. 'He seems so exhausted and not wanting to battle on.'

'Exhaustion seems to be half the problem, Frau Spann. Then there is his arm and foot. He was probably hungry and thirsty, completely worn out from fighting in the battle and then struggling to get here with his wounds. I feel that he needs rest more than anything.'

It surprised both women when their patient attempted to sit up. He lifted his head, his lips moved and he whispered, '*vandens.*'

Frau Spann quickly fetched another pillow and placed it under his head. 'What did he say?' she asked.

Frau Wehlau shook her head. 'I really didn't hear it, but I don't think he was speaking German.'

'But he was fighting for the Prussians. He surely must be German.'

'No, not necessarily. The armies in Europe today are made up with men from the lands the powerful countries control. They could be Polish, Danish, or Lithuanian and there could even be Russians fighting in the Prussian army. And then he could be speaking a German dialect we don't understand. I'm sure a German, from Berlin say, speaking high German would have trouble understanding the farmers around here. I know the pastor does.'

While speaking, the pastor's wife had not forgotten her patient but had held a beaker of water to his mouth from which he was drinking thirstily. He stopped and when she was about to take it from him he stayed her with his good arm and drank some more. He smiled and said in a language they all understood, 'Thank you. Thank you.'

His mouth moved as though wanting to continue speaking but Frau Wehlau put her hand to his lips and said, 'Hush. Say no more. Let those few sips of water refresh your being. Say no more "thanks" for I can see gratitude written in your eyes. Close them now and be at peace. We shall be here when you reawaken.'

With those reassuring words he closed his eyes and relaxed.

The women looked relieved that he had responded so well to the drink of water, but Frau Spann frowned and asked. 'And fever? Are his wounds likely to bring on fever?'

'Yes, that is often the biggest problem. If it does set in, and we will know within a day or two, we can only hope that our good Lord will be merciful to him and grant him healing.'

'And the poor boy is so young. I'm surprised that he's old enough to grow such a wild, red beard. And then to be a dragoon.'

'We will have to leave him to sleep, Frau Spann. That will probably help him more than what we can do. I will prepare some soup so that when he awakes we will have something to feed him with. I'm sure he won't be able to chew anything tough with that slashed skull and cheek.' Then she gently placed her hand on his head and continued, 'God rest you, Soldier.'

The two women, both shaking their heads sadly, made their way out of the room leaving the soldier alone.

Down the hallway in another bedroom three other Prussian soldiers were discussing their situation. They had turned up at the parsonage the day before seeking safety from the French victors. They were infantrymen who had fled unwounded when the cohesion of their unit was breaking apart.

When they, together with many others in their company, could see what was happening they threw down their knapsacks and rifles and, freed of this weight, made quick their escape from the battlefield and death. They had hidden in the pastor's attic as the French cavalry came through the village searching.

They now felt that they could breathe more freely, but realised they could not stay in this village. They would need to move on to re-engage with their comrades. The recent battle was still on their minds.

'Had we been ordered to move up behind the cavalry

when they had forced the French back to that village of Hassenhausen we would have routed those French bastards.'

'Why didn't someone give that order? We were just sitting there waiting.'

'That was the problem. There was no one there to give the order.'

'But we were moving along the road and someone told us to halt. Who was that?'

'And does anyone know why?'

'Someone said we were waiting for General von Wartensleben's second division to arrive to strengthen our centre.'

'I think too many of the top people were worried about Brunswick being shot. And that chap — Schornhorst, wasn't it? — that took over our division when old Schnettau was hit didn't know what to do.'

'They say that the king took over after Brunswick was shot.'

'I've heard that too. But what sort of a general is he? He's had no experience of leading troops into battle. There's a lot who don't even like him as a king.'

'No, most would prefer the queen.'

And the three of them laughed.

'Good leader or not, the king had all those reserves waiting. Why didn't he send them forward? That would have made all the difference.'

'No good worrying about what should have happened. We were routed. Napoleon will now be in control of our country and what can we do about it?'

'More importantly, what will the king and queen do? Napoleon won't be very happy that they decided to go to war against him. He's sure to be very hard on them. And that means us too.'

'Let them work that out for themselves. Right now we have ourselves to worry about.'

'I think we have to try to get back to our fortress at Magdeburg.'

'But that's a long way!'

'It won't be too bad. We marched down here with all our gear in four days so we should make it back in about the same time not carrying anything.'

'And food?'

'We will have to beg or steal that along the way.'

'What? With the French everywhere, that won't be as easy as you might say.'

'That's true, but we must try to get back. We are in deep trouble if we are found here doing nothing.'

'OK, let's tell the good pastor and his wife that we will be leaving in the morning. Maybe they will give us a little bit of food to take with us.'

'Yes, and they will probably be glad to see us leave. They have a badly wounded dragoon to look after. The poor beggar, I hope he will survive. He really must have struggled to get here. And if he does recover how on earth will he ever get back home or to his regiment, wherever that might be?'

CHAPTER XXI

Strength to Travel Home

Next morning the pastor's house in Spielberg was a hive of activity. The three infantrymen were preparing to leave, saying their goodbyes and expressing thanks for the secure roof they had found there. They also showed concern for their wounded comrade and insisted they meet him and wish him well.

The night's rest in a comfortable bed and the helping of soup which Frau Wehlau had prepared during the night and fed to him at daybreak, worked wonders. Vadimas felt revitalized in body and mind. No longer were thoughts of dying uppermost in his mind, but they were now dreaming of being with Kinischken friends and family in far distant Lithuania. He was further uplifted by the visit from the three Prussian soldiers who presented a very positive face.

'Have courage, Brother, and forget our defeat. The time will come when Napoleon and his soldiers will face a stronger, better organized army than what they have just encountered. We will rebuild.'

'Yes, we are on our way back to the fortress at Magdeburg to join our comrades there. French blood will flow when they come and try to chase us from there.'

'Our king and queen will be relying on all of us to restore Prussia's pride. Recover quickly, you brave dragoon! Go back and join your regiment and look forward to our next encounter with the invaders.'

The pastor and his wife as well as Vadimas had to warm to the enthusiasm shown by the three soldiers who only a few days ago were running for their lives and hiding.

'God go with you and protect you on your way back to Magdeburg. With soldiers like you our king and queen can be confident that Prussia will not remain under the control of the French emperor for very long.'

The soldiers saluted their benefactors, waved farewell to Vadimas, took up the food packages which had been prepared and moved out. Pastor Wehlau turned to their other guest whose face now looked strained. He was alarmed at the change he noticed there. Was this a reaction to the forced optimism he had shown to his infantry comrades?

'My Dear,' he began, 'this man is in severe pain. You can see it on his face. We must see how we can help him.'

'Yes,' his wife replied, 'I have not really looked to see where his injuries might be. Last night I just wanted to give him some food and water. We should now examine more closely where he is hurting, knowing that he is able to understand us and converse with us.'

'You have already saved my life,' said Vadimas, looking sincerely into the eyes of the pastor's wife. 'If you had not taken me into your home like you did, I would have died. And you knew that the French soldiers would punish you if they found out. I must thank you.'

'I have done little,' the woman replied. 'That is at the heart of my husband's and my Christian beliefs. We should help those in need.'

'Even so, you are kind and generous,' he replied with feeling as he raised his crippled arm to his blood-streaked face and winced in pain.

'Oh, I see you are in great pain and we have not really done anything about it. My husband took your boot off last night. I see now that your ankle has become quite blue and swollen. How on earth were you able to walk here all the way from the battlefield? You must have been in agony.'

'Indeed, it pained very dreadfully, Frau Pastor, but I managed. I could not remain there and die with the many other dead.'

'Yes, the body can do wonderful things if it has the mind and determination to do them. Hopefully it has not been broken,' said Frau Wehlau, gently massaging the painful-looking foot.

'If it has not been broken and after resting it for a few days it should not be a problem. It is probably throbbing now but that will disappear with rest and healing.'

'But I cannot be a trouble to you all that time.'

'Have no worry, my son,' came in the pastor, 'we see it as an honour to our country to help our soldiers. I fear, however, that your other injuries may pose more problems.'

'Yes,' replied Vadimas, 'both my head and my arm are causing much pain to me.'

'Hopefully we shall soon be able to attend to that. The lady who was here last night should soon be here again with some herbal mixtures she uses to wash cuts and get rid of the blood. And old farmer Egbert claims he can heal broken bones.'

'I shall be thankful for all of this. How will I ever be able to repay you?'

'Do not worry about such things. For now, close your eyes and rest if possible. We must wait for Frau Spann and old Egbert.'

For the next week, Vadimas wavered on the edge of death. Despite the efforts of all of those involved in helping and encouraging the sick man it was only after his body threw off the last bout of fever that they could breathe more freely.

Old Egbert did determine that his left arm was broken and twisted into an unnatural shape. No matter how hard he tried, often with Vadimas crying out in pain, he could not align it correctly. It remained abnormally bent. Egbert finally admitted defeat. Vadimas appeared relieved, accepting now that he would spend the rest of his life with an arm that would never be fully useful.

Frau Spann's herbal mixtures did help clean the gash in his head and cheek. It exposed the severity of the cuts bringing gasps of amazement that a man could survive such damage. Their location made it very difficult to bandage which would help in shutting and healing the wounds. But all this care and attention was not able to ward off the fever which soon wracked the soldier's body.

The whole village was anxious to hear of any improvements. Every morning, news of his condition — improvement or lack thereof — would be quickly circulated. Teenage girls would turn up each morning asking whether they could help. The pastor's wife surmised — probably correctly — that they were only interested in looking at the bearded, young man. At the Sunday church service, the whole village joined in prayers asking for recovery for their patient. The pastor and his family, and he suspected many others as well, offered up daily prayers for his recovery.

After a week of uncertainty the village awoke to the news that the fever had broken and the dragoon was on the way to recovery. After another few days he could be seen sitting on a seat in front of the parsonage. A few more days and he was limping around the farmhouses on a walking stick, talking to the villagers who had done so much to aid in his recovery.

By the beginning of November he was becoming restless and wanting to start heading home. This caused great concern for his new friends. The warmth of late autumn had disappeared and the chill of winter was making its appearance.

'You cannot leave now that winter is almost upon us,' Frau Wehlau appealed to him.

'I love you all for what you have done, Frau Pastor, but I must start heading to my home. I would become a burden for the village if I stayed here.'

'You need more time to regain your strength and your ability to combat the cold.'

'Cold worries me not at all,' Vadimas replied. 'In my village of Kinischken up in Lithuania the cold becomes very bad. I am used to the very bad cold.'

'And how will you travel?'

'My legs are now good. I will perhaps find a horse. People will help me. The French will be in winter camp and not looking for Prussian soldiers. I will take each day as it comes.'

It seemed that no argument, no amount of persuasion could stop Vadimas from setting out on his journey back to his homeland.

Finally with sufficient clothing given him by the village people, with one of the knapsacks which had appeared mysteriously after the battle, with food and a little money, he set off on the long journey home.

CHAPTER XXII

Concern in Crémieu

It was a cold, windy Saturday morning and many of the stallholders at the Crémieu markets were wishing they had stayed in the warmth of their homes. Customers were few and most of those who had arrived quickly purchased what they required and left. Hardly any were interested in standing around gossiping and passing on the latest news. All in the square knew that Mayor Maillard and his son, Gustav, had arrived and their eyes followed them as they moved from one stall to the next.

The mayor as usual was immaculately dressed, perhaps a little overly so for a Saturday morning visit to the markets where rough working outfits were the norm. His son also stood out in his brightly coloured uniform of a cuirassier captain. Their noble bearing and confident stride perfectly complemented their chosen dress for this outing. The mayor, belying his short stature, walked tall and proud as was his custom while Captain Maillard moved as if on parade. They cheerily greeted all those whom they met.

'Where's your horse, Gus?' came from a young man standing beside a table piled with onions and pumpkins.

There was a short burst of laughter from those who had heard what was said but no follow-up comment, as was probably expected, by the young stall attendant. Gustav did nothing to cause the comment to be added to. He looked towards its source, smiled at the young man whom he did recognize and stated in a very friendly manner, 'Good morning, Louis. No, on foot today. Need the exercise.'

Gustav and his father did not stop and start up a conversation with Louis. Gus and Louis had been good friends in earlier years but their interests and expectations changed as they grew into early manhood. People who knew them both very well were not at all surprised to see this happening. A captain in the French cavalry and the son of a struggling village farmer had little in common, even after the revolution.

They did stop at the wine stall which Henrí Natalier was now operating himself since Bernard had been called off to serve his emperor and his country. Anton Maillard and Henrí had retained their friendship throughout their lifetime. There were times when they had serious disagreements which led to heated arguments but they always respected one another's opinions. This long-held respect was one of the few things they had in common. Agreement on most topics, they both realised, was unattainable — except perhaps acknowledging a good wine.

'And which of these would you recommend on this cold morning?' the mayor asked, indicating two bottles standing at the front of the display table.

'For you, Anton, neither,' Henrí indicated, 'but I do have something here which should suit your palate. It's a new blend, nice and heavy, which I have been working on, and I am very close to being satisfied. Just the thing for a cold morning. Tell me what you think.'

The winemaker then poured a pair of generous goblets and handed them to his friend and his son, Gustav. They both then spent time sipping, tasting, commenting, agreeing that it was a wine well worth drinking. With more positive comments they placed their empty goblets in front of Henrí who felt obliged to fill them up again.

Topics of conversation turned to different matters during a more leisurely tasting of Henrí's second offering.

'Yes, I was at Jena when we came up against the Prussians,' Gustav was relating in response to a question. 'My company was held back in reserve. We were not needed so I did not see any real action.'

'Were the Prussians not able to hold firm?' asked Henrí.

'We were told that they were very disorganized and that Napoleon took them by surprise. The night before the battle he was moving his troops around getting them in position while the Prussians were apparently sleeping.'

'Do you know whether Bernard's company of cuirassiers were there?'

'We have such a large army that it is not easy for someone like me to know where other parts of the forces are located. I mean a captain is not really a high-ranking officer, and so I have no idea what is going on everywhere.'

'So do you have any idea at all?' Henrí was looking for some answer from Gustav. He and his wife and many friends in the village were worried for they had heard nothing from Bernard. They saw in Gustav someone who might be able to supply some answers. Word had reached them that Napoleon had achieved another great victory; that the Prussians had been defeated. But at what cost? Such details remained unknown. How many paid the price for the victory, and who were they?

'I could be wrong,' began Gustav, 'but he was probably with Davout's Corps which encountered the enemy north of where we were stationed.'

'And what happened there?'

'All I know is that the Prussians crumbled there too. There was some very fierce fighting but in the end they fled the battlefield. I have heard that a number of our cavalry units were sent out trying to round up isolated groups of King Frederick William's forces. Bernard's unit could have been one of these. As for Bernard himself. . .'

Here the mayor interrupted the other two for he could see that his son was not giving Henrí any real encouraging news.

'So he is probably somewhere in Prussia. If he were a casualty his family, I mean you, would have been notified.'

'Yes, Dad, I'm sure they would have been,' Gustav confirmed. 'Apparently our emperor is very insistent that all French casualties are identified and that their families are notified. It is that which helps make him so popular and our country great.'

'Possibly somewhere in Prussia,' mused Henrí.

'Yes, and you must be positive. Bernard is carrying out his duties as a Frenchman somewhere in Prussia.' The mayor spoke as if closing that topic and continued by asking, 'And Henrí, have you ever heard what might have happened to that Bacot boy who went missing after being called up to join our forces? Same time as Bernard went away, wasn't it?'

Henrí was surprised at this sudden change of topic. The mayor's question about Nicolas Bacot made him feel somewhat apprehensive. Why after all the time that had passed was it mentioned again? There had been a lot of speculation at the time it occurred but soon people forgot and just regarded it as something that had happened. Most were quite sympathetic towards the boy for it was widely known that he was very shy and retiring.

Now the mayor was raising the matter again. Did he suspect his friend of being somehow involved? Had some facts recently come to light? If so, how could that have come about? Anton Maillard knew that Henrí had no great love for Napoleon but that was a different matter. Helping someone to evade call-up was a much more serious matter. Only Nicolas' parents knew of Vivienne's involvement and they would never divulge that his wife had helped them.

'That shy boy, Nicolas? No, I've never heard a word. There was a lot of talk at the time as you probably well remember. Everyone was amazed that he would try to disappear, let alone do it successfully. It's been months now and, well, I've not heard what might have happened to him.'

'How have his parents handled it? You see Eugene Bacot quite a lot, don't you?'

'Yes, he has some good vines and is very knowledgeable about wine. We often have ideas to share. I have never asked him about his son. I know a lot have and in a very unkind manner. I've seen how these unwanted comments have upset him. I suppose his wife too; probably more so. And if they knew something I'm sure they would keep it to themselves. We all would if we were in their situation.'

Mayor Maillard nodded.

'Our colonel,' joined in Gustav, 'says that it is Royalist groups that are helping some of these absconders and deserters evade capture. He says they are everywhere. You would be surprised.'

Henrí didn't like the direction this conversation was taking. He would have liked to say nothing but he wanted to know what the mayor was thinking and so he said, 'I can understand that there would be such groups in the cities, but I doubt if you would find organized groups in the rural areas. We don't have such groups here, do we Anton?'

Mayor Maillard looked at his friend. 'I hope not, Henrí. I know that you do not agree with everything our emperor is doing. But then I remember that before the revolution, you, like a lot of us, did not agree with everything the king and his advisors were doing with the country and its citizens. But we did not join the revolution. To be honest, at times I do hear rumours which suggest that there are some here who would like to help restore the monarchy, but as for a group of organised Royalists, I really don't know. I sincerely hope there is not one.'

To Henri's relief they were interrupted by a couple of prospective customers who wanted some advice on the wines for sale. He excused himself from the mayor and his son, who then moved on to talk to others, and attended to these new arrivals.

A worrying thought remained with him. How much did the mayor really know? And if their group should somehow be exposed would his friendship with Anton be strong enough to avoid any serious repercussions for him and his Royalist friends?

CHAPTER XXIII

A Merry Christmas

The cold had come early to Kinischken. Most residents gritted their teeth and accepted the added burden nature had delivered to them, complaining bitterly nevertheless. Old Grandad Grigas nodded contentedly. He had predicted this would be the case and was not surprised. When asked how he knew, he simply smiled and answered, 'The storks left early.'

For almost six months of the year — the warmer summer months — storks were part of the daily lives of the residents of this village in far eastern Prussia. This was the case throughout most of northern Europe and not only here. They were not permanent residents. The birds would arrive during late March. It had become somewhat of a village honour to be the first to spy a returning bird.

The storks would return to the nest in which they had raised their three or four young the year before. Once back in their summer home they would immediately begin repairing the damage it had received during the winter storms. Over the years the nests would grow to quite a huge size as the birds kept adding to them.

Kinischken was only a small settlement but was proud of the six, large, untidy, stork's nests which it claimed as its own. Three were built in forks of high pine trees and the other three were situated on the tops of barns. Some regarded it as an honour to have a stork choose their building on which to build a nest. Valter Mazeika had even affixed a couple of stays beside the nest on his barn's roof to give it added protection. Now that Herr Schulte had purchased the farmstead it was expected that he would continue caring for the nest. He accepted this task willingly.

Each year it was normal for the same pair of birds to return to occupy their nest of the previous year. There were times when a pair would not return. This was soon noticed and was regarded as a bad omen.

The idea of bad luck happening in the village when a pair of storks failed to return developed years ago when unfortunate events coincided with unoccupied nests. There were three instances in consecutive years: a house destroyed by fire, the accidental death of a child, and a severe crop failure. As a result of these coincidences — or were they? — a local myth was born.

Secretly, each person hoped for the return of all the birds for this would forecast a happy year.

The cold of winter had returned but Vadimas Zukas had not. Most in the village were very sad and downhearted. Grandad Grigas remained optimistic. He reminded everyone that all the birds had returned this year, and this would indicate there would be no tragedy. He will come home. We have only to wait. This was his message of hope.

Not everyone shared his optimism. Christmas was approaching and still no news about their missing son. His parents had approached the regiment's headquarters in Tilsit but the officer in charge could give no definite information. He was missing; that's all he knew. He was one of many of their regiment who was either confirmed dead or noted as missing. Most did realise that "missing" was a euphemism of deceased. The present mood at the headquarters contrasted greatly with the spirited show of optimism that was evident when war had been declared.

Five months ago, Vadimas and his dragoon comrades had ridden so proudly from their barracks. The streets were lined with townsfolk cheering and wishing their soldiers well. How eagerly they rode off to war.

And how relieved were the civic leaders and governmental officials to see that Prussia was finally making a stand against the "Corsican upstart" who had been plaguing Europe. For years their king, Frederick William III, had stood aside and watched idly as Napoleon subjugated and reorganized German states — indeed most of Europe — for his own benefit. He had taken away their autonomy and compelled them to dance to his tune.

This created much alarm and anger among the Prussians. Many of the landed gentry of eastern Prussia had close ties with the German states to the west. They found it difficult to stand by as they became vassals to the emperor.

If only *der alte Fritz* was still alive, was the plaintive cry of many. He would not have allowed Prussia's reputation for bravery to be questioned. He would have marched his army against those French invaders and sent them running.

Memories of *der alte Fritz* as the subjects lovingly called their King Frederick II (Fredrick the Great), who ruled half a century ago, remained. Those were times when Prussia was feared and respected throughout Europe. Times had changed. Now the present king, hardworking and dedicated indeed, but lacking the flair and acumen of his famous predecessor had hesitated in upholding the pride of Prussia. Despite the urging of his wife, Queen Louisa, as well as many of his senior advisors, he remained neutral, tolerating the excesses of Napoleon.

Then in mid-1806 because of some relatively minor disagreement over Hamburg in Northern Germany, he declared war and his armies were mobilized.

Finally, it was to happen. Throughout the Prussian regions the soldiers and their officers celebrated. The infantry, the cavalry, the artillery, grenadiers and fusiliers, dragoons and hussars, all prepared to uphold the might of Prussia. Their country would again be great. But this did not happen. Jena and Auerstedt saw them defeated.

Now a week before Christmas and Kinischken was depressed. The only joyous sounds were coming from two Petronis boys who were skating on a frozen pond and chasing one another. Getting back on his feet after being pushed over by his older brother, one of them pointed into the distance and cried out, 'Hey, look!'

'Look where?'

'There, down the road. There's someone coming.'

'That's not a person. That's a cart.'

'I know that; but there must be someone in the cart.'

'It's the old Jew coming to sell his stuff. Let's go and tell Mum.'

They pulled off their skates, put on their boots and ran off back towards their house.

Excitedly they shouted, 'Hey, Mum, Mum, guess who's coming down the road?'

'How should I know. Who is it?'

'It's Old Osher, the Jew, in his red wagon.'

'That's right, he usually comes before Christmas. He's later this year. Probably because of the cold.'

The boys pulled their mother out to watch the wagon approaching. She looked at the bright, red wagon as it made its way down the road.

'He seems to have someone with him this year,' she noted.

The boys had raced off towards the cart yelling, 'Osher! Osher!'

More doors were opened, and heads peered out quietly watching the hawker's cart coming closer and closer. The silence of the winter's day was suddenly shattered by a scream coming from Herr Schulte's house. It was Frau Schulte's young helper, Marija Zukas, shrieking again and again, 'It's Vadi! It's Vadi!'

Soon the whole village had surrounded the red wagon, ignoring Osher and his wares, having eyes only for his passenger.

Dragoon Vadimas Zukas had returned home.

CHAPTER XXIV

Eylau

The battles at Jena and Auerstedt had resulted in a demoralizing defeat for the Prussian army, many killed, many more captured and many fragmented units fleeing throughout eastern Europe to avoid capture.

Did peace follow these battles? No.

The Prussian king, Frederick William, refused to meet with his conquerors to discuss peace terms. With the French forces approaching, he and Queen Louisa, had fled the capital, Berlin, and sought refuge in Königsberg in East Prussia; later even further east in the small town of Memel bordering Lithuania.

Prussian citizens were living under very trying conditions with the war against France not diplomatically concluded and with the French soldiers ravaging the countryside. Their situation, especially those in rural communities was rendered even more perilous because a large Russian army was still campaigning in eastern Prussia. Unlike the Austrian emperor, the Russian tsar had not concluded any peace treaty with Napoleon after his army (together with the Austrians) had been routed at Austerlitz two years previously. His army had merely retreated east towards their homeland.

This force still posed a problem for Napoleon who could not claim to have conquered Europe while enemy forces were still on the move.

It also posed a problem for the populace of those areas through which these foreign armies were moving. The campaigns of the Russian army could be more devastating for her allies than for her enemies. Being so far from their homeland the difficulties of keeping these thousands of men supplied was enormous and in winter impossible. Providing fodder and care for their horses — there were always large cavalry attachments — was even more difficult.

Should the supply wagons not arrive or be unable to keep up with the movement of the military units, the stores of grain and fodder of local farmers was simply commandeered, their stock herded away. Farming land was left a wasteland, the farmers left with an uncertain future.

Napoleon was determined to confront the Russian forces in eastern Prussia. While a section of his army was consolidating its control in Berlin and western Prussia, the other sections were endeavouring to force the Russian commander, Benningsen, to face them in battle. Their armies were somewhat fragmented and while there were lesser skirmishes between smaller sections of each army, never was Napoleon able to confront Benningsen's full force. Military intelligence was never able to accurately discover his movements.

Until at Eylau, a small village on the vast plains of Prussia. Here on the 7th and 8th of February 1806, 75,000 French soldiers confronted a similarly sized Russian force which also contained a number of Prussian units.

Here over two days was fought one of the most brutal battles of the whole Napoleonic era.

In a blizzard with driving snow and temperatures below zero wave after wave of half-starved, frozen soldiers advanced and retreated, advanced and retreated, again and again, each time leaving behind blood-red snow and frozen, mangled bodies.

At the end of the second day of slaughter, it was fatigue, hunger and cold rather than either side claiming victory that resulted in both armies withdrawing. The only result was the many thousand dead.

That such a loss of life was in vain, resulted in both commanders shaking their heads in disbelief. That the sword should keep devouring without an end was a situation to be avoided again. Both sides sought winter quarters to recover.

Did peace follow this battle? No!

Come springtime, sufficiently rested, both armies were again on the move. Napoleon was mobilizing his forces, bringing in reinforcements, so that he might finally compel the Russians and their allies to see the benefit of ending the war and concluding a peace treaty.

CHAPTER XXV

In Berlin

The bugle had sounded for parade, *non equo*, and Bernard and a few other members of his company were strolling towards the parade ground. They seemed very happy with life, chatting and laughing as they went. They were surprised by the appearance of their sergeant.

'On the double, you lazy peasants. Can't you move unless you are sitting on a horse? Forget what your legs are for?'

'Fair go, Sarge, don't want to turn a fetlock.'

'Fetlock, be dammed. Soldiers in my army do not move slow to parade. It certainly does not mean that you are to drag your arse on the ground when you are not sitting on a horse. Now move!'

'But the captain's lady friend hasn't left yet,' one soldier said quietly to his mate.

'I heard that. Insolence! Horseshit for you, Gagneau. For a whole week. Now move, you lazy donkeys.'

'Come on, Sarge, it's too cold to move any faster.'

'Cold? Too cold, you say? You violets don't know what cold is. You weren't at Eylau like me. That was cold.'

'You're in Berlin now, Sergeant, Sir. Come, walk along with us and enjoy the cool, fresh air.'

'Enough! Listen! If you smart-arses are not at the parade ground before me you all will be shovelling horseshit for a week.'

With that he took off, running towards the parade ground. Unfortunately, he was newly appointed to the company in Berlin after being slightly wounded at Eylau. He still had not fully recovered and had forgotten that he could not move as quickly as when he was fit. He also was not fully acquainted with the men in his company. In this case he had challenged four of the fittest members. They were up to the challenge. They raced off after him and reached the parade ground entrance ten metres ahead of him.

They stopped and smiled at him expecting the worst.

He glared at them but then his face softened into a slight smile. 'I'm a fair person,' he said, 'and you have been lucky this time, soldiers. And I shall remember you when I have some urgent messages to run.'

'Thank you, *Sir*.'

Ignoring the sarcastic "Sir", he continued, 'Now be ready to fall in!'

The four stayed talking.

'*Non equo*? What's that supposed to mean?'

'Well, we know what we have to do when we hear it; turn up to our parade without our horses.'

'It's probably Latin some smart sergeant — no, probably officer — worked out. In the past it's just been used to give us some information, strange as that may seem. We are usually kept in the dark and don't know from one day to the next what we are going to be doing.'

'Maybe we are moving somewhere else. That's OK by me. Anything for a change. I've had enough of duties here in Berlin, patrolling the streets every day.'

'The trouble is you don't know whether someone is going to shoot at you or not. And I would like to know what these local Germans are shouting at us as we ride past. It certainly doesn't sound very friendly. No, I must say, the Berliners don't seem very happy having us here.'

'There were two chaps shot from Company C only yesterday. Slowly riding along, they were, when all of a sudden out of nowhere, bang! bang! They never could catch up with those who shot at them. It's a bit scary.'

'Yeah, I think I'd rather be charging off into battle. At least you know then that someone is going to be shooting at you.'

'You know, fellows, I don't fancy that much either. I can feel a little bit sorry for the people here. How would you feel if we had Prussians back home patrolling our streets and telling us how to run France?'

'Well, some might do a better job than our mayor back home. He just looks after himself and his family. Half the village works for him in his clothing and leather factories. And his son is a cavalry officer. He couldn't even ride a horse back home and suddenly he's made a captain. Tell me how that happens?'

'You seem a little jealous, Bernard. Would money have anything to do with it? But at least we can say that our captain and the lieutenant can ride. They led the charge back there in Auerstedt, or wherever it was. What about the new sergeant? What do you think of him?'

'Yeah, I reckon he would be out in front. Bet he won't be challenging us to any more races.'

Their conversation was interrupted by the bugle sounding "On parade". Then all the soldiers sprang into action. That was essential in their training. When the bugle sounded they were to jump into action; no waiting, no deciding to react or not, no slowly carrying out instructions. Whether marching through the countryside, forming up on parade or in battle a quick, complete reaction was required; was demanded.

'Attention!'

The company's captain rode on to the parade ground on his white charger. Many thought many things, but no one moved.

'Soldiers of the Empire, brave Frenchmen, cuirassiers. Orders have arrived instructing us to move out and join our division in the field. Our emperor has lost patience with the Prussian king and his queen who have refused any peace arrangements;

and with the Russians who continue to snub their noses at us. It is reported that their armies are mobilizing. It is time to teach them a lesson they will not forget. We shall shortly be leaving our quarters here in Berlin and moving eastward. Your sergeant will give you specific orders.' With that he turned and rode off the parade ground.

Once he was gone, the company sergeant took centre stage. 'Stand easy and listen up. You are about to become soldiers again. You lucky men. Say good-bye to your gentle rides along the streets, your picnics along the Spree and in the Tiergarten. No beerhalls where you are going, and no gambling dens. Kiss adieu to your painted ladies in those shady streets. Tomorrow, you polish and pack and remember once again how to act like a soldier of the French empire. Day after tomorrow, parade at 7.00. Then we move out. Attention! Dismiss!'

CHAPTER XXVI

Into Battle Again

Having left Berlin, Bernard and his company were moving east across the plains of northern Europe. Village, farmland, forest. Village, farmland, forest. This repeating pattern was the background to the boredom of riding in column day after day. Small lakes and swamplands did provide some relief from time to time but did nothing to lift the spirit of the cuirassiers. Bernard, riding beside his friend Pierre, who had recovered from his injuries received at Auerstedt, and other of their companions were approaching another village. They looked ahead expectantly. Perhaps this one would offer something different. They arrived and were disappointed for they had seen it all before: unfriendly villagers, hunger and poverty.

The further they rode from Berlin, the closer they came to the possibility of being engaged in another battle. This played on many minds.

Bernard and Pierre accepted that what lay ahead was out of their hands and decided to try to avoid thinking of what might happen. The further they rode from Berlin, the more they learnt about Napoleon's last major battle (the one in the blizzard at Eylau) and the more they learnt about their sergeant who had come to them in Berlin. Stanislaw Kowalczyk was his name.

Sergeant Kowalczyk had become obsessed with Bernard's horse, Terror, and was determined that the beast, as he called him, should get to like him.

Bernard was honest with him. 'As long as you keep thinking of him as a beast you have no hope of becoming his friend.'

'That is ridiculous. You speak as though the beast knows what I'm thinking,' replied the hardened sergeant looking from Bernard to his horse and then back again. He chose not to notice how Terror lifted his head defiantly when the word "beast" was spoken.

'Cuirassier Natalier, you are trying to make me look like a fool.'

'No, sergeant, Sir,' replied Bernard innocently and taking the conversation a little further continued, 'I feel that my horse does not like you because you are Polish.'

'You are insane. What are you trying to tell me?'

'I think Terror must have had a Polish owner; one who mistreated him. He has a dislike for Poles.'

'He's probably a Prussian horse,' suggested Pierre who also liked to annoy the sergeant in a friendly manner. 'Sarge, why don't you say something to him in Polish and see how he reacts.'

'Bloody ridiculous,' grumbled Kowalczyk, but then standing directly in front of the horse's head said loudly, *'ty glupia bestia patrysz na mnie.'*

Terror's reaction was startling. He snorted and jerked his head up and down and pulled away from the man standing in front of him.

Kowalczyk looked suspiciously at Bernard sitting on the horse. 'What did you do to him to make him behave like that?'

'I did nothing,' replied Bernard innocently. 'That was Terror's reaction to what you said to him; whatever it was. It was garble to me but he clearly understood what you said. What did you say? I mean in words that Pierre and I can understand.'

'I merely asked the horse to look at me.'

'Just that? Now what exactly did you say? The exact words?'

'Well, I said, "You stupid beast, look at me." That's all.'

Pierre looked — actually pretended to look — stunned. 'You said that! No wonder poor Terror reacted as he did.'

'I'll catch you two out sooner or later,' said Kowalczyk.

The friends smiled and Bernard decided to change the subject. 'Sergeant Stanislaw Kowalczyk, and you speak the Polish language. . .'

'And bad French,' Pierre butted in.

'Yes, and French,' continued Bernard. 'You are a Pole from

Poland. Why then are you fighting in Napoleon's army? We have to be here for we were called up in the *levée;* but why you?'

'Pole. Polish. Poland. There is no Poland. I speak this language because that is what my parents spoke. I fight because I am a soldier, for the wages which I usually receive and for the spoils of victory.'

'Fighting for France has been good?' asked Pierre.

'Good? Yes, so far. We have been winning the battles. It is not that I love Napoleon or hate the Russians or Prussians. I am a soldier who fights for the one who pays me.'

'And the battle at Eylau earlier this year in February? Did you earn your money there?' asked Bernard.

'Eylau was not good. There was not a winner; only many, many dead and wounded soldiers.'

'You were lucky?'

'Lucky, you ask. Having to charge into a blizzard in freezing temperatures. Is that lucky? Seeing your friends being mowed down by Russian cannon. Is that lucky? Having your horse shot from under you; being slashed with a razor-sharp sabre. Is that lucky?'

'But the doctors fixed you up. That was lucky. I'm sure they were not able to treat everyone.'

'Doctors? No! No way! I did not seek torture at the hands of the field doctors. I wanted to keep my arms and legs. Kept out of their way and struggled out of the battlefield by myself.'

'But you are alive and are now here with us, Sarge. That is lucky.'

Kowalczyk said nothing as he rode ahead to do whatever a

sergeant of horse has to do when on the move.

'Why do they choose to become soldiers?' asked Pierre.

'Perhaps there is nothing in their village to occupy them and they do not realise what it really involves,' suggested Bernard. 'They probably see only the positive side of being a soldier.'

'Positive side? Is there one?'

'For some there is, if they survive long enough. You saw how some of the old professional soldiers lived while we were in Berlin. They would just take whatever they wanted. No way would they have lived back in their home village like that. That is what Sarge called the spoils of victory. Oh, and then what can be gathered after a battle has been won.'

'Can't say that we got any spoils after fighting down near Bad Kösen,' complained Pierre.

'No, we are just new, and you were in the hospital, remember? We do all the fighting and get no reward. Not like those who have plenty of money, the privileged class who can buy what they want.'

'You mean the officers. I see what you mean,' agreed Pierre.

'Yes,' said Bernard, 'there is this good friend of mine back in my hometown. Well, he used to be a good friend, perhaps not so much these days. He chose to join the army and is a captain now. His father is the town mayor, owns some factories and is very rich. I'm sure Gustav, that's his name, is where he is because of his family's influence and wealth.'

'Has he been to any battles?'

'Yes, he has. Austerlitz was the first and then there was Jena, so maybe he deserves to be captain. He is also a cuirassier. We might meet up with him when we get to wherever we are going.'

And their column rode eastward, step after step, kilometre after kilometre. Often, they would be riding through countryside already picked clean by units which had preceded them. Many villages appeared deserted, the inhabitants having moved to where they might be able to find food and keep alive. Perhaps they remained but stayed hidden behind closed doors when they were aware that a military column was approaching.

Soldiers on campaign were worried, unhappy beings, riding into an uncertain future. Many were riding to certain death. Communities caught up in campaigns were sad communities. The poor became poorer and the hungry, hungrier.

CHAPTER XXVII

Battle of Friedland

In the months following the battles at Jena and Auerstedt the French army remained in Prussia in eastern Europe. Bernard and his company had been sent to Berlin to help maintain French control there. Other units were directed to Prussian fortified cities to overcome the resistance emanating from these strongholds. The main section of Napoleon's forces was attempting to engage the Russian army which still had large numbers of troops campaigning in eastern Europe. There had been minor skirmishes but Napoleon had been unable to defeat the Russians. The armies kept moving, attempting to outwit each other.

Winter had arrived with its freezing temperatures and raging blizzards. Both commanders saw the foolishness of continuing activities in the extreme weather and the French and Russian armies went into winter cantonments. The men were undernourished and over-exhausted after months of campaigning, weary from fighting and longing for home. Napoleon himself had been away from his home in Paris for nigh on five months, but rather than return there for the remainder of the winter he chose to reside in the Finkenstein Palace, a palatial estate home forty kilometres south-west of Eylau. From here he directed the rebuilding of his forces, preparing them for the recommencement of hostilities in spring.

During this lull in conflict, the intendant-general of the campaign had an uninterrupted opportunity to ensure that the army's shortages were rectified. Replacement horses had to be requisitioned from allied cities as well as voluminous supplies of fodder and grain necessary to keep the cavalry in fighting fitness. Added to this were the requirements of the army of many thousands — fighting men and their support — which could not be left unattended. Cash, uniforms, shoes, ovens, cattle and sheep, tents, sheeting and bedding, arms and ammunition; the list seemed endless.

Towards the end of May, anticipation was mounting along the banks of the two East Prussian rivers — the Passage where the French were encamped and the Alle along which the Russians had spent the winter. Both commanders, Napoleon and the Russian, Benningsen, determined that the coming months would finally see a conclusive victory for their forces and an end to the campaign. Manoeuvres had begun.

Benningsen thrust first, engaging Marshal Ney's Corps at Guttstadt and succeeded in forcing the French back. However, he was hesitant in taking advantage of his initial success. Afraid of overextending and being caught between advancing reinforcements he retreated to a heavily fortified position at Heilsberg on the Alle River.

The huge redoubts which the Russians had erected during the winter did not deter Napoleon from moving against the entrenched enemy. From early morning until close to midnight there was attack and counterattack with neither side willing to concede defeat. Eventually both sides recoiled in horror at the sight of dead and mutilated bodies, at the screams of pain and anguish and they ceased fighting. Death had claimed victory.

The war continued.

Rather than stay in the defensive position at Heilsberg, Benningsen retreated north along the Alle River, heading towards Königsberg where there were stores and reinforcements.

To reach Königsberg his army would need to cross the Alle River. Benningsen headed for the town of Friedland where there was a bridge crossing the river. Napoleon had anticipated what Benningsen was planning and he also realised that there was a bridge crossing at Friedland. He ordered one of his Marshals, Lannes, with his reserve Corps to hasten there to obstruct the Russian retreat.

The French arrived at the small town with the Russians across the river on the right-hand bank. Lannes was alarmed for he realised that he had encountered the whole of the Russian army. Benningsen was surprised at his luck for he realised that he had met up with only a single corps of the French army. This was his chance to inflict a telling defeat on the foe. His plan was to move his troops quickly across the river, defeat Lannes' Corps, then retreat before reinforcements could arrive. He poured his troops across the Alle, even erecting three pontoon bridges to hasten the crossing. Soon the majority of his 85,000 troops was in position to overwhelm the French. Batteries of canon fired from across the river and the infantry and cavalry moved against the French.

His plan had initial success and the French were in danger of crumbling; but they did not. The Russian commander had underestimated Lannes' ability to absorb the continual attacks and to reform always being ready for the next wave. This gave Napoleon time to arrive with reinforcements and assess the situation. They soon halted all Russian advances.

In the early afternoon fighting appeared to have ceased. The soldiers rested, wondering what the morrow would bring, for neither side had claimed victory. No retreat had been ordered.

For many, very many, there would be no tomorrow. At five o'clock three salvos from a battery of French canon signalled the advance of Napoleon's massed troops. Benningsen watched in horror from the tower of the church in Friedland as the countryside to the west became alive with marching troops, their bayonets glistening in the late afternoon sun.

Advancing with the infantry were two batteries of French canon. They unlimbered and fired mercilessly into the Russian lines at 500 metres. Then moving forward, they repeated the attack at 250 metres. The Russians were unable to break through to disable the guns which continued firing. Then they moved forward another 100 metres firing now at blank range. The carnage continued.

The Russians were defeated and they attempted to retreat.

Without fully realizing it at the time Benningsen had placed his army in a very precarious position when he had them cross the Alle. He had erected his pontoon bridges near the permanent bridge at Friedland leading directly into the town which was located in the inner bend of a meander. Now having to retreat in the face of an artillery charge, his whole army (or what remained of it) had to stream through the village towards the bridges. This was their only route of retreat. The town began burning and the army was caught in a bottleneck, attempting to reach the bridges which were now also under attack.

The Russian army was completely routed.

Three days later Tsar Alexander and King Frederick William approached Napoleon with the white flag. Napoleon was now in complete control of Europe. His army continued moving east to the Nieman (Memel) River. The three rulers met in the town of Tilsit to discuss peace.

CHAPTER XXVIII

French Victors in Tilsit

Barely a week after his decisive victory at Friedland Napoleon arrived in the eastern Prussian town of Tilsit. The citizens were expecting his arrival for they had watched in disbelief as the remnants of Benningsen's Russian army had passed through their town, struggling to reach safety from pursuing French soldiers. They were now left in no doubt that the defeat of Prussia and Russia was complete and Napoleon's power absolute. His path to dominance, a red trail of blood, led over the slain heroes of battlefields and the economic ruin of once happy and prosperous regions. He had crumbled the resistance of nations and could now dictate their fate. This would happen in Tilsit.

Since the arrival of the French army, Tilsit had undergone a remarkable transformation. The once dour, orderly streets of this Prussian town were now alive with the shouting and rowdy celebrations of their unwelcome visitors. Not one of the streets escaped the colourful parading of the soldiers of the victorious army. Long into the summer night they spurned the whole idea of the peace and quiet once enjoyed by the local citizens. These now stood and looked grimly at their uninvited guests or sat indoors and contemplated sullenly this sudden change of their circumstances. Many sadly remembered the last time the streets had witnessed such celebrations — their own celebrations. That was when the city farewelled their dragoon regiment as it moved out to confront Napoleon.

Hermann Schulte had hurried to Tilsit when word of the defeat at Friedland reached him in Kinischken. He had concerns for Martha and Manfred and how they would react to French officers who would come and demand to be billeted in the house. He arrived to find them in a very anxious state.

'You have no idea what our city looks like,' said Martha after Hermann had settled her down on his arrival. 'All sorts of beings dressed in all the colours of the rainbow, parading up and down our streets.'

'Many look very splendid, I have to say,' added Manfred, 'with all their war medals cluttering their chests.'

'Yes,' went on Martha, 'there is this daily cavalcade of marshals and generals, colonels and majors, and whatever else, walking along our streets.'

'You spend a lot of time looking out of the window at them,' commented her husband, 'and I must admit that the officers do carry themselves with dignity. As for the lowly foot-soldier, his behaviour is quite different. He probably realises that he can never rise to be such an officer.'

'And what about those who have decided to make this their present home?' asked Herr Schulte.

'Huh!' grunted Martha.

'They are clearly men of good breeding,' answered Manfred. 'Well mannered. But you should hear the distain with which they regard our city. They call us a frontier town lacking all the comforts and amusements which might make it livable.'

'And they ask me where all the beautiful houses are,' continued Martha, 'and the theatre and entertainment. And what is more,' Martha was now appearing quite miffed and aggrieved for she regarded herself as a very competent cook, 'they asked where to find a kitchen staffed by chefs who know how to satisfy a discerning palate. I tell you, Herr Schulte, I have a good mind to put some poison in their beef pies.'

'I don't think you should do that,' advised Hermann. 'I'm sure Emperor Napoleon would not be too forgiving towards a Prussian who poisoned some of his officers because they did not appreciate the good cook they had.'

Martha smiled and blushed at the same time. 'No, I would not really do that. But how long are we to suffer them being in our home? How long are we to tolerate those who see themselves as being sent by God and us here as their servants?'

'Don't worry, Martha,' consoled Hermann, 'I'm sure they will go back to France once they have concluded their meetings here with our king and the Russian tsar. They won't want to stay in our backward village longer than necessary. Their throats will be yearning for the rich wines of Burgundy.' And he laughed.

'I must tell you about the visit I had from your manager at the timber yard,' said Manfred, changing the topic.

This got Hermann's full attention. 'Oh?' he queried. 'Not bad news, I hope.'

'The yard was visited by a number of officers from Napoleon's Guard Artillery. They requisitioned a quantity of logs and planks. It seems they are building a pavilion on a raft in the middle of the Memel. The peace discussions are to be held on the raft. It is neutral ground, they say, between Russia and Napoleon's Europe. Nothing is said about Prussia. Have they forgotten us?'

'There was nothing much poor old Fritz down at the yard could have said. Whatever they wanted, they would take. He is clever enough to know when to be quiet. I have a good idea of what he would have liked to have said to those French officers.' Hermann seemed to take the news very philosophically, and he continued by asking, 'That's all they were interested in?'

'I think so. Yes,' replied Manfred. 'Fritz said he kept them away from the back storage shed.'

'Good man,' murmured Hermann relieved.

'And we were right about those two strangers who we thought were spies. They have become very friendly with some French officers from Napoleon's personal guard. Probably telling them what they have discovered. I have no idea if they found anything,' related Manfred.

'Yes, we shall have to be very careful and keep well out of the way of the French. I did see several French patrols while I was coming down from Kinischken. One stopped my carriage and asked where I was headed and why.'

'The war is over and they should not be allowed to go roaming around wherever they like,' said Martha. 'Our king should not tolerate them going wherever they want to.'

'I feel he is able to do very little about it,' said Hermann, slowly shaking his head. 'We have been thoroughly defeated and must now live with the consequences.'

'Oh, and I hate to tell you, Herr Schulte. . .' began Martha.

'Yes? What is it, Martha?'

'Your bedroom. The officers have taken that too. They would not listen to Manfred and me when we told them that you would need it. They simply took it and expect me now to keep it clean.'

'Oh, dear,' said Hermann, 'then I shall have to sleep somewhere else.'

'Yes,' said Manfred, 'we have made up one of the servants' rooms for you. I hope it will be suitable.'

'Thank you. I'm sure it will be. As I said, we must not do anything to set them against us. It will be better if we, especially me, stay unnoticed. Napoleon and his army will not be staying here in Tilsit for very long, but you can be assured that we will have French officials telling us what to do for a long time after the emperor leaves.

'Yes,' agreed Manfred, 'no doubt until we are able to battle back our independence.'

'God protect us,' sighed Martha.

C H A P T E R   X X I X

Treaty of Tilsit

Hermann Schulte and two of his close business associates were standing in a back corner of the grain market in Tilsit trying to look inconspicuous. It was not a very difficult task to accomplish for the square was jammed full of people, pushing and jostling, all wanting to satisfy their curiosity as to what was happening. Word had travelled quickly from Napoleon's headquarters that the major event everyone was waiting for was about to take place. The three rulers, Napoleon, Tsar Alexander of Russia and King Frederick William of Prussia were to meet on a barge in the middle of the Memel River to work out a peace agreement. The whole town, so it seemed, was anxious to see how this historic moment would unfold in detail.

Reinhardt Müller, the owner of a clothing and fabric emporium in *die deutsche Straße*, was looking around at the number of people crowded into the square. 'It surprises me to see so many people here. But I suppose everyone knew that something important was about to happen.'

'And happen out in the middle of the river,' replied August Pfeiffer, whose butchery was also located in the main street of the town. 'I'm sure everyone was wondering what they were building out there. I think that most are very excited that three important rulers are here in our city. They want to see them.'

'This is a great change from the last few weeks,' observed Reinhardt. 'Our local civilians have been seen less frequently since our visitors have arrived. I believe it to be a good thing too. Our womenfolk especially do well to confine themselves to the four walls of their homes. It would be insanity for our young ladies to venture unaccompanied into the city. It has sadly been taken over by these foreign soldiers. Can they be trusted? I think not.'

'Not only our young ladies,' said Hermann. 'They treat us all with disdain. I arrived at my home to find that I am not able to sleep in my own bed. Poor old Manfred felt so embarrassed to tell me he had to arrange for me to sleep in one of the servants' rooms.'

'Yes, Hermann, such behaviour is not at all surprising. It seems that these officers take their lead from their own leader. I believe Napoleon has treated our own king and queen with the utmost discourtesy,' Reinhardt noted, sadly shaking his head.

August agreed. 'Yes, the rudeness he has shown to our monarch, and not only to him, but especially to our Queen Louisa has upset many of our leading citizens. To make matters worse he seems to have formed some friendship with the Russian tsar. It is hard to understand. One day they are fighting one another, sacrificing thousands of lives, and the next they are embracing and attending dinners, balls and concerts with each other.'

'And that this should be happening in a Prussian town makes it even harder to accept,' added Hermann and then he continued. 'But we can do little, or nothing about it.'

'Hopefully we can continue to make our little contribution once they have moved on,' said Reinhardt, referring, as the other two men recognized, to their smuggling operations.

Their conversation was interrupted by a brass fanfare coming from an army band positioned on a platform beside the river. This was followed by loud army instructions and then the sound of rifle fire.

'What is happening?' asked August. The other two looked at him blankly, for they also did not know as they were unable to see to the river from where they were standing. Finally, word reached them. Napoleon had arrived at the riverbank and was travelling over to the barge. "And he is by himself" was a message being passed along the crowd.

'When will the other two arrive, I wonder?' asked August.

'Probably when he calls them,' suggested Hermann. 'He wants to make them realise that he is the one in charge. Fancy that! Being so powerful that tsars and kings stand and wait to be bidden.'

A break had temporarily formed in the restless crowd and Reinhardt could see through to the activity on the river. He gazed at the pavilion for a moment and then cried out in excitement, 'Look at that pavilion there! See that elaborate cloth?'

'Well, no, Reinhardt, we can't really see it all from here. Only the top section.'

'Well just imagine it then. The finest that could be obtained. English cloth that is. And do you know where they got it from?'

'I think that you are now going to tell us, Reini.'

'You are right. From my store. Some of those haughty officers came in and acted as though they owned it and packed up whatever they took a fancy to.'

'And did they pay you a fair price for what they wanted?'

'Pay a fair price! They paid nothing. Just took it.'

'At least you will have the last laugh.'

'Last laugh? What do you mean? It is nothing to laugh about.'

'What I mean,' explained Hermann, 'is that you will know that the great Napoleon will be signing treaties in a pavilion made from the finest English cloth. Cloth made by his enemies and then smuggled into the country against his orders. That is something to tell your grandchildren. I'm sure you will be able to replenish your stocks. And Reinhardt, you are not the only one who has a reason to complain.'

'No, you are right, Hermann,' said August, 'There are many here in Tilsit who have suffered loss because of the French army and their needs.'

'Yes, indeed,' said Hermann. 'I should know, for you are looking at another one right here.'

'What? You Hermann?'

'Yes. All those logs and planks used to make the rafts for the pavilions came from my yard. And I wasn't even there to say "goodbye" to them.'

The band which had been playing was suddenly interrupted by wild shouting and cheering.

'Who's coming now? Can you see, Reini?'

'Is it our king?' asked Hermann.

'No, it must be the Russian tsar. He's a tall young man dressed in a green uniform. Looks more like some young officer in the Russian Guard. He is being rowed over to the raft surrounded by officers. A colourful sight it really is. But no one has seen our king,' reported Reinhardt.

As everyone's attention, including that of the columns of soldiers lining the streets and the bank of the river, seemed to be directed towards what was happening on the river, Hermann and his two friends had moved closer to the riverbank and now had an unimpeded view of the proceedings.

'He does seem a handsome young man,' exclaimed August, now that he could see him clearly. 'And I can now see your pavilion, Reinhardt. My, it does look very plush.'

'Yes, indeed,' agreed Hermann. 'But look at those decorations at the entrance to the salon. There is an N for Napoleon, I presume, and an A for Alexander the tsar, but no mention of our king. Where is the FW?'

'More importantly, when is he coming?'

The crowd waited for the person they most wanted to see. They waited and waited. An hour passed and finally word was passed to those waiting that the king and his entourage had also been waiting beside the river upstream from where they were. He had been waiting for Napoleon's invitation to come to the barge, but none had been forthcoming. He also was left waiting.

'It appears that Napoleon has snubbed our king again,' remarked August.

'Yes, he seems to have taken a liking to Alexander. There must be a reason behind that. I wonder what they have decided to do with Prussia?' asked Hermann of no one in particular.

'And how will it affect our bringing goods into Russia from England?' asked August. 'Will the Russians still be wanting to buy from us? The tsar might now make his subjects do what Napoleon wants.'

'We will have to wait and see. It will be very dangerous for us to operate in Königsberg and here as well, but I do have a good, reliable group working up where I am. I'm sure they will keep going. The way Napoleon has treated Prussia will make me even more determined to work against him.' Hermann spoke quite passionately.

'Let's hope everything runs smoothly for everyone,' nodded Reinhardt.

C H A P T E R   X X X

Ambush

'Sarge, why were we chosen to stay on in Tilsit while most other units are heading back home?' Bernard asked his sergeant who was riding beside him.

'I suppose because we are the lucky ones.'

'Lucky?' asked Pierre.

'Sure. I ask you, who gets to live in the cavalry barracks in town while our comrades sleep out with the mosquitos and beetles?' explained Sergeant Kowalczyk.

'I would rather be travelling back home. It's time we had leave from army duties,' said Bernard.

'Remember, cuirassiers, you can't have all the luck. Perhaps this is our punishment for arriving at Friedland after the battle was over.'

'Yes, that was good luck,' agreed Pierre. 'At least we are still alive. But tell me, when do we get to go hunting elk like the other units?'

'When the captain decides. Right now, he has decided that we patrol this area while he and his friends hunt elk,' answered the sergeant.

'Yes, I suppose we should be happy riding around the countryside with no worries. I can't imagine there would be any smugglers in this area. All we've seen are old farmers with their broken-down wagons, half loaded with hay or a few bags of grain being pulled by a couple of weary-looking horses. Not like Terror here.' Bernard gave his horse a friendly slap on its shoulder.

'And the peasants here seem half asleep,' added Pierre, 'and they certainly don't like us pulling them up to look in their wagons. The looks they give us!'

'Independent buggers,' agreed Sergeant Kowalczyk. 'I suppose this is the first time they had to do what someone tells them.'

'There is someone heading over to that clump of trees,' Bernard pointed out. 'We had better go and check him out.'

The small troop of French cuirassiers left the road and headed towards a slowly moving wagon which was accompanied by a couple of horsemen. It didn't take long before they overtook it. Bernard had ridden in front of the wagon, loaded with fodder, to signal the driver to stop when a volley of gunshot came from the nearby trees.

'What the?' shouted Pierre as another volley rang out from a group riding directly towards the French. Disregarding a couple of their comrades who had been shot from their horses, the remainder caught so unprepared, turned and fled. The local group followed the fleeing Frenchmen, but it soon became obvious that they could not catch them. They gave up the chase.

'Well, there are two of the bastards who won't be causing us any more problems. It's a pity the others got away but we can't risk chasing them all the way back to Tilsit or wherever they have come from.'

'Yes, it is Tilsit. I've heard that a couple of their cavalry companies have taken over our barracks there.' It was Vadimas Zukas who provided this information.

'That is where you trained, isn't it, Vad?'

'That's true, but it seems so long ago and I'll never be a dragoon again with my crippled arm. Right now, we have something more important to worry about,' replied Vadimas. 'We have just shot two French cavalry men and we cannot leave them lying there. We need to go back and get rid of the bodies.'

At this the group of local villagers made their way back to the place where they had ambushed the French patrol. They were part of a network of part-time smugglers, organized by Hermann Schulte from his home in Kinischken, carrying goods coming from England to Russian contacts. In his bid to weaken the power of his enemies in Europe Napoleon had forbidden trade to take place between England and the continent. Whereas he was able to enforce this at major ports, many illegal smuggling routes had been established to frustrate the emperor.

The French authorities were aware of this and patrols were constantly on the lookout for smugglers who might be operating in the area. These patrols were aware of the dangers of being in unfriendly territory but never had a unit been attacked here in the Tilsit region.

'There they are, and there is that black horse that didn't run off with the others. Who would like a fit-looking French cavalry horse? Only don't let the French catch you with it.'

They rode over to the two French soldiers who were lying in high grass beside the track.

'This poor beggar caught a bullet right in the neck. Half his throat is blown away. We will take him to the sexton, or whoever, and get him to organize his burial. Then he can talk to the French if they come looking for their mates, which they definitely will. You mark my words. Especially for this fellow. He's not just a private. I would say he is a sergeant.'

'What about the other one? Where did he cop it?'

'Just a minute. There's a lot of blood here. His arm is twisted into a funny shape and. . . Wait, I think he's still alive. We might have to finish him off.'

Vadimas remained sitting on his horse as the others inspected the two fallen Frenchmen. After his experience on the battlefield he found it unsettling to be handling bodies. His attention was drawn to the black horse with a white flash on its forehead. It was very upset and restless and kept stamping around making it hard for Vadimas to obtain a clear look at it.

'Peter, can you get hold of that horse?'

'I'll try.'

Peter approached the horse which stared at him with fierce eyes and then backed away. He grabbed hold of the bridle reins which were hanging in front of the horse. It reared up and Peter was lucky not to be caught by flying hooves. He threw the reins aside and quickly backed away. The horse then turned towards those who were kneeling beside the wounded man. It stood looking at them very menacingly.

'I wonder,' began Vadimas as he dismounted and made his way over to where they were attending to the man. 'Could it really be? Let me have a good look at that man.'

His friend looked at him wondering what he had in mind.

'Well of all the...' he began as he looked at the French soldier lying close to death. 'I think I recognize this man from the battle in Auerstedt back in October last year.'

'Are you sure? How could you possibly remember anyone in the heat of battle and it's almost a year ago, isn't it?'

'You are right. Just over nine months. That's the day I nearly died,' Vadimas had to admit. 'I can't be absolutely sure that it's the same horse. I'm sure if it isn't it is very much like the one the cuirassier was riding then. I remember this great black beast with a flash on its head. I thought it was going to trample me to death. I was lying pinned under my horse that had serious injuries. I was getting ready to put it out of its misery so that I could wriggle my leg out from under it. I looked up and saw this rider, a cuirassier, coming at me with his sword drawn. But he didn't strike as I had thought he would. He sort of saluted me and then rode away.'

'And this is the horse? And this could be the rider?'

'I'm pretty sure it is. I only had a brief glimpse of his face, but this fellow certainly reminds me of him.'

'Whether it's him or not, we still have to decide what to do with him.'

'I think we should give him a chance,' said Vadimas. 'Our wagon will be unloaded. We will go and get it and put him on it and take him back to my place in Kinischken.'

'And the black horse? I'm certainly not going near it again. It would probably kill me. Fancy having a beast like that.'

Vadimas looked at his friend and then said, 'We will just have to leave it to look after itself. The French will probably come and round it up.'

It wasn't long before the small wagon was headed back to Kinischken with the Frenchman lying on some straw in the back. Vadimas had tied his horse to the back of the wagon and it was happily trotting behind them. When he looked back shortly after leaving the site of the ambush he noticed, not only his own horse, but the black one also following.

'I must save this man,' he thought. 'He must have something special to have formed such a relationship with his horse that it would follow him like this. And if it really is the man who spared my life, then I know that he does have something special.'

CHAPTER XXXI

Nursing the Enemy

A state of suspense and uncertainty pervaded Kinischken in the following days. This resulted in the villagers displaying all manner of emotions. They were all soon aware of what had happened — in general terms — but were at a loss to know where Vadimas' decision to bring the wounded French soldier back to their village might lead them.

The condition of the wounded cuirassier was not of great concern to most of the people. They had no contact with him and so he remained merely a captured enemy, a foreign soldier who had been part of an occupation force, a trained cavalry man who had fought against, and probably caused the death of Prussian soldiers. If the truth were known most would have wished him dead. Many had expressed this opinion to members of the Zukas family despite Vadimas' strong desire to save the man, and his attempts to convince them to see the situation from his point of view.

To some of the people however, the Frenchman's situation of whether he lived or died, was of grave concern. Vadimas was stricken with remorse. He had been a member of the ambush party which had shot at the French patrol. Was it the bullet from his rifle which struck the man from his horse and caused his life-threatening injuries? How would he ever forgive himself if it transpired that he had caused the death of the person who had opted, those many months ago at Auerstedt, to give him a chance to live?

Ponia Zukas and Marija were aware of the turmoil their son and brother was experiencing. They had accepted the responsibility of doing everything within their power to restore the patient's health. This was surrounded by problems, for they knew how injuries, especially internal ones, and one which in this case appeared to be very serious, could quickly lead to death. Many aspects were completely out of their control. They were further hampered in their efforts because the patient was unconscious and unable to give them further information than what was visible to them.

The gunshot wound to his right shoulder was obvious. They could see where the bullet entered his body, just above the breastbone, and where it exited. They were able to stop the external bleeding and realised that if there was internal bleeding, they were powerless to do anything. They were all experienced enough to know that wounds such as this would bring on a fever which most times resulted in death.

His left arm appeared to be broken for it was dangling in a most unnatural position. They would have to ask Grandad Grigas how to approach that, for he had attended to broken arms and legs in the village previously. There appeared to be no further major injuries although blood was seeping through his breeches below his left knee.

The Zukas family had readily accepted the responsibility of caring for the Frenchman. Day after day there was always someone by his side, bathing his wounds with herbs steeped in honey and wishing for his recovery. He remained unconscious. If only they knew more about how to heal a person.

The senior men in the village, including Hermann Schulte, were concerned about other unknowns. It was only after much heated argument that all agreed that he could remain. Everyone could appreciate their main worry. Would the French arrive, and if they did, would the village be able to hold onto its secret? Not that the majority particularly wanted this injured man to stay. They realised they could not surrender the wounded man without implicating themselves and bringing the enemy's wrath down upon the village.

They waited in suspense. When will they come looking? How can the wounded man be hidden should they want to search through all the houses and buildings? And that black horse. They needed some plan. To give the village a better chance of evading French retaliation and hiding incriminating evidence Hermann sent his son, Nikolaus and another young lad to two locations on the main thoroughfare from Tilsit to Memel. They were to keep their eyes open and report on any French movement.

The search parties did come as was expected. They were working north from Tilsit and were gradually drawing nearer. On the evening of the second day one such group looked across the meadows and swamplands to the forests of Kinischken.

'What is that?' they demanded of a couple of labourers cutting wood.

'Kinischken,' was their brief reply.

'Kinischken? What is Kinischken?'

The labourers shrugged their shoulders and smiled. 'A few struggling farmers trying to live in the middle of a swamp. Never been there myself.'

'A few? How many?'

'As I've just said, I've never been there. Never had a reason to go. Maybe ten. Perhaps less. Or there could be more.'

'How can we get there?' the French wanted to know. 'Through the fields here?'

'No way through from here. Those reeds sticking up over there are the beginning of a swamp. At this time of year it would be very full and your horses would get stuck.'

'And I'll tell you something else, Captain,' commented the other man, 'if that storm coming up is as bad as it looks you would be like the Egyptians in the Red Sea.' Both labourers laughed at their comment.

The French officer was becoming impatient. These were not the first local people he had to question, and none were eager to give out information. He pointed his finger at the pair. 'I need no Bible lesson from you two. Any more of this rot and you will feel my sword across your arse. Now tell me; Is there a road to the houses?'

'Sorry, Sir. Yes, Sir. There is a causeway half an hour further on. It starts in that patch of trees you can see ahead there.'

The sky had become darker. The lightning flashed menacingly, and the thunder cracked in loud bursts. It had begun to rain.

The French soldiers looked at one another. After a brief discussion they turned and headed back to another village through which they had passed. Shelter from the oncoming storm seemed more important at this time of evening than approaching "a few struggling farmers in the middle of a swamp".

The two axe men shrugged, looked at the approaching dark clouds, agreed that a downpour was imminent and moved towards a temporary shelter which had been built for occasions such as this. The two local men were correct in their initial assessment of the storm. The heavens opened. The landscape was drenched. Swamps flooded, fields became lakes, ditches overflowed. Roads became rivers. Access to Kinischken was lost as parts of the causeway became submerged in the overflowing swamps.

Next morning when the French search party moved to reach and search the isolated village their path was flooded. The only way in had become lost in a sea of brown water. Nikolaus Schulte later brought news to his father and other anxious people that the French searchers had moved on. Would they return? He did not really know.

Hermann looked at his co-conspirator and neighbour. 'You know, Antanas, my life has revolved around rain and water.'

'How is that, Hermann?'

'Well, my business in Tilsit depends on the water in the Memel River to bring the logs down from Russia. Then I was able to come and live here because the previous owners of my farm were drowned in a flood after a storm. If you think about it, we have improved our farms here because we have dug canals and controlled the water to some extent. And now, the biggest miracle of all. That storm last night has protected us from the French.'

Antanas shook his head wondering at his friend and how he had interpreted natural events happening around him. He pointed towards his house. 'I hope the storm has hastened the healing of the fellow lying in there. If only he would wake from his coma. I'm sure he would then be in a better position to fight his infections. He just lies there.'

'He's getting water, isn't he?' Hermann asked but Antanas could not decide whether he seriously wanted to know or was attempting to be humorous.

'Edita and Marija kept his mouth moist with liquids of one sort or another. Edita claims that her broth will restore the weakest of people. The trouble is that he is not eating any food. Well, he can't, I suppose, being out to it. If that doesn't change he won't last much longer.'

'The fever has passed, hasn't it?' asked Hermann.

'I believe so. The women are saying that today is the day.'

'Does the patient know that?'

'He probably does for they are talking to him all the time. I told them he does not want to wake up because he doesn't want to listen to them talking all day long.'

Ignoring Antanas' comment on the talkative women he lives with, Hermann asked, 'Do you think they would allow us to have a look in on him now?'

Antanas knocked on the bedroom door and before waiting for an answer they both entered. The drawn curtains caused the room to be quite dark and it took a moment for the two men to adjust to the surroundings. There was very little in the sparsely-furnished room for them to see. Marija was seated on a chair beside the patient's bed. She was holding a moist sponge to his mouth. Apart from the bed, a large cupboard, painted in a red and green design and a similarly decorated bedside cabinet were the only other pieces of furniture. A black and white sketch of a group of trees decorated one wall. A small fireplace stood in the centre of the other side wall.

On entering Antanas immediately walked to the window and drew one of the curtains back slightly.

'If he wakes up the poor bugger will think that he is in some dark dungeon,' he commented before the women had time to speak.

'How is the patient?' Hermann directed the question towards Edita Zukas who was standing at the foot of the bed, bending over a black and blue, badly swollen ankle.

'The poor boy. Look at his foot. We had no idea it was hurt until we saw it swelling up and turning black. It must have been caught in the stirrup when he fell off the horse.'

'Hmmm, it doesn't look good. He won't be walking on that for a while.'

'We have been managing it with some lotion Grandad Grigas gave us,' replied Ponia Zukas. 'He said they used it when he was a soldier. Had them up and marching in no time, he reckoned.'

Hermann smiled. 'But don't forget that the soldiers were much tougher back then when he carried a rifle. But he has probably told you that already.'

And the patient lay still and quiet.

C H A P T E R   X X X I I

Bernard Awakes

The following night witnessed another storm sweeping across the already flooded landscape. Kinischken was in its direct path and needed to endure once more the strong wind and driving rain. It was sometime during this evening that the injured French soldier moved, groaned, blinked and tried briefly to grasp the muddle running through his mind. He attempted to open his eyes and hoped that some understanding might come. What he saw — dim images and bright flashes — meant nothing to him. With the forces of nature still raging, he closed his eyes in frustration and drifted back into a shallow sleep.

The still gloom of the room was disturbed by the shrill wailing of the wind as it battered against the windowpanes, found no entry and continued whistling around the corner of the house. The glass squares rattled constantly, threatening to break free of the old wooden frames holding them in place. The rain, driven almost horizontal by the power of the wind beat relentlessly against the windows. How much longer would they survive? The branches of an adjacent pine tree scratched at irregular intervals at the glass creating their own cacophony of ghostly sounds.

The light from the small lamp burning on the bedside table, doing little to dispel the gloominess, did however reach the window, painting in it an eeriness reflecting the surrounding noises.

The patient tossed, turned and woke once again to the sounds of the outside storm. In terror he looked up but could see nothing but the dark glow of the ceiling. He attempted to move but pain shot through his right side forcing him to stop. He painfully turned his head towards the source of the frightening sounds. He saw the dark shadows moving against the windowpanes. They scratched. He shuddered. He tried to move, sit up, but his body would not respond. Some invisible force seemed to be holding him down, anchoring him to his bed.

A thunderclap rattled the windows.

He shouted in fright, '*Oh Papa. Oh, mon Papa.* Some monster has grabbed hold of me. He is hurting me. He won't let go!' He feels the strength of his beloved horse under him, speeding him through the wind and rain. The ride is not smooth. It is rough and painful. 'Terror,' he cries out, 'Terror! Put me down!' But his steed races on. Each mighty leap has them soaring through the air into empty space, into darkness.

He continued struggling trying to get off his back but the pain forced him to abandon any hope of moving. He cried out again. He then lay exhausted.

Finally, a feeling of peace settled over him. A bolt of lightning flashed, the room became brighter and he sensed movement. Or did he see it? He struggled to keep his eyes open and he watched as a white, flowing figure placed a bright candle on the unlit fireplace.

This figure was immediately joined by another figure with long blond hair also carrying a light.

'Oh, my God,' Marija said to her mother, 'what has been happening here? Did you hear the shouting too?'

'Yes. I think that we should be thanking God, for I believe that our patient has awakened from his long sleep.'

They both approached the bed and looked down at the sick man. His eyes were wide open and they could see that he was glancing suddenly from one corner of the room to the other and then from one woman to the other.

'There, my son,' said Ponia Zukas as she placed her hand on his uninjured arm, 'have no fear. We will do you no harm. You are in no danger.'

She smiled and was sure that she felt his body relax.

'We have been nursing you back to health,' Marija added.

The patient said nothing. His eyes once again surveyed the room. His mind was wandering. Where was he? She is nursing me but this is not a camp hospital. They do not have women there.

And she is not Michelle. This is not a room in a real hospital. And these two are not in uniform but seem to be wearing night dresses. They are not nurses, and she is not my mother. Where am I?

Finally, he asked, 'Where am I?' It was one of the many questions running round in his mind. The wind was still whistling and the lightning created grotesque shapes in the room. He did not realise that this was a natural event passing the house but felt that there were strange forces reacting in his body. He remembered who he was. He was Bernard Natalier, a cuirassier in the French army. He could remember his mother, his father and the girl he so often thought about during the long cold nights lying on the ground or a hard floor. They appeared so far away and dim, drowned out by the frightful noises, bright flashes so near to him and the pain throughout his whole body. Yes, they had been part of his life. And these women?

One of them had touched him and he felt kindness. This person now spoke again. 'You are in our home in a village here in the Memelland. You were injured and someone brought you here for us to care for.'

'Yes,' added Marija, 'we were so worried for you but now, thank God, you are recovering. You are safe here.'

So many questions but already he was feeling tired and his mind fading. Sleep. His eyes and body were begging for sleep. He relaxed and closed his eyes.

'Come, let him sleep,' Ponia Zukas said to her daughter. 'And us too. We hope that tomorrow will bring with it nothing but happy tidings.'

For Marija, the rest of the night brought anxiety, tossing and turning and little real rest. Finally with the sun peeping through her bedroom window she could wait no longer. She dressed and went into the other room. Her patient was sleeping peacefully on his back, eyes closed, breathing evenly, but his face appeared strained and fatigued. She sat on the bedside chair looking at him, waiting. She suddenly jumped from the chair.

'Vadi. I must tell Vadi,' she cried out as she ran from the room.

Vadimas was still asleep on his temporary bed in the barn. The family's horse gave her a friendly toss of its head as she ran past him. She had to shake her brother quite roughly before she had his attention.

'Vadi! Vadi!'

'What the hell! What are you doing?'

'You have to wake up.'

'Funny girl. I am awake. You've just woke me up. What's happening? Is it flooding?'

'No,' she shouted, 'your soldier friend recovered consciousness last night. Perhaps it was the storm that did it. Mum and I both heard his shouting. In a dream probably. His eyes were open when we went in to see what the trouble was.' She was so excited saying this and then she went on saying something else that Vadimas had trouble understanding.

'Is he awake now?' Vadimas wanted to know.

'Well, no. He wasn't when I left him. Come with me now and you will be there when he does wake again.'

Vadimas could not show Marija's enthusiasm so early in the morning, but he was soon following her into the house. He had convinced himself that this was indeed the man who had spared his life. That this was not the case was a possibility he had not really thought much about. Running through his mind now, however, was this very perplexing thought: What if this is not the same fellow? Horses can look the same and a quick glance at that person when I was wounded and scared for my life can lead to a wrong image. Well, he would soon find out.

To their surprise and relief, the man's eyes turned to them and followed them as they walked into the room. As his father had done the day before, Vadimas walked to the window and drew one of the curtains back. Light flooded into the room. He then moved to the side of the bed and looked down at the soldier who was staring back at him.

'Redbeard,' came quietly from his lips. Was it a question or a statement? It was merely a word.

'Frenchman,' Vadimas replied. 'You are that Frenchman!'

'You lived, Redbeard. Thank God.'

Marija gave a squeal of delight. She threw her arms about her brother and gave him an all-embracing hug. 'This is wonderful!'

Then she bent down and kissed the French cuirassier who could do nothing to stop her.

CHAPTER XXXIII

Homecoming in Lyon

The cavalry led the parade. How proudly the returning heroes sat astride their mounts. These represented some of the best of Napoleon's mounted forces — carabinier, cuirassier, dragoon, hussar, chasseur. Each knew who he was. Each was proud of who he was and of the uniform he wore. Most of those lining the streets of Lyon shouting a welcome home above the stirring music, saw only brightly-dressed soldiers on horseback. They cared little whether the man in grey trousers was a hussar or a cuirassier.

The tide of colour trotted past on the backs of blacks

and bays, browns and chestnuts, and the occasional white, generating a wave of pride and shouts of *Vive la France* and *Vive L'Emperor*. Who cared that the colourful plume standing erect on a black shako distinguished a chasseur from a dragoon, or the pelisse with its row of red chevrons belonged to a dragoon? Who cared that the breeches were green or grey, or the pompoms red or purple? Most spectators just wanted to be part of this spectacle celebrating victory for France and remembering the continuing victories of her *Grande Armée*.

There were some however who were attending the parade for a special reason. They were welcoming home loved ones. Their son, or their brother, rode on a chestnut mount with a cream and grey saddle cloth. His tunic was red, breeches black. They knew he was a hussar. They were there to cheer for him, to see once again the young man who had gone off into battle many months before. Their eyes were for him and him alone.

And the shouts of joy, the sighs of relief when one of his family could shout out, 'There he is! There's our Anton!'

The regional city was crowded. Local citizens lined the streets standing shoulder to shoulder with country folk. These people came from the small towns and villages surrounding Lyon to welcome home the heroes who had earlier been taken from them by Napoleon's war machine.

They had also come from Crémieu. The mayor was there, not in his mayoral robes, but immaculately dressed in an afternoon suit. He had been notified that his son, Captain Gustav Maillard, would be leading the cuirassier contingent.

This parade could certainly improve his standing in his town as well as advance his business interests in the district.

Henrí Natalier had travelled down with his wife and family. Vivienne, his wife, had struggled down with a basket of her home-made delicacies which Bernard always loved. Henrí had added a few bottles of his own wine, his best wine, for, as he said, 'Nothing but the best for our boy.'

Michelle had convinced her family to also be a part of the celebrations. It had become clear to them since Bernard's last departure that there was more than a teenage friendship between him and their daughter.

The parade was nearing its conclusion. Contingents of horsemen had trotted past to wild cheering. Surely Bernard must soon be coming. Captain Maillard passed with his unit of cuirassier. Bernard was a cuirassier, but he was not seen among them. The final contingents were approaching and still no sign of him. Where could he be?

The street was alive with excitement whereas Henrí and his family were becoming more and more concerned. They were standing looking blankly at Michelle's parents shaking their head in disbelief.

Michelle came running up to them. '*Oh maman, maman,*' she sobbed, 'he's not here. Bernard has not come home. But he must be here!'

She ran immediately down the street again, chasing the parade. Grasping the arm of the first soldier she came to she looked frantically into his tired, drawn face. 'Please tell me. Have you seen Bernard?'

'I know no Bernard. Let go child!'

She ran further. She asked. She pleaded. No one could answer her.

She grasped the bridle of a cuirassier.

'Let go, girl. You will be trampled on.'

'You must know Bernard.'

'All I know is that a battle takes many. Now let go.'

'Please! Please!'

'Ask the captain.'

Michelle looked desperately around. Embracing families welcoming home their loved ones looked only to themselves. They did not want their happy reunion to be interrupted by a stranger. She ran further up and down, becoming more and more frantic; but she received no happy response. Sometimes nothing. Mostly a mere shaking of the head and a sad "no".

Perhaps, from those showing more concern, "I know of no Bernard from here," or "Many stay on the battlefield, my child".

In desperation she threw herself down on the steps of a building. People watched as she cried out in grief. It was here that her mother found her.

She went up to her and put her arms around her. 'Have you seen Gustav?'

'*Maman*, I do not want to see Gustav! I want to see Bernard.'

'I know, my dear. We all want to see Bernard. His family wants to see him. I do. You do. But we have not seen him. He is not here. He has not returned.'

Michelle's father approached. She rushed over to him. He put his arms firmly around her. 'Come, my child, we cannot remain standing here. We will need to speak to Gustav. He may know where Bernard is.'

The main street in Lyon remained abuzz with excitement long after the parade had passed. The music had stopped, and the soldiers were now returning to reunite with their families. Amid all the noise and excitement there were groups which could not hide their sorrow. Bernard and Michelle's families stood together trying to grasp their disappointment.

After being approached Anton and Gustav Maillard were happy to stay and discuss the situation, with Gustav keen to give any information which might help give Michelle and Bernard's family some hope. He was able to tell them that Bernard was a member of a French patrol that had been attacked by local outlaws. He had not returned.

'Our search parties combed the area, asking questions, forcing answers from the local peasantry, but to no avail. He had simply disappeared. There was no sign of either Bernard or his horse.'

'But he can't have disappeared. Surely you went back to where he was shot?' Henrí asked.

'Was Bernard the only one unaccounted for?' Michelle's father wanted to know.

'No, there was one other cuirassier shot. The smugglers — we think they were smugglers — had taken his dead body to the local church and he was buried in the cemetery there.'

'Could that person have been Bernard?'

'No, the priest, or whoever, could give a good description of the fellow to be buried and it definitely was not Bernard. We did know who it was. He was a sergeant.'

'From what you are saying, it seems that Bernard was not shot and killed by these smugglers? If he were dead, they would have taken him to be buried like the other soldier.'

'Yes, that's what we thought too, but there was no trace of him. If he was shot from his horse he would have been badly injured. Can't imagine him getting back on his horse and riding off somewhere to hide. The other members of the patrol thought that he had been killed.'

'Could some local people have taken him away? And his horse too?

'Possibly, but unlikely in my mind. The locals were not friendly types, especially to French soldiers who had just defeated them in a battle. They would be more likely to put a bullet in him and let him lie.'

The questioning and discussion continued with Gustav casting doubt, or pointing out the impossibility of every suggestion brought forward as to what might have happened to his long-time friend. He was forced to admit that in his mind, and he pointed out, also in the mind of the regiment officers in Tilsit, Bernard had been killed. He assured them that the regiment had exhausted all avenues of finding him.

Michelle had been standing to the side with her mother, face buried in her bosom, as the men were talking with Gustav. She was listening to what was said. When Gustav had finally conceded that Bernard must be dead she pulled away from her mother and screamed. Then she ran up to Gustav and began pounding him on the chest with her clenched fists.

'How could you?' she shouted. 'How could you let that happen? He was your friend. How could you let him disappear?'

'Michelle, please listen, I . . .'

'Murderer! I hate you. I hate you!'

Michelle's mother had approached them and tried to grab hold of her daughter's arms.

'Darling, Gustav is not to blame. There is nothing he could have done.'

She pulled free and pushed her mother aside and continued her attack on Gustav. 'Why did you come home? Go away! Go away!' She suddenly turned away and looked towards the sky, 'Oh, Bernard, Bernard. Where are you, Bernie?'

And she ran. No one follow her. They all stood and looked at one another.

CHAPTER XXXIV

Michelle's Distress

For weeks Michelle could not be consoled. She lived in a world dominated by her grief, a world into which none other could penetrate. This was not the person that the town had known. Throughout her teenage years she had a close group of girl friends who had grown up together in the village. They had become inseparable. Even after they had found employment as household helpers, farm labourers, shop assistants or cleaners they still would meet to share their recent experiences, their joys and disappointments. Michelle, once the prime mover, and now most in need of the support of her friends, was usually absent from their get-togethers.

They were well-aware of her predicament but she ignored all attempts which were made to have her share her sorrow. When they were in the market square Michelle was locked in her room at home. When they were spending time walking along the banks of the village stream shouting challenges to boys who were making unwanted advances, she was sitting on the crumbling town wall throwing pebbles at sticks. It appeared she did not want to be reached.

Her parents and younger brothers and sisters were unable to have any sensible conversation with her. She avoided them as much as possible. Her siblings were baffled, and her parents distressed. If she suspected that they were about to talk to her about Bernard and suggest what she might do, she would shout "Leave me alone" or "Why Bernard? Why Bernard?" and run off.

Unable to work out what they could do, her parents approached the village priest seeking his advice.

'It is impossible. We really do not know what we can do,' confessed Monsieur Rosset. 'We are unable to talk to her,'

'It must be very difficult for you,' agreed Père Maurice.

'You must know, mon père, before all this it was always a joy for us to come here for mass,' said Madame Rosset. 'We would sit with our children and feel so united. And Michelle had such a beautiful voice. She would lift us all. Now she usually refuses to come near the church and when she does come, we feel the tension. This is not good. We fear for her soul.'

'Yes, I have noticed that Michelle is often missing. I shall offer up prayers for her.'

'Your prayers, yes; but what else should we do? She has often left the house and gone off somewhere, we feel, to grieve,' explained Madame Rosset. She clasped her hands and looked up at the image of the Blessed Mary in a side alcove, her sorrowful eyes offering up a prayer of supplication. Tears could be seen running down both cheeks.

Her husband spoke, arousing her from her spontaneous meditation and bringing her focus back to their spiritual helper. 'Père,' he said looking at the priest and then turning to include his wife, 'my dear, we must find a way, work out a way— anything— to bring our daughter back to her cheerful self. She cannot continue like this. She is harming herself. Oh, that we could be a happy united family once again.' He paused and then added, 'If only we had realised!'

Père Maurice looked at Monsieur Rosset questioningly. 'Realised? Realised what?'

'Realised that she had such strong feelings towards Bernard. She gave us no indication. We thought that she was just part of that group of friends, yes, boys and girls, that enjoyed one another's company.'

Père Maurice nodded knowingly. 'Have you spoken to Bernard's family? Were they aware that the young couple had such strong feelings towards each other?'

Madame Rosset answered. 'Yes, we know them very well and have spoken to them. They are as puzzled as we are. They thought that Bernard was more interested in horses and getting up to mischief with his mates that having a serious girlfriend.'

Père Maurice was at a loss to know what to say, what practical advice to give them. He had joined his religious order at a young age and had no personal knowledge of advising young women on affairs of the heart. Being asked to help in easing Michelle's pain and distress was very much out of his comfort zone. He could only remind them of their religious faith.

'We must place this matter in the hands of our Lord and Saviour and his Blessed Mother. We must ask that they look kindly on this confused young person and ease her pain. She must never forget that in all things they are ready to help her. This must be a comfort to her. Knowing this should give her the strength to move from her disappointment and allow her friends to help her move back to a normal life. You and your family must never stop showing her your love and concern so that when the good Lord has eased her burden, she will have her family to help her move forward. I pray that he will also comfort you and your family during this difficult time.'

'Would you also be able to talk to her too, mon père? She may listen to you. Telling her to put her trust in the Lord for help would be better coming from you than from us. She has often told us in the past that for a priest you were a very likeable man.'

Père Maurice smiled, picturing the cheerful, young teenager who would always accompany her parents to mass. That had ceased however and for the last few months he barely saw her. When he did, she had not acknowledged him. That had concerned him and he had so often mentioned her in his private prayers.

'I shall certainly try, dear friends. She may still feel friendly towards me for old times' sake. I'm not so sure whether she has many friendly feelings towards the church, or indeed towards Him I work for.'

'I'm sure the beliefs, the attitude and faith she learnt growing up will not have completely deserted her.' Madame Rosset seemed quite convinced that this would be the case.

Père Maurice had been the priest in Crémieu for the previous fifteen years. He was a friendly man, well-liked by the townspeople whether they regularly attended mass or not. He was tall and athletic and were it not for the clerical dress he always wore he could well be mistaken for a hard-working farm labourer. He was also a skilled rider and had never lost his love of horses.

He owned no horse of his own but was a regular visitor to households and farmsteads which contained horses to his liking. As a result, he was often seen riding in and around the town, alone or in the company of others. He was easily recognised for he insisted on riding in his cassock, clerical collar and hat, with the black and white cincture around his waist ensuring that the flying robes would not hinder his view. When he was riding a likely mount, he was not averse to challenging the local young lads to a race which he more often than not would win. On the other hand, he was often seen slowly riding beside someone in deep conversation.

He had often ridden with the mayor's son, Gustav, Bernard and others of their friends. This group also included Michelle and a few other girls who had been raised where horse riding was an accepted part of life. Now a plan was forming in the priest's mind. He must convince Michelle to go riding with him. In the thrill and excitement — perhaps even a small race — of cantering along country lanes she might forget her sorrows and be open to a discussion. Monsieur Rosset had told him when Michelle would be engaged in looking after the horses; it was her regular responsibility. He arrived at the Rosset home on his borrowed horse, just as Michelle was finishing the grooming.

She was watching him approach. 'Père Maurice, where on earth did you find that nag?'

'God's greeting to you, Michelle. Don't smile for this is also one of God's dearly loved creatures. Maybe not the most handsome but still loved.'

'I can see why she has not been taken off to Napoleon's wars like so many of our best horses here in the district.'

'And what of your lovely beast there? Do you think he would like to bring you along for a gallop with me and my horse here? It's been a while since I've been riding with you young folk from the parish.'

'And whose idea is that; that I should go riding with you?'

'To be honest it's my idea to go riding. Sure, your good parents have been talking to me about your sorrow, but a while out in the open air with your fine beast there would certainly not do any harm.'

'On one condition, mon père.'

'And what would that one condition be, if I may ask? That I don't beat you in a race?'

'I wouldn't worry about that! No, that you don't start preaching to me about how I should be thinking and what I should be doing. And also, that you don't start making me say prayers with you.'

'For goodness sake, child, what makes you think that I would be doing that?'

'I know you, mon père. And you are a priest of the church, after all. That's what you are supposed to do, isn't it?'

'I can't argue with you there. I am to console my flock and say prayers for them. In this case, Michelle, I shall be as silent as the deaf mute himself, unless you should wish otherwise.'

'OK then. Just wait while I put some harness on my pet here.'

The priest smiled contentedly to himself. *Dear Lord, he thought to himself. Dear Mother of Jesus, thank you for this opportunity. Come with us and help me ease this child's sorrows.* Then he started humming a favourite medieval chant while his mount was showing some impatience by stamping the damp ground. It appeared they both were anticipating some hoped-for happy results.

Michelle had quickly saddled her horse and disappeared into her house to re-emerge in an outfit more appropriate to riding. Soon they were ambling along a path through the town forest which led to open fields. Once here they increased their pace and were soon galloping beside a field of grazing sheep.

'To the end of the lane!' Michelle shouted a challenge as she heeled her horse into a faster pace.

Her companion was caught unawares but soon had his horse stretching out trying to lessen the gap widening between them. He knew he stood no chance. His poor old hack did not easily accept defeat and strained to keep contact, but to no avail. Michelle had stopped and was laughing when they caught up with her at the end of the paddock. They moved on with Michelle admitting that she took an unfair advantage at the beginning of the race.

They talked about the grazing sheep and the birds seeking food in the green pasture. They stopped and talked to a local farmer whom they knew and who was now slowly walking home after digging ditches. They watched the clouds, seeing animals emerge and disappear as breezes moved them across the sky. They were approaching a low hedge bordering a field when Michelle turned to the priest and said, 'Are you ready?'

'Ready? What for?'

'Another challenge.'

'Well, OK.'

'See you on the other side of the hedge.'

Suddenly Père Maurice realised what she meant. 'Michelle, no!'

But Michelle had spurred her horse into a fast gallop heading for the hedge. The priest urged his horse forward, shouting, 'No! Stop! Don't!'

To no avail. Michelle was racing towards the green barrier intent on jumping over it. She knew her horse could do it. He was a jumper and she had cleared obstacles much higher than the hedge ahead of them. But a few metres before taking off, her horse propped and swerved to the right sending its rider flying and landing in the tangle of the hedge.

'Oh, God! Oh, sweet Mary! What have I done?' The priest murmured as he reached the accident site.

Redbeard and the Frenchman

Antanas and Vadimas Zukas were wanting to follow the recovery of the patient in their house but finding it difficult. Ponia Zukas and Marija, who were nursing him, resisted any outside interference in what they were doing. Whenever the men suggested that they might pop in to see how he was faring they were met with "No, he needs his rest and cannot be disturbed", or some such comment. While he remained bed-ridden, they had trouble even gaining access to his room.

'I think it would be easier to break into the Bastille than

to get into that bedroom to see our Frenchman,' Vadimas complained over the fence to Hermann Schulte.

'It's a woman's nature to be protective,' commented Hermann in reply, not being very sympathetic towards their cause.

'But why? Do they think we would start fighting?'

'Hardly, for they know that you did bring him home here rather than leave him die in the grass somewhere.'

'It would be interesting to have a good talk with him and find out what he thinks about all this fighting the French are doing.'

'Ha! There's your answer. It's discussions like that which might get him upset and that certainly would not help his recovery,' Hermann pointed out.

Vadimas had to concede that some discussions might not help his recovery. He still felt that his mother and Marija were being unreasonable. 'And I don't know his real name yet,' he complained. 'They call him Bernard, but I still only know him as the Frenchman.'

'Be patient, Vadimas. I'm sure the novelty of looking after him, and the time they spend with him, will become tedious. They will then be pleased for you to take over his care and talk to him as much as you please.'

'You are probably right, Herr Schulte. I can see that Mum is already becoming less enthusiastic, but Marija. . . She seems to be with him all the time.'

'What would you expect? She's a young woman and he is probably a handsome young man.'

'A young woman?' protested Vadimas. 'She is my sister. She

is still a young girl.'

'Indeed.' And Hermann left it at that.

At that moment they were interrupted by the very girl they were discussing.

'Vadi, Vadi. Oh, there you are. Good morning, Herr Schulte.'

Vadimas turned around. 'Yes, what do you want?'

'Mummy and I think it's time for Bernard to spend some time sitting on the front porch in the fresh air. We would like you to help him walk out there.'

Vadimas turned back to Herr Schulte, raised his eyebrows and said quietly, 'Now they want me to help.' Then he replied to his sister, 'Shall I just lift him up and carry him out like a baby?'

'Don't be ridiculous, you silly man. He would be embarrassed. Just let him lean on your shoulder. But walk on his left side for his right side is still very sore.'

'Yes, nurse.'

'Well come on. He's ready to move now.'

A new chapter was about to begin in the saga of Bernard's sojourn in Kinischken.

No longer was he hidden away, lying injured in a room, the passive recipient of medical care from two caring women. He was now open to public view at the front of the Zukas house. People quickly became aware of this. Everyone in the village was anxious to see this foreign soldier who had ended up with them.

'Are there always so many people walking past your house?' Bernard asked Vadimas, who was sitting beside him a few days after first being seen on the front porch.

Vadimas laughed. 'And they certainly are not in a hurry to get where they are going. No, I think everyone is anxious to see what our enemy looks like. I hope Marija washed your face this morning.'

Bernard half smiled. 'Yes, she has done so much for me. Is she like this with everyone?'

'Everyone? How many French soldiers do you think come here to be fussed over? No, old Hermann next door thinks that she is falling in love with you. And he is an astute sort of a man.'

The sick man sat up so quickly on hearing the remark that he hurt his wounds and cried out in pain.

'The idea is not that bad, is it?' joked Vadimas, seeing the pain on Bernard's face.

'How could he think that? She has been with me a lot, I know that, but it is good to be able to talk to a man once again. I haven't been able to for ages. Or so it seems. Before I was shot I only ever spoke to men; my comrades.'

'What? No girls?'

'A lowly cuirassier like me does not get to speak to many girls. You should know that. It's different for the officers.'

'Yes, I suppose it's the same in all armies. We get to shovel the shit and the officers get the champagne and crumpet.'

'Don't be offended if I tell you, however, that your sister is much more attractive than you.'

'Marija? She is just my little sister.'

'Yes, you are right, but you will soon have to realise that there are young fellows who regard her in a different light.'

'You Frenchmen! Is that all you think about?'

The more they talked, the more they got to like and respect each other. They acknowledged, but mainly left unsaid, the fact that each had been responsible for saving the other's life. What made this more remarkable was the fact that it was done in the most unlikely circumstances — done to a so-called enemy. That was now behind them, but it was a strong bond. Their friendship developed. None of their individual beliefs or opinions caused the other to be offended although they came from a completely different cultural background.

At first the conversation centred less on politics and warfare and more on local matters. Vadimas was so proud of his little village and loved telling his captive friend about Kinischken and its people.

Old Grandad Grigas walked slowly past looking intently at them. Vadimas was surprised that he did not come up onto the porch and begin a conversation. Or was he still a little wary of this French enemy? Perhaps he had very pressing business elsewhere.

'Now, there is someone you will soon get to meet.'

'Oh?'

'Yes, Old Grandad Grigas.'

'A village elder?'

'You might say that. He's an old soldier who was a grenadier in the Prussian army when we were winning battles.'

'So he won't like Frenchmen?'

'Especially any branch of the cavalry. I remembered that when he discovered that I was training with the dragoons he said to me: "Not much of a bloody soldier if you need a horse to help you fight your battles". Or something similar.'

'Sounds like a likeable old character.'

'Yes, everyone loves him. I warn you, however, not to get him started on the advantages of a bayonet at the end of a rifle over against a cavalry sabre, especially if there is a broom or stick handy. He will be dancing around poking and jabbing and if you are not careful you will have a broom handle shoved into your stomach. Tell him you are a dragoon, like me, and he's more likely to accept you. Don't mention cuirassier or anything French for it will get him going.'

'He went into the house next door. Marija had often mentioned Herr and Frau Schulte, your neighbours. Does she work for them?'

'They are the real Prussian family here. Only arrived ten years, or so, ago. They are much respected by everyone here. He's quite a rich businessman who also has a timber mill down in Tilsit. I often go to him for advice. There is much more to him than meets the eye and he always seems to know what is happening in the district. Yes, Marija used to spend a lot of time in their house teaching Frau Schulte our language.'

'So should I stay clear of him?'

'No, he can become a true friend.'

'Will I need true friends here?'

'You can count me as one. It seems like Marija is also one.'

'And others?'

'Frenchman, the way things are going now in our country it is more important than ever to have good friends and to know whom you can trust.'

Michelle and Gustav

Père Maurice would allow nothing to arise which might hinder him from paying his weekly visit to the Rosset family. He felt responsibility — partly if not fully — for Michelle being flung off her horse into a hedge some weeks ago. Monsieur and Madame Rosset had assured him that in no way was he to blame for their daughter's spill. Michelle also assured him, time and time again, that it was not his fault that she had been sent flying through the air, but the horse's.

He was now sharing a glass of wine with the family on a chilly afternoon.

'In spite of that unfortunate accident (he always referred to it as "that accident") I think it was the beginning of your recovery, Michelle.'

'How do you come to that conclusion, mon père?' asked Madame Rosset.

'Well, while we were riding out to the farmlands, I could feel some of her old lively spirit returning.'

'You could feel?' repeated Michelle, emphasizing the word "feel".

'Perhaps not feel but see a slight sparkle of *joie de vivre* in your eyes. It's difficult to explain.' The priest seemed to be searching for the right words.

Monsieur Rosset then turned to his daughter. 'Did you feel some of your old spirit returning like Père Maurice suggested, Michelle?'

'I can't really tell what he might have seen or imagined. I remember him concentrating very hard to keep in the saddle. I probably should have been doing the same.' Michelle smiled at the priest as she said this. 'I do agree that I enjoyed that ride.'

The priest enjoyed her gentle humour. 'And I am so happy that you have kept going out regularly. I am also quite relieved that now it is not with me. You have no idea how stiff and sore I was after that ride. It took me at least a week to recover.'

They all laughed sympathetically at this misfortune and then allowed Père Maurice to continue. 'I'm sure Gustav is a better rider that I ever have been, and I know that he would be far better company.'

Michelle blushed.

'Yes,' said Monsieur Rosset, 'we have much to thank Gustav for. It is something that previously I would not have thought possible, for we have never had a high regard for the Maillard family. That is no longer the case. Being in the army has certainly changed him. Before going away he appeared to us to be very self-centered. Now he seems totally devoted to our Michelle.'

While Père Maurice and her parents continued to talk, Michelle's attention and thoughts drifted.

Initially she realised that she had been running around in emotional circles. *Oh, Bernard, should I be spending so much time with Gus? But you are not here. What am I to do? I cannot sit inside and sob all day. He had coaxed me out of that bad habit. And he has been so kind to me in spite of how I shouted at him and abused him when he first arrived back home, and you didn't. I blamed him for what had happened to you. Bernard, where have you gone? And now I am leaning on him more and more. Can you blame me for that? Oh, forgive me, Bernard, but you are no longer occupying my mind from daylight to dark as you once did. I am sitting daydreaming and I suddenly realise that it is Gustav Maillard that I am thinking about. Captain Gustav Maillard. Oh, Bernard, what is happening?*

She faintly heard how her father was struggling to explain how at first there seemed to be a great void within her. How an emptiness seemed to swallow all their attempts at guiding her back to a normal existence.

Oh, Daddy, she thought, *Oh Mummy! You were so desperately trying to help and I would just shout at you and run off crying.*

But you did not give up. You must have been so disappointed and worried. I should now tell you how much I love you for being so patient through all of that.

They were all startled by a loud banging on the front door.

'Oh!' gasped Michelle jumping up and running out of the room to the front door.

The other three sat and looked at one another.

'What's she forgotten now?' asked Madame Rosset of no one in particular. 'Of late, she has become very forgetful.'

'She must have other things on her mind,' Père Maurice came up with the suggestion with a knowing nod and a smile.

'Yes, I agree, mon père,' said Madame Rosset, 'but I have a feeling that it is not Bernard who is continually occupying her mind and causing distress. Recently it has been a much calmer forgetfulness.'

Their visitor was raising his eyebrows questioningly when Michelle and Gustav came into the room, smiling broadly and holding hands. His question was being answered.

'I had forgotten that Gus and I were to go riding today,' announced Michelle. 'I thought it was tomorrow.'

Gustav greeted the parents and the priest who had all looked up as the two young people had entered looking so happy. Their minds were asking questions but they were saying nothing.

'It was tomorrow, I have to admit,' Gustav then acknowledged, 'but I thought it would be nice if we could go today as well.'

'It seems a good plan,' said Père Maurice. 'I suppose you will have to be going back to your regiment soon and you want to do as much riding as you can before you go?'

'We officers were given very generous leave after our success at Friedland and our emperor's meetings at Tilsit. It appears that peace has finally arrived in eastern Europe.'

'And everyone is happy with the outcome?' asked Madame Rosset.

'The Prussians are very unhappy. They feel that they have been too severely dealt with by our emperor,' explained Gustav. 'We will have to have troops stationed throughout their country for some time to come. I am waiting to see where exactly I shall be sent to. I do know that it will be somewhere in Prussia.'

'Will the campaigns ever end?' asked the priest.

Michelle had been standing listening to the others talking. She finally interrupted, 'Are we going riding today, Gus, or not?'

He looked at her embarrassed. 'Oh, I'm sorry. Yes, we must go.'

'And keep away from hedges, Michelle.'

She laughed and skipped out with her companion.

CHAPTER XXXVII

Questions in Crémieu

Everyday life for Michelle and her family was emerging from a dark, worrying period. It was becoming more and more obvious to Michelle's parents that her relationship with Bernard was petering out and that she now saw her future happiness tied to Gustav Maillard. They were happy that she was returning to the cheerful, carefree person she had previously been but at the same time saddened by her change of heart for they had always regarded Bernard very highly. They understood Michelle's attitude, for a young lady could not wait indefinitely for news of her missing beau. They watched, without interfering, as the relationship between Michelle and Gustav quickly grew.

The Natalier household was experiencing nothing that was able to lessen their worry and sadness. The opposite was the case. Where was Bernard? Concern for their missing son had not diminished but was becoming more and more frustrating as time wore on. Added to this was a military investigation in the town which was causing them grave concerns. Two senior officers of the French army had suddenly arrived and began asking questions about possible Royalist sympathisers and *levée* evaders.

Thinking that they were bringing news — good or bad — of their son, Henrí and Vivienne Natalier had welcomed the first visit of the two officers.

Yes, they were aware that the whereabouts of their son, Cuirassier Natalier, was a mystery, but no, the main purpose of their visit to Crémieu was not specifically about that. This statement had surprised Henrí and Vivienne. If they did not come to give them some information about their son, why then were they there?

To their credit, the officers had expressed their sympathies and suggested how proud they must be to have a son who was willing to give all for his country and his emperor. But their conversation had quickly taken a more sinister turn. They indicated that their main enquiries centred on tracking down Royalist groups in the area and specifically their anti-republican activities in helping young men evade the *levée*.

Their questions at that time were general in nature

indicating that they had no detailed evidence involving Henrí and his wife. The fact that they were one of the few families visited and questioned was of concern.

Henrí and his friends lived in fear of another visit. And it did eventuate.

That previous visit seemed not to have satisfied the investigating officers and they were once again in the town.

Vivienne Natalier answered the firm knock on her front door to be greeted by the same two officers who had previously been questioning people in Crémieu. She could do nothing but invite them to come in.

'We were hoping to speak with both you and your husband.'

'Is it about our missing son, Bernard?' asked Madame Natalier very excitedly.

'No, I'm sorry to say, Madame, his whereabouts still remains a mystery. But your husband? Do you know where he is?'

'Henrí? Yes, he went out to one of his vineyards at Montouvier this morning.'

'When are you expecting him to return?'

'He planned to come home for lunch. When you knocked I thought for a moment that it could be him. But that would be quite unusual for he normally comes to the back door.'

'Do you mind if we wait until he returns?'

'Well, I suppose if what you want to tell us is so important.' Vivienne was somewhat hesitant in her reply, fearing that their being at their home could mean trouble. She quickly composed herself and played the friendly hostess. 'May I offer you a glass of wine to enjoy while you wait? After all my husband is a vigneron, and he does produce very good wine. Many in the village think so, anyway.' And she laughed.

'Thank you very much. We would appreciate that,' replied one of the officers.

Vivienne moved out of the sitting room into the adjacent kitchen where she selected a bottle of what Henrí regarded as one of his better vintages. A good wine, she thought, would aid their cause much more than something less drinkable. She had just finished pouring two generous glasses when her husband walked in. He looked at the two glasses of wine and not knowing for whom they were poured asked his wife, 'What are we celebrating?'

'They are not for us,' she hastened to reply quietly. 'The military officers have returned. They are waiting for you in the sitting room.'

'Oh, hell! That's not good,' he murmured. 'Have they asked you anything?'

'Not really, but they are not here with news of Bernard. They are waiting for you to return home.'

'We must be doubly careful with what we say.' Henrí poured a third glass for himself and with his wife carrying the other two they moved into the sitting room to be interrogated by the officers.

Courteous formalities were soon dispensed with and the officers began asking questions.

'Where have you come from now?'

'I was at one of my vineyards checking on the progress of some relatively new vines.'

'That was here in Crémieu?'

'No. I do have a couple of small holdings nearby, but today I went out to Montouvier.'

'By yourself?'

'What do you mean?'

'My question is quite clear Monsieur. Were you out at Montouvier by yourself or were there other people with you?'

'I'm sorry, I thought you wanted to know if I travelled out there by myself. I did, and then I talked to two of my workmen while I was there.'

'Your workmen?'

'Yes. There are two men whom I have employed for years. They happened to be working there today.'

'Their names?'

Henri was becoming annoyed at all these seemingly purposeless questions. He did not know where the officers' questions were really leading. Were they aware of the Royalist meetings which sometimes were held in the shed out there? Or were they compiling a list of his associates, hoping that they might correspond with a list of suspects which they probably had in their possession. If they were here asking questions again then they must have been made aware of some "treasonous" activity in the town. He must however remain calm.

'Their names? Yes. There's old René Carrier and Isaac Hubert.'

'Are they local men?'

'Local? Both René and Isaac have lived here in Crémieu all their lives.'

'Are they trustworthy men?'

'Trustworthy? What do you mean?'

'That's a simple question. Do you trust them?'

'They have worked for me for many years now and I have never had cause to doubt their honesty. I have never heard anything bad spoken about them in the town.'

'Then you would be comfortable sharing personal details with them?'

'I'm sorry. What are you asking? They are my workmen, not my confidants. We have always had a good relationship but they have never become my personal friends.'

'What about Monsieur and Madame Bacot? Do you know them?'

'Yes.'

'And their son?' The officer looked at a paper in front of him. 'Yes, Nicolas. Madame Natalier, do you know him?'

Vivienne had her mind on other things and had not been following the interrogation closely. When she heard her name mentioned she jumped. 'Oh, I'm sorry. Did you ask me something?' She was blushing with embarrassment.

'We were asking about Nicolas Bacot. Do you know him?'

'Yes, I do. He is Eugene and Beatrice's boy.'

'What do you know about him?'

'That's a strange question. What do I know about him? Well, he is a very quiet, shy boy. He plays the violin very well. He worked in one of Monsieur Maillard's factories. And everyone in the town knows that he ran off somewhere when he was called up to do his military service.'

'Yes, that's the man. Were he and your son, Bernard, good friends?' The officer looked from Henrí to Vivienne, but it was Henrí who answered.

'Yes, they knew one another. Everyone does in this small town. But good friends? I would have to say no. Nicolas kept mainly to himself even when he was with the others. He and Bernard were in a group which was often seen together. Had been ever since their school days. But I'm quite sure Nicolas was not one of Bernard's best friends.'

The officers nodded. Then they turned to Henrí's wife and directed a completely different question at her. 'Do you, or your husband, have friends or relatives in Switzerland?'

She was taken aback by the question and was undecided how she should answer it. Why ask her about Switzerland? Did they know something about what she had been doing or were they just stabbing in the dark, seeing that Switzerland was relatively close to where they lived and was the obvious place to flee to if one wanted to escape the *levée*.

'Switzerland?' she asked in order to gain more time.

'Yes, Madame, Switzerland,' the officer repeated.

Her husband came to the rescue by suggesting an answer in her place. 'Didn't a distant cousin of yours marry a Swiss man and move over there years ago?'

'That's right, officer. That was years ago. It was a cousin of my aunt in Lyon. I did not really know her.'

'What does all this have to do with Bernard or even young Nicolas?' asked Henrí.

'It's just inquiries we are making, Sir. We know that many

deserters escape to Switzerland and there are people helping them to do this.'

'Are you saying that you suspect us of doing this? Our Bernard was serving his country at Auerstedt, in Berlin, at Friedland and then again at Tilsit. He is not a deserter. He is not that sort of person. He has probably died for his country and here you are suggesting that he is a deserter!'

'Please do not become too upset with us for asking these questions, but we need to follow up on information which we have received, and I am not suggesting that your son is a deserter. About this woman in Switzerland. Do you know her married name?'

'Oh, dear. I don't remember hearing it, even when she was first married. After all she was a very distant relative living in Lyon and we never had any contact with her.'

'So you are saying you have no idea?'

'I have heard my aunt talking about her. It could be a name beginning with "B"; Boucard. Bouton, or something like that. No, I really do not know.'

'Would your aunt know?'

'Yes, I'm sure she would. Unlike us, she did have some contact with her.'

'And would you know where they moved to in Switzerland?'

'No,' replied Vivienne.

Henrí also made a reply. 'You must realise that although we knew of the woman, we did not really know her. We have never travelled to Switzerland. Where she is living there, or if indeed she still is there, heaven alone knows.'

'I'm sorry we are upsetting you, Monsieur, but we need to ask you these questions if we hope to make any progress in our investigations. Another thing: getting back to your vineyards out at Montouvier. Do you have any buildings there — storage sheds, packing sheds, machinery sheds?'

'Yes,' replied Henrí.

'Do you ever meet people in any of the sheds there?'

'Yes, from time to time throughout the year I invite friends and businessmen to come out and sample my wines. It's a good setting to do this. Then there are times when my neighbours, from out there and from here in Crémieu as well, arrive unannounced and we enjoy a few glasses of wine in the storage shed.'

'Quite a number of different people then?' one of the officers noted.

'Yes,' replied Henrí and smiled. 'There are many in the town here who enjoy a free glass of wine or two.'

Then for the first time since they had arrived the senior officer smiled as he took up and finished the last of the wine in his glass. He placed it back on the table and said, 'I can understand that. But that probably answers our questions for the time being. We may have to come back to you after speaking to a few other families here in Crémieu.'

With that, they stood up, thanked their hosts for the wine — which they admitted was very good — and the information they had received. They then bid them a very official "good-bye" and left.

This left Bernard's parents shocked and very worried.

'Oh, Henrí,' Vivienne burst out, 'what do they know?'

Henrí shook his head. 'I would suspect nothing definite, or they would have dragged us both off with them. But what rumours have they heard? And from whom have they heard them?'

'And you will have to be careful with your meetings. Better stop them completely for a while.'

'Yes, it is a worrying situation. I am going to Lyon next Tuesday to see my wine merchant there. I will attempt to contact the Royalist supporter there who works with our group and see if he has learnt anything.'

'But please take care, Henrí. These are dangerous times and in working against the emperor we are doing very dangerous things.'

A Slow Recovery

Bernard was slowly recovering from the injuries and subsequent fever which had taken him to the edge of eternity. It was mainly the efforts of Edita Zukas and her daughter, Marija, which had prised him from the clutches of death and accompanied him on the road to recovery. Others in the village watched.

His health was returning but what was this place into which his misfortunes had thrust him? Where was he? Who were these people? At night his sleep was often interrupted by the sounds of war and even during the day he found himself thinking of the bloody scenes of carnage at Friedland and Auerstedt. At night he would awaken screaming and during the day he would turn around violently on hearing a sudden sound behind him.

'Why is he so moody, Mama? He can smile and be so happy to see me but the next time I go towards him he turns away as if he doesn't want me near him.'

'He is probably very worried, my dear. Unsure about what has happened, what will happen to him next and what he can do about his situation.'

'But we are always so kind to him.'

'Yes, we are and I'm sure he realises this; but remember what he has been through. There must be so much going on in his mind.'

'But what have I done, Mama, to have him treat me like this? What can I do?'

'It's nothing you have done, or not done, my daughter. He is a confused young man caught between two worlds, divided by the trauma of war.'

'But I must be able to do something while he is recovering; something to make him happier; something to get him out of these moody periods?'

'Just be kind. Be his friend.'

Day by day Bernard's health kept improving but his mind remained confused. He could be happily dreaming of those bucolic days, laughing with his teenage friends back in Crémieu, with Michelle, then as he limped along a village path a pain would stab through his side and arm. Then he heard the cannons firing over his head and the enemy's bullets whistling past. He had escaped the bullets there but might a local bullet here among friendly enemies strike his heart. He was unsure.

But wait, he thought, how could Redbeard, who may have shot him in that ambush, his doting sister and their fussing parents, and even the other simple folk in the village, be his enemies? These were not the familiar faces of home, but there was a remarkable similarity in the way they approached their work, their friendships and their life generally, that time and time again Bernard felt himself warming to them.

Marija had a reputation for aiding the infirm and so everyone accepted that she should attend to the star patient. Soon many noticed that the care she was showering on him was more loving than they would have expected. The village folk watched this developing relationship with curiosity, her parents and brother with anxiety.

They did see how Marija and the Frenchman were walking together along the paths of Kinischken. They did not see everything.

'You must do more walking to gain strength,' pleaded Marija.

'Let me be. Where is your brother? I want to speak to him.' At times Bernard appeared to be very rude. Some of their walks lasted only a short time and ended unpleasantly.

Marija was easily discouraged and disappointed. Could the wounds and memories of war cause some to lose their civility, she wondered? At these times she felt that she did not like this Frenchman.

Then she remembered back to when Vadimas had first

arrived home. He also was very moody at times — completely unlike him — and this was when he was over most of his war wounds. Bernard, on the other hand, was in the early stages of recovering from his ordeal. But even at these capricious moments she was forgiving for she discerned a spark of warmth in his coolness. Too often, however, he would limp on ahead leaving Marija with a worried brow and tears of disappointment slowly trickling down her cheeks.

Running back to her house, Marija went to her room and threw herself down on her bed. Ponia Zukas stopped what she was doing and followed her into the bedroom only to find her daughter lying stomach down sobbing.

'My daughter, what has happened?'

'Bernard hates me!'

'Hates you? Why do you think that, child?'

'He walks off even when he knows that I am upset. He won't let me help him,' stammered Marija.

'But you have done so much to help him. You have sat beside him and spent hours bathing his wounds. He knows that.'

'But why is he now upsetting me?'

'Probably, Marija, he wants to have some time alone. Perhaps he feels that he is too close to you. He is hurting — not only his head, his arm and his ankle. It seems that his soul is overcome with pain and anxiety. You must remember that he is away from his family and loved ones.'

'What do you mean, Mama?'

'He is having difficulty living here. He is a Frenchman living with Prussians, with the enemy. You need to give him a little more space so that he can work out who he is. We know nothing of his memories of his home that may be playing on his mind.'

'What should I do now?'

'Just be there as his friend who is always ready to help him.'

The days passed. Bernard's body healed and Marija sensed that he was enjoying more and more the small pleasures of life: listening to the birds, walking beside the river, laughing with Vadimas.

Without realizing what was happening he began looking at her in a new way, not as his nurse, but as a companion, a woman companion. Was she aware of this? And what were her real feelings towards him? Was her kindness and attention simply her way of repaying him for sparing her brother?

She wasn't beautiful, as he always understood the term, as the beauty he had seen in Michelle. He recognized that her beauty was more than just her face. And she had a real smile — a smile that reflected her love of the simple life — uncomplicated by political tensions, by the world beyond the near horizon.

And her skin was clear with just a few freckles matching her long, untidy hair. It was red like her brother's. No, not really like her brother's. It was much more refined, a subtle strawberry blond.

When she hurried ahead, encouraging him to step more briskly, his eyes would follow her, resting on the small of her back and the gentle sway of her hips. Her slender body was firm from the physical work which had to be done, but it had a femininity which Bernard sensed. Her simple country dresses hung loosely over her thin frame but reflected the contours of her maidenly breasts.

All in the village watched intrigued as an indifferent Bernard was nursed back to health, and life, by a dedicated Marija. But he remained, seemingly, aloof from her advances. Was it because he had a sweetheart back home in France that he was reluctant in showing any fondness towards her?

All were eagerly waiting for some change to occur. Whereas nothing was obvious to the onlookers, Bernard found himself looking at her more and more often and finding pleasure in what he saw. The warmth within him became more noticeable and he found himself deriving some sexual pleasure when there was some physical contact. It seemed to him that ofttimes their contact was not accidental; but was it she or he who initiated it?

Hermann Schulte was particularly interested in Bernard's progress, both physical and emotional. Where is all this heading, he thought to himself? We cannot carry on our smuggling operations with a Frenchman living with us. It was probably from selfish motives that he cultivated a friendly relationship with the guest. He wanted to be in a position to direct Bernard's reaction should he ever find out what was happening in their village. Encouraging him to become emotionally involved with village life and the people there would certainly help.

'The village is growing to like you, Bernard.'

'Yes, Herr Schulte, most are very friendly,' Bernard replied.

'You are also recovering your health very well.'

'Yes, I am becoming stronger every day. But I am not very happy. I was nearly killed.'

'You are a soldier,' Hermann reminded him, 'and soldiers lead a very dangerous life.'

'Yes, I know that. And not only when in battle I've found out. Now I don't know what I should do.'

Herr Schulte looked at the young man with a degree of concern. 'Do not spend your time agonising over the past, Frenchman, my friend. It has gone and nothing you can do will change what has happened.'

'But Herr Schulte, if only. . .'

'No, listen. Forget the past. Nor should you imagine what tomorrow might bring. It is the here and now that you should be addressing. Don't hinder your future recovery by being negative. Accept the friendships which are offered you here. And another thing.'

'Yes, Herr Schulte?'

'I don't want to hear Marija complaining about how moody you are.'

'Oh. How can I . . .?'

'Well, she's coming out of her front door now and no doubt she will come and talk to us. Smile and show her that you are happy to see her.'

CHAPTER XXXIX

A Horse's Help

Marija approached the two men with a smile on her face and a spring in her step.

'Good morning, Herr Schulte. Oh, hello Bernard. We were wondering where you were.'

Hermann could see a frown beginning to appear on Bernard's forehead, and so he quickly phrased a response that would intercept it.

'Marija, how great to see your smiling face.' He put a slight emphasis on the word "smiling" and turned to Bernard as he said it.

Bernard clearly got the message for he smiled as he looked at the young woman and gave his reply. 'Don't worry, Marija, I'm still here. I still have a sore arm for you to care for. Herr Schulte was just telling me what a wonderful person you are.'

Marija blushed. 'Don't be silly, Bernard. You wouldn't be saying things like that would you, Herr Schulte?'

Bernard continued speaking before Hermann could answer, 'Yes, how you helped his wife. How you work so hard in the fields. How you help all the wounded soldiers who are brought to your doorstep. How...'

At that stage Marija stepped right up to Bernard and intended to give him a friendly push but she stumbled and was about to fall. He was aware of what was about to happen and caught hold of her. For an embarrassing moment they were locked in one another's arms and they both looked towards Hermann Schulte who was standing there smiling. Bernard felt their connection right down to his toes and a strange sort of shiver raced through his body. One part of him was telling him to push her away while another was urging him not to break the contact. Soon they both moved away after, in Hermann's mind, just a little longer than he would have expected. Also, a little more quickly than he would have hoped.

He could sense that his presence there was not really needed. 'I will leave you two. I am sure that I have a lot of work to do somewhere.'

'Thank you,' Bernard called after him as he walked away.

Marija looked at him. 'Why did you thank him?'

'He gave me some good advice,' answered Bernard.

'Good advice? Giving a Frenchman advice?'

'I shall ignore that. Yes, he told me not to be so moody.'

'I've told you that a number of times, but you have never thanked me.'

Bernard looked at her and smiled. 'Thank you, Marija, for always telling me how moody I am.'

'You. . .You. . .' She took a step towards him and was about to push him once again but stopped not knowing what to do.

'Why don't we go and visit Terror?' Bernard broke the silence.

'Your horse?'

'Yes, my horse. What else could I mean?'

Visiting his horse had been an emotional outlet for Bernard during the first weeks of his recovery. When he felt lost and alone, he would slowly hobble to the stables, to Terror, who would stand quietly and listen to him as he opened his heart. What a pity he could not saddle up his friend and together they could discover the village pathways thinking of happier times. But that time would come, he promised.

His horse naturally had always been happy to see his master. He had few visitors. His reputation for being unwelcoming was well known throughout the village. One person would come and see to his water and food but he would do what had to be done and then quickly leave. Vadimas was aware of what the horse was capable of. There were no kind, soothing words from him.

He now pricked his ears, awakened from a semi-slumber. His master was approaching. Not only could the horse sense his presence but could distinguish his voice.

But he is not alone. Who is talking and laughing beside him? I do not know that voice.

The stable door opened and Terror stepped forward to welcome his master. He lowered his head to allow Bernard to wrap his arms around his neck. Marija stood and marvelled at this show of companionship. She noticed also that the horse was watching her closely.

After having rubbed the horse's neck and murmured what must have been some equine words of affection in his ear, Bernard stepped back.

'Come and meet Terror.'

'He won't kick and bite, will he? Vadi says that he is a monster. And he was looking suspiciously at me while you were hugging him.'

'He was probably wishing that it was you hugging him and not me,' laughed Bernard. 'But don't worry. If I am with you, he will be as quiet as a kitten.'

A little hesitantly, Marija put out her hand to stroke the horse. He sniffed her hand and then lowered his head, as he did for Bernard, and Marija assumed that she was to give him a hug. She did while all the time thinking, 'Why doesn't Bernard let me hug him?'

'You are now friends. Whether I am with you or not, he will know you and not harm you. But I warn you: If he feels that you are wanting to harm him, or even me — perhaps I should say especially me — you will see another side of him.'

'What a wonderful creature!' sighed Marija.

'Go to the feed-room and bring back a handful of grain. You

will love the way he nibbles it out of your hand. You will feel a thrill run up and down your spine. It is surprising that such a large creature can be so gentle and sensitive.'

A short while later Marija returned with her two hands cupped in front of her carefully carrying a wheat treat for the horse. She was thinking how this would surely cement their relationship. As Bernard turned to watch her come into the stable, Terror gave him a friendly nudge in the back — something he would often do. Caught unawares, Bernard stumbled forward into Marija. Wheat flew everywhere as she threw up her hands to protect herself. To no avail. She ended up on her back in the straw on the floor with Bernard sprawled on top of her.

A brief moment of embarrassment was followed by another moment when some electricity flowed between them, and they relaxed to enjoy the enforced closeness.

Unaware of the mishap he had caused, Terror was intent of snuffling around in the straw trying to locate the scattered grain. In his eagerness to claim as much as possible his nose had pushed against Bernard and Marija's legs. Bernard recognized the compromising position in which he found himself and immediately pushed himself up off the poor girl.

He struggled to his feet and looked at her still lying there. 'No,' he thought, 'I cannot. I must not.'

She clutched his good arm which he had reached down and he pulled her back onto her feet. Was it relief or disappointment he saw in her eyes?

'I'm sorry. Did I hurt you?' stammered Bernard.

'No, I've fallen over before. I only spilt the wheat. Terror was probably more hurt that I was, for he did miss out on nibbling my hands. Did you hurt your sore shoulder?'

'Not really. I had something nice to land on.'

Marija blushed. 'I do love your horse in spite of what he did. If you are able, we should go riding together some time,' suggested Marija. 'I would like to do that.'

'Yes, I think Terror would like to do that as well,' replied Bernard.

'And you, Bernard?'

'Yes, Marija, I would also like it. Very much, I think.'

They began riding together, Marija on her father's old mare and Bernard on Terror. They traversed the paths and laneways which surrounded the village. Bernard was used to the chatter of his soldier companions where riding was a company experience. Here at his present home, there were only the open spaces, the wide skies, the occasional cry of some passing birds or the silence of the frogs alarmed by the approaching danger of horses' hooves. Beside him here was a quiet companion, not attempting to invade his solitude but finding pleasure in his presence.

Then one day, after returning from an outing, Marija left her horse standing in front of their house and she ran in crying out to her mother, 'Mama! Mama!'

'Yes, what is it? Where is Bernard? Has he had an accident?'

'No, Mama, he did not come back with me. He rode off to where Herr Schulte is working in the far paddocks.'

'So why are you so excited?' asked her mother.

'He kissed me. The Frenchman kissed me!'

'You mean he kissed you?'

'Yes, Mama. That's what I said. He kissed me. Oh, Mama, for so long I have wanted him to do that.'

'Yes, Marija, I was aware of that. Was it his decision to finally kiss you?'

'Well, not quite,' Marija had to admit. 'We were standing beside the river watching the dragonflies hovering over the reeds. It was so lovely there that I suddenly threw my arms around his neck and kissed him.'

'Oh! And?'

'Well, at first he was a little surprised, but he did not push me away. Then he put both his arms around me and pulled me close to him and kissed me so. . . so. . . Oh Mama, I am so happy.'

'I am happy for you too, my child,' said Ponia Zukas; but her slight frown indicated some doubt.

'And he did say he loved me,' added Marija.

'He really said that?'

'Yes, Mama, and I'm sure he meant it.'

The mother chose not to express the many doubts and worries which were running through her mind. Her daughter was happy. She must not spoil the moment.

Water Meadow in Kinischken

Bernard was sitting alone with his back to the river looking across the lowlands. The whole scene was exactly as Herr Schulte had described to him. Herr Schulte, his neighbour for the last few months. Herr Schulte, a Prussian citizen living in a Lithuanian village far from the centres of power on the European continent. Was this person an example of the Prussian people his Emperor Napoleon had insisted they hate? He could see no reason why anyone should hate this man. He was a hard-working farmer earning money to provide for his family.

A short number of years ago, Herr Schulte also had sat here

listening to the tiny creatures as they croaked and chirruped in the sodden meadows. He had watched the long-legged storks with their hungry chicks to satisfy, treading silently and cautiously across the fields surprising the unwary. It had been his favourite spot. Time and time again he had gazed across the verdant swards watching the scene similar to that in Bernard's view, activities which had been enacted and re-enacted since the ice age millennia ago.

Bernard could see a section which differed from the normal, a section which had been changed because of Hermann Schulte's initiative. He could still see the pride when Herr Schulte had explained it all to him; how he was initially unreconciled to these watery lowlands being completely in control. This situation could not continue. He was intent on putting this land, part of his holdings, to his use, to his benefit.

The plan forming in his active mind was a product of his business experiences. He knew that there had been large areas of swampland downstream from the river town of Tilsit where he had lived before moving to Kinischken. The farmers there had interlaced the area with ditches which drained the excess water and created arable land from what had previously been the domain of the elk and the stork, the frogs and insects.

Surely, he had reasoned, similar techniques could be employed here. Were he to get his neighbours to see the benefits of his scheme, they would all benefit. No longer would the land beside the river be so unpredictable, reacting solely to the vagaries of the weather.

Bernard had seen how the local community had accepted

the newcomer Schulte's ideas and how they had profited from adopting his suggestions. Antanas Zukas had often commented on Hermann's contribution to the village's prosperity. This was the Schulte, the Prussian, whom Bernard had grown so fond of during his time in the village. Herr Schulte had explained to him how he loved these lowland sweeps of nature.

Bernard now sat looking out across the sodden meadows. It was impressive in its way but he felt little of the connection which Herr Schulte expressed. Here, there was none of the varied beauty of the hills surrounding Crémieu. There the hills gave variation and character to the landscape and the seasons painted changing portraits of it. No, that does not happen here. Winter comes and turns the green vistas to scenes of frozen emptiness.

In spite of the future Herr Schulte painted for him here, Bernard wanted to be home. He wanted to wake to the trilling of the larks and the finches. He wanted once more to see the squadrons of ibis silhouetted against the rosy evening sky. Above all he missed the company of his childhood friends, the love of those who knew his real self.

During the last couple of years changing circumstances in the life of the quiet vintager's son had taken and clothed him in varying layers of camouflage, temporarily cocooning the boy who had previously happily sold wine at the village markets. Emperor Napoleon's military machine had taken the boy and wrapped him in the colourful uniform of a cuirassier; colourful but feared by his opponents. In most cases it was this outer layer which caused the fear rather than the intimidation of a struggling beard or the palpitating heart hidden within the uniform.

After the successes of the battles at Auerstedt and Jena the uniform had taken on the role of policeman and oppressor of the Prussians. When on patrol duty and being abused by the local citizens of Berlin, Bernard could console himself by thinking it was the role he was playing rather than him as a person whom they were decrying.

And now in Kinischken another layer of identity had enveloped him. He was seen by some as a danger; a wolf lying in sheep's clothing waiting his time to cause havoc. He was seen as someone who could bring severe repercussions down on the village, probably imprisonment and death to some individuals. Most, he felt sure, had modified this feeling but it remained etched on the memories of the locals who had always been suspicious of outsiders.

The people of Kinischken had also accepted him as another human being, to whom although coming from an opposing camp, their humanity could relate. He was accepted as a person, but also as a horseman, a soldier, a cuirassier, a French policeman, but mainly as a chivalrous knight who had saved one of their own. They reached into various layers but there was only one person who came close to unravelling and ignoring his many layers of identity and seeing his true self. That person was Marija Zukas.

His feeling towards her had strengthened as time passed. Often in the last few weeks when he was idly sitting, he suddenly became aware that he was thinking of Marija, thinking of her very affectionately. But I must not betray

Michelle he thought. We made a promise and I must not break it. I must get back to her. As his affection towards Marija grew, his desire to travel back to Crémieu became more pressing.

Oh, how he wished he could unburden himself of those rings of responsibility that had recently enclosed him. Had his recent severe wounds and subsequent recovery at the hands of new friends expunged these imposed obligations or must he remain true to his role as a soldier of the emperor?

He sat listening to the river's quiet rippling, to its gentle melody. How wonderful to be here at one with the river and its accompanying trees and bushes, with nature. Even the screams and thunder of battle had not reached here, drowned out by the quiet and peacefulness of the river. What could drag him away from this bucolic isolation?

It was clear to him that there were worries. There were forces which he could not ignore. He was staring across a Lithuanian landscape and seeing the hills of Crémieu. His eyes were fixed on a green embankment built by Hermann Schulte or one of his workers to keep the waters at bay. But he saw the crumbling stone walls of Crémieu, built to repel enemy attacks. He was becoming part of this caring community beside the lowly Minge River. His body had responded to their medicines, herbs and curing hands, but his heart still yearned for his homeland. It was Crémieu and the people there rather than France that was calling him home. Napoleon's army had taken him far away from Crémieu, but Crémieu had not left him. It could not be ignored. It could not be resisted.

'Bernard, there you are. We have been looking for you.' A

voice drowned out his reminiscences and focused them on the adjacent willows. He turned to see Marija approaching.

'Looking for me?'

'Yes, Mother was expressing some concern for you. She saw you leaving the house but for a long time you had not returned.' She sat down beside him and kissed him. Then she lay her head on his shoulder.

'Don't be alarmed. You see that I am here beside your Minge River and not on my way to the French soldiers in Tilsit or to Paris.'

'Paris? You are wanting to go to Paris?' Marija seemed quite alarmed.

'No, my dear Marija, I do not wish to go to Paris. Why should a person like me wish to go to that big city?'

'I'm sure there would be many nice girls there to entertain you.'

'Marija! How can you think something like that? No, I think your mother feels that I want to go back to France, but not to Paris. Yes, I must agree with her, but I would like to go back to my village of Crémieu.'

'Crémieu. Yes, that is a strange sounding name for a village. Is it Crémieu you want to go back to or someone in that strange-sounding town?'

'The town and all the people there whom I miss very much. My parents must be very concerned that I have not returned home. Others would have returned, and they would be wondering if I were still alive.'

'And maybe a special friend?' asked Marija somewhat shyly.

'Yes, there are many who would be missing me selling my father's wines at the village market. The wine I sold was very special.'

'No, you silly Bernard. I mean a special friend who would be still dreaming about you. A girl friend perhaps?'

'You are my special friend here, Marija. You have nursed me back to health.'

'Am I more special than Vadimas? I know that he is your friend, but he is a man. I would thank God to be a better friend to you than my brother. Would you miss me if you went back to your. . . how do you say it? Your Crémieu?'

Bernard did not know what to say. He sat and looked at this bare-footed girl with long blond hair scattered around her shoulders and piercing blue eyes searching him for a response. When his eyes settled on hers, she began blushing with embarrassment and looked away. She quickly changed the subject.

'Does it look like this around your Crémieu?'

'No, Marija, it is so different. There are hills and mountains and so many different colours. But nowhere there can you see as far as we can here.'

'And you often sit and see those hills and mountains?'

'Yes, I was seeing them when you came. They were making me quite sad. But come, we shall go back to the house or your mother will become more worried.'

CHAPTER XLI

Decision Time

The Zukas family and Bernard were sitting around the large kitchen table enjoying Edita's stew, thick with pork fat, Swede turnip chunks and cabbage, washed down by beer brewed at nearby Memel. The warmth of the summer days was being replaced by the chill of an approaching autumn and this made the meals even more enjoyable. Antanas and son Vadimas ate large meals for they needed the energy to complete all the necessary work before the onset of winter. Their guest, Bernard, was enjoying his meals more and more as well, with his health returning to normal. Vadimas had jokingly commented how he would soon be able to work hard enough to earn his keep.

Ponia Zukas and her daughter, Marija, were proud to be able to provide their menfolk with such hearty and enjoyable meals. Tonight, however, with a polite "No, thank you," Bernard declined a second plate full of hot stew.

'Come on, Frenchman,' said Vadimas, 'what's wrong with you? If you don't eat you won't be able to keep up with me doing the jobs I have planned for you tomorrow.'

Bernard smiled and looked at Vadimas' plate of steaming food. 'Do not fear, Redbeard my friend, I shall have more than enough energy to keep up with a dragoon with no horse.'

During Bernard's recovery period he and Vadimas had become firm friends. Everyone in the village referred to them as the pair of crippled horse riders. They continued to call each other by the names they used when they first met on the battlefield at Auerstedt. Vadimas reserved the right to refer to his saviour as "Frenchman" and Bernard always called his former enemy "Redbeard". All others in the village accepted this special bond which united these two young men.

Bernard then turned towards Ponas and Ponia Zukas. He began, 'My friends, there is something I must talk to you about. It's something I'm sure you realised would come up sooner or later.'

'Yes?' was a tentative reply from Edita Zukas.

Marija wriggled around in her chair and looked a little uncomfortable. Was he going to tell them how much he loved her?

'I have to start preparing to go back to my family in France.'

Everyone at the table turned quickly to look at Marija as she cried out, 'Oh, no!' She then jumped up and ran out of the room sobbing. This was not what she wanted him to talk about.

'Leave her, Edita.' Antanas Zukas caught hold of his wife's arm as she was about to rise and follow her daughter. Then he looked at Bernard. 'Yes, I think we all knew that this day would have to come, although some of us, I know, hoped that day would never come. Most like you, soldiers finding themselves left in a foreign country, eventually want to go back to their homeland. Mind you, I have been told of French soldiers who are buying a passage on a boat and crossing over to Sweden. But, I suppose, they are real deserters. You are not like them.'

'I was forced to join Napoleon's army and was never a really dedicated soldier. I suppose Redbeard here should be happy about that! I am still a Frenchman and still have my pride and I know that my family and friends will be missing me. I miss them too. And my home village.'

'And the cuirassiers? Your battalion?'

'No, I'm sure my wounds would prevent me from continuing in the cavalry. My one arm is almost useless. And believe me I don't really want to continue being ordered about in the army.'

'I will be sorry to see you go, my good friend, and so will most others here in the village.' Vadimas finally said something. 'I know that there are a few here who will be worried when they hear that you are going back to France.'

'Worried? How do you mean?' Bernard was surprised. 'I thought they would be pleased to see me go. I know some of the older men still see me as the enemy.'

'Yes, that's my point. They are worried what you might talk about when you get back home. Or who you might talk to. If the authorities, or your former military leaders hear about what happened to you and what is happening here, we would be in serious trouble.'

'Yes, I am aware of that. And I wouldn't like to end up floating head down in the Memel. But I can assure you, I would never put any of you in danger.'

'What plans have you made?' Ponas Zukas wanted to know.

'None really. I just wanted to tell you first that I have this in mind. I want to talk to Herr Schulte about it. I'm hoping he will know people who would be able to help me. What I don't want to do is suddenly turn up at the French barracks in Tilsit. That would really have them asking questions.'

'Schulte, yes. Good idea. Old Hermann will probably dress you up as a Jewish raftsman and send you off to Russia somewhere! But you've really upset my sister, Frenchman.'

'Yes, I imagined that she would take my news badly, but I had hoped not so badly. She has been so kind to me right from the very beginning. I thought it was because I had not killed you at the battle. She spent so much time nursing me back to health. That's probably why I am as well as I am today. And I was sure she would understand that I had to go back to my friends and family in Crémieu. I know now that her feelings go much deeper.'

'Perhaps,' said Ponia Zukas, 'but underneath she was hoping that you would choose to stay here. She has grown very fond of you. I think I could say that it's even more than that. She has grown to love you. I am her mother, after all. We women can see these things. Surely you had some idea as well.'

'Oh, dear Mother of Jesus! What have I done? I just didn't think.' Bernard shook his head in despair.

'Go out to her,' suggested Ponia Zukas.

Bernard turned pale and remained seated. Someone who had been trained to charge into an on-coming barrier of enemy swords or attack a square of firing carbines found it very difficult to confront a young girl who loved him and who now saw him abandoning her. His head was spinning. What would he say?

He could imagine what she would say for she was one who would not hide her feelings. She would call him a horrible monster and he could not blame her. But was he wrong to want to go back to his home and to the girl he had promised to marry? No, his error, his foolishness, lay in always being too close to Marija, in allowing her attractiveness to draw him away from his fiancée back in Crémieu. Could a person be blamed for falling in love with a second girl? As a young man he was certainly aware of her attractions. And yes, there were times when his thoughts went a little further than seeing her as his friend's sister, and they had often kissed. But these were his private thoughts. How could she know?

And Michelle had always been on his mind, and he could not betray her. It had been months since he had last seen her but at that time on brief leave from his duties in Berlin, they had reconfirmed their love for one another. She was not just his personal dream, someone about whom he romanticised to keep his mind off his unpleasant duties in Berlin, but someone who he knew would be back home waiting for him; someone wishing for his safe return. Their commitment went much deeper. How could he convey this to this sweet child whom he now also loved, this girl who had given him back his life and his desire to live? What he was slow to realise, was that her concern for his health had gradually turned to devotion and then inevitably to love.

He rose from the table and slowly made his way to the front door. He could see Marija leaning against the birch tree at the front of the house sobbing. She must have sensed his presence for she turned, looked searchingly at him for a few moments and then raced towards him. She threw herself against him embracing him tightly.

Marija cried into his shoulder, 'No. No. No. You can't mean it. Why do you want to leave us? Why do you want to leave me? I love you and you said that you loved me.'

'Oh Marija,' Bernard began, 'I do not want to leave you, but this is not my home. My home is still back at Crémieu in France.'

'I can . . . I mean . . . we can help you make this your new home. You are becoming part of the village here and everyone likes you so very much.'

'Yes, you have all been so very kind to me and I do love you all for that but as Vadi keeps reminding me, I am the Frenchman.'

'Vadi especially wants you to stay. You are brothers and I . . .I . . .'

Marija threw both her arms up around his neck and pulled

Bernard's head towards her pleading lips. Both she and Bernard were unaware that Vadimas had come out of the open door and was standing looking at them.

'Frenchman, what are you doing with my little sister?' His question was friendly and not at all aggressive.

They both spun around in surprise.

'Don't you realise that you are breaking her little heart? She has lived and breathed you for the last few months. We can all see that she is so in love with you. Can you not see that? Has falling off that black brute of yours affected you so much?'

Bernard pulled away from Marija and stood shaking his head. 'Oh, my God! What has happened? What have I done? What am I going to do?'

CHAPTER XLII

Back Home

The forces struggling within Bernard were becoming unbearable. He had doting parents and a family back in Crémieu whom he knew loved him dearly and would surely be missing him dreadfully. Even more than that, he assumed that they would be living in the heart-wrenching uncertainty of not knowing what had happened to him. After all this time they might have assumed that he had been killed. But no, he knew his parents well enough, especially his mother, to know that they would still be clinging firmly to the possibility that somehow, somewhere, their son would still be alive and unable to contact them.

And Michelle. He still thought of her constantly, perhaps less now than previously, but she was still very close to his heart. What was he doing to her?

Was his commitment to his homeland, to his family and friends, and especially to Michelle compelling enough to break the loving relationship which had developed between him and Marija here in enemy territory?

So many questions. So many unknowns were burdening Bernard. He needed advice so he went to Hermann Schulte for whom he had the highest respect.

'Yes, my boy, I understand the predicament in which you find yourself. I believe the whole village has been watching how our dear Marija is becoming more and more attached to you. Even my older daughter had jokingly said how she would like to be next in line if Marija did not win your heart.' Here Hermann stopped and smiled as Bernard was shaking his head.

'And I haven't noticed this?' replied Bernard.

Now Hermann Schulte began slowly shaking his head. 'Of that I am not so sure. I think your feelings towards her have been gradually changing. You have recognized this but have found it hard to accept.'

'But. . .' began Bernard.

Hermann did not allow him to continue. 'I see you, Bernard, as a most loyal man. I respect that in you tremendously. You have often indicated to me that you are a true Frenchman and that your loyalty is to France rather than to your emperor, Napoleon. There were times when I wished that you were not so outspoken especially when old Grandad Grigas was listening.'

'Well, yes it is true and. . .'

Again Hermann showed that he had not yet finished presenting his opinion. 'And your loyalty is not only to your country. I am absolutely convinced — and stop me if you disagree — that it is also to your family and, dare I say it, to that sweet girl, Michelle.'

'But I hardly ever. . .'

'Hardly ever! No, Bernard, you have referred to her so often that it has become clear to me that you miss her very much.'

'Yes, Herr Schulte, you are most probably correct. You seem to know more about me than I do myself.'

'I wouldn't say that, but I do not have the emotions inside me pulling me one way and another. I can stand back and assess what is happening.'

Bernard then asked the question of Herr Schulte, although he was sure he knew the answer which would be given, for he was becoming more aware of the answer which he himself would give. 'What should I do?'

'We all in the village here would be very happy for you to remain — some perhaps less than others. However, I believe that you would never be content until you had returned to your own country, to your own town and to your loved ones.'

'It will be a difficult farewell.'

'Yes,' agreed the older man, 'and do not forget also that it will be a difficult journey. It is a long way, a way with many dangers. But a way I feel you must make.'

'Thank you for what you have said, Sir. It is what I believe I should do. I would ask this of you however: May I come to you for help and advice as I make my preparations?'

'Bernard, I would be very disappointed if you did not do that.'

Many weeks later a solitary horseman sat on the brow of a hill gazing towards the west. He was no longer a French cuirassier in his colourful uniform riding a well-groomed horse, resplendent in military harness. Weariness was written clearly on both horse and rider. Many kilometres of arduous travel had taken their toll on these two overtaxed bodies. The man's eyes, however, still sparkled with the light of a dauntless spirit which had brought them this far and which was anticipating the joy of uniting once more with loved ones.

The rider watched as a squadron of ibis, silhouetted in the rosy-orange glow of an approaching evening, made its way to the safety of the birds' nesting grounds to the safety of their home. His mind was racing. I too, he thought, will soon be in the safety of my home. No longer will I need to evade the ubiquitous military patrols and never-ending stares of suspicious villagers. No longer will I have to bed down with only my faithful Terror for warmth and company.

Oh, *mère et père*, I will soon be home. Michelle, soon now I shall be holding you in my arms. Thank you, oh thank you, Herr Schulte, for your advice. Thank you for your help, for your generous money which has made all this possible!

Yes, one more day and his journey would be over. He would be back home.

People on the streets of Crémieu stopped and stared at the tall, bearded man, poorly dressed, riding on a mud-stained black horse. They assumed that some vagabond had found his way to their town. What could he want in their closely knit community?

Others watched as he made his way to Henrí Natalier's house, dismounted and knocked at the front door. Some had a strange thought: Could it be? But how could it be possible?

Bernard was puzzled that no one opened the door of his house. He knocked harder. It remained closed. A neighbour appeared and walked towards him.

'Excuse me, are you looking for Henrí and Vivienne Natalier?' he asked as he approached Bernard.

Bernard turned around when he heard the man asking and was about to reply when his neighbour let out a loud scream, 'Oh, my God! It can't be! It's Bernard!'

He ran up to him grabbed him by the arms and peered into his face. 'Oh, my God! Is it really you, Bernard? You're not dead. Oh, blessed Mary! Margot, Margot!' he shouted more loudly to his wife. 'Margot, it's Bernard. He's not dead. He is here!'

Bernard was completely overwhelmed by this greeting but baffled that his parents had not made an appearance, considering the noise his neighbour was making. Other people were appearing in the street disturbed by the loud shouting, but not his parents.

'My parents? Do you know where they might be?' he asked.

The neighbour stopped his joyous shouting. 'Oh, don't you know?'

'Don't I know what?'

'Of course not. You wouldn't know. You have just arrived.'

'Tell me Louis. What is it that I don't know?'

'Oh, Bernard, your parents are not here. I don't know where they are. Some military officers came and took them away.'

'What?'

'People say that they have been arrested.'

'Arrested? *Oh, mère. Oh, père.* What have they done with you?'

With that he pushed his way past his neighbour, swung up into the saddle and spurred Terror off in the direction of the town hall.

Once more people stood amazed at what appeared to be a madman galloping wildly through the streets of their quiet town. At the steps of the townhall he jumped out of the saddle leaving Terror snorting loudly and raced into the building.

'The mayor! Mayor Maillard. Where is he? Where is the mayor?'

The office workers in the town hall were very disturbed by this man who had rushed in. One had run off to fetch the town constable.

'Oh, my Lord! It's Bernard Natalier,' someone said. 'And everyone thought he had been killed or had run off and deserted.'

'Yes,' said another, 'and now he comes home to discover that his parents have been arrested.'

'I want to see the mayor. Where is he?'

Everyone was looking at Bernard and did not see the door

to the mayor's office opening. Then Mayor Maillard walked directly up to Bernard. He took him by the elbow,

'Bernard, I think you should come into my office. I will explain everything.'

CHAPTER XLIII

Adieu

'Treason? They were accused of treason?' shouted Bernard throwing his arms in the air. 'How can you believe that? What were they supposed to have done to be accused of treason? And what did you do to help them? I don't believe this. What did you do?'

'There was nothing I could do, Bernard.'

'Nothing? But you are the mayor. You and my father have always been good friends. Surely you could have done something.' There was accusation in Bernard's voice. 'Do you just stand and watch idly as your citizens are dragged away?'

'No, Bernard, believe me. I did ask what was happening, but the officer answered my question with a wave of his arm and told me it was none of my business. Our constable and I could do nothing. The whole thing was conducted by army officers who were in control and who would tell us nothing.'

'Nothing? But surely you were told why they were arrested? What sort of a country do we live in? Is that what I have been fighting for? We are not still in the revolution, you know! The army just can't come into your town and carry people off without explanation. Didn't you demand answers?'

'Yes, we did keep asking, but not demanding. That would not have been the right thing to do. Eventually they indicated that it was treason, working against the republic, and the emperor.'

'Treason! My dad and mother are no traitors. Dad may not agree with everything that the emperor is doing but that does not make him a traitor. You know that!'

'I agree with you, yes. But they must have discovered more than just a few comments your dad has made from time to time. And then that they should take your mother as well. I just don't understand that.'

'Do you know where they are?'

'Not really, no. I would think that they would have been taken to Lyon. I know they hold trials there and . . .'

'Oh, Lord! What can I do? Should I go to Lyon and try to find out where they are and why they are being held there?'

'Don't rush off to Lyon, Bernard. Think of your own situation. You might meet with serious trouble.'

'My situation. What do you mean?'

'Gustav has been in contact with his senior officers to ask about you and they have discovered that the commander of your regiment thinks that you have deserted.'

'Deserted? How could they think that?'

'Well, they could not establish that you had been killed on that patrol. You had simply disappeared, and they assumed that you had become a deserter. You should know that many French soldiers do that. They disappear and find a life somewhere else: Russia, Sweden, Switzerland perhaps, or even in isolated areas here in France. You might have trouble explaining where you have been the last few months.'

'It's my parents I'm worried about. What can I do to help them?'

'At the moment, nothing, I'm afraid. I suggest you take time to rest and recover from your travels wherever they may have taken you. You are very tired and stressed. You will be able to think more clearly after you have slept and eaten. Will you do that? When you have done that, you can tell me what happened to you after you disappeared while on that patrol at Tilsit in Prussia. Then we can decide what can be done here to help you and your family.'

'I suppose you're right, Monsieur Maillard. What else is there for me to do? I'll go to my home and calm down and rest for a while.'

'Take care, Bernard,' said the mayor as a distressed young man turned and walked away shaking his head.

Bernard was outside the town hall and just about to mount his horse which was standing waiting for him when he heard his name being called. He stopped and looked around.

'Bernie!' The call came from his friend Guy L'Espenard, who was walking quietly towards him. He grasped both of Bernard's hands. 'Bernard, so it is you. I'm so glad to see you again. We all thought that you were dead.'

'Guy, my old friend, it's so good to see you; but I may as well be dead. My mother and dad have been taken away. The mayor just told me. What has been happening around here that I should have to hear news like that?'

Guy shook his head sadly. 'You look all in. Come with me to my home and rest. We will be able to sit comfortably and you can tell me all about your adventures. Yes, and I will be able to tell you what has been happening here in Crémieu.'

Bernard nodded his agreement, looked at his horse and said, 'Come, Terror.' Then he and his friend walked off towards Guy's house with the black horse following closely behind.

Madame L'Espanard always thought of Bernard as a "dear boy" and couldn't fuss over him enough when he and Guy arrived. She immediately prepared a hot bath for him, insisted he use it while she fetched a set of Guy's clothes to wear once he had cleaned himself thoroughly. While sitting in the bath he had time to consider the fate of his parents. What had gone wrong? Who may have spoken a careless word? What did the officials really know? Who else had been arrested? Did his misadventure and the fact that they thought that he was a deserter, cause the military to look more carefully, more suspiciously at his parents and their friends? Guy's parents were clearly not caught up in the investigation. And Michelle's parents?

Oh hell! You thoughtless, unfaithful friend. Some lover you are! All this time I have been running around concerned about myself and my parents and not once have I stopped and given a thought to Michelle. Thank you Madame L'Espenard, at least I will not smell like a horse and goodness knows what when I take her in my arms. All these months away thinking about you and now that I am back home near you what do I do? I forget all about you.

'Guy! Guy!' he shouted.

'Yes, what's the trouble? Want me to scrub all the dirt and smell off you?'

'Bring those clothes, I must hurry. How selfish I have been. Not once, until now, sitting there in the bath have I thought about Michelle, my dear Michelle. Where are those clothes?'

'Here inside the door. I shall wait for you in the sitting room.'

Bernard quickly dressed and joined his friend who was waiting with two glasses of wine already poured.

'Yes, that looks and smells better,' greeted Guy. 'Now come and sit down and have a glass of good Natalier wine with me.'

Bernard looked hesitant, wanting to get quickly to his loved one.

Guy insisted. 'Please, it's already poured. And I have something to tell you while you are here.'

'Fine, but only because you are my friend. Has something unfortunate happened to you or your family and you need to tell me about it now?' asked Bernard.

'No, we are fine. It's about Michelle.'

'Michelle! What about her? She's OK, isn't she? She's not

sick or something?'

'No, not sick. She's OK, but . . . Oh, how can I say this? Bernard,' Guy paused and looked at his friend, 'she has married Gustav Maillard.'

Bernard jumped up, his wine spilling over the carpet. 'Married Gustav Maillard?'

He could not believe what he was hearing. 'She is married? And married Gus Maillard? Married him!'

'Yes, Bernard, our friend Captain Maillard. She was so upset when you were not at the home-coming parade in Lyon that she went crazy with grief. He was around to comfort her when no one else could. She seemed to rely on him more and more. And he was always there ready to help, take her riding, go walking, just sit with her. Then it was no surprise that she married him.'

'That lowdown, sneaky bastard! I always knew that he had no sense of honour, no decency. Wait till I lay hands on him. He'll regret it.'

'Bernard, be careful. After all he is a captain in our army and the mayor's son. Don't do anything stupid.'

'Damn them all to hell! Oh, what have I come home to? First my parents. Then the mayor telling me I'm wanted as a deserter, and now this!' He threw down his glass smashing it on the floor, turned on his heels and made for the door.

'Bernard . . .'

There was nothing Guy could do to stop his friend from leaving the house, swinging into the saddle and galloping away.

Shortly later Michelle's mother answered the loud knocking

on her front door. She was shocked to see Bernard.

'Bernard, what a surprise. We all . . .'

'Where is she?' he demanded.

'I'm sorry, Bernard, but . . .'

'Where is she?' shouted Bernard once again.

'Michelle and Gus are living in the mayor's house until . . .'

Bernard did not wait to hear Madame Rosset finish her explanation but swung away and headed back to his horse kicking the gate shut behind him. He sprung onto a surprised Terror who was soon racing through the streets again with his rider urging him to go even faster.

Michelle and Gustav were sitting on the front porch of Mayor Anton Maillard's house when they were startled by the horse and rider which raced to a stop in front of them. They watched in silence as a tall, bearded rider jumped off and strode up to them.

Michelle suddenly stood up. 'Oh Gus, it's Bernard!'

Gus Maillard looked more closely at the man coming towards them and recognized him as well. 'Bernard Natalier! How on earth . . .'

He was unable to finish, for Bernard had grabbed him by the throat and threw him back onto the wicker chair. The table stopped it being knocked over completely. Bernard was standing over him.

'You sneaky bastard! You poor example of a human being! How could you do this?' and he punched him hard to the side of the face. Gus tried to stand up to defend himself. He was halfway to his feet when a blow to the other side of his head sat him back down on the chair.

Michelle had recovered from the shock of seeing the man she had loved and threw herself between the two men. 'Bernard, stop. Please stop!'

Bernard pushed her aside with his left arm and struck out at Gus again with his right causing the head of his cowering opponent to snap backwards. 'Keep out of this Michelle.'

'You won't get away with this, soldier. Striking a senior officer will land you in the lock-up for a very long time.' Gus was trying to gain some dignity by using his military rank.

'Senior officer, bah! You cur,' shouted Bernard in his face and raised his fist once again.

'Stop all of this immediately. Stop it!' Mayor Maillard had arrived on the scene. 'What on earth are you doing, Bernard? I will call my constable and have you taken into custody. I will not tolerate this behaviour in my town.'

'Your town. Your son. Your constable. Keep them!'

Bernard turned, kicked the front gate open and vaulted onto the waiting Terror. An angry, distraught young man rode away from the girl he had always loved, the girl he had ridden across Europe to be with and to marry.

An hour later, in response to his enquiries, the town constable was told that a rider on a black horse was seen leaving the town, heading south.

CHAPTER XLIV

A New Sunrise

The man on the black horse was riding south out of Crémieu but to where was he headed?

Bernard realised that he had made an unwise decision in attacking Gus Maillard. His anger and unsettled emotional state were no excuse. It had happened and he was now suffering the consequences. He would be hunted down by the authorities. His only option was to flee.

His immediate instinct was to seek safety in Switzerland. That would add extra dangers. Were he to leave Crémieu travelling east towards Switzerland the authorities in those areas would soon be on high alert. His chances of reaching safety over that border would be almost nil.

However, it was general knowledge in these southern regions of France, that one route of escape for deserters (and it seemed that he was now branded as such) was to head to the Mediterranean coast and find passage on a boat heading to North Africa or Lebanon and Palestine. The plan forming in his mind was to head south to give that impression. Then after passing through a few southern villages, he would change direction and slowly make his way to the safer grounds in Switzerland.

Now riding away from all that he had hoped for, and more importantly the immediate danger, he was attempting to comprehend the disappointments that fate had ascribed to him.

Bernard patted Terror on his shoulder. 'Yes, my old friend, it's just you and me again now. I'm sure things will turn out well for us. Well, I hope they will. Oh, the uncertainty of it all.'

He thought back to the time when he had decided to leave Kinischken and travel back here to his family and friends — especially Michelle — in Crémieu. Hermann Schulte had said to him then that the journey home would be long and difficult, fraught with many dangers. He had been correct in that. What he had not mentioned — and was not to know — was the disappointment, sorrow and anger that awaited him there.

What a homecoming he had received! Now after those totally unexpected hours he and Terror were on the road again. He was in no doubt that this journey, wherever it may lead him, would be even more difficult and fraught with greater dangers. Mayor Maillard had not made an idle threat.

Luck, friendly farmers, personal deprivation and the strength of his horse saw him eventually cross the border into Switzerland. He had little trouble tracing down his friend, Nicolas Bacot in Chellex, who was now accepted as a permanent resident of the village. On arrival he was physically and mentally unable to make any sensible decisions. Once again in his short life he was nursed back to health by the patience of unselfish people.

It was here in Switzerland, staying with Nicolas Bacot and his newly-made circle of friends that he made the decision to travel back to far-distant Kinischken. Bernard and Terror recovered, and although weighed down with a heavy heart, Bernard was ready to face the future. He rejected the invitation of Nicolas' host of staying and making a new life for himself there. Those distant friendships, smiling, carefree faces and happy memories were calling him back to the flat meadows beside the Minge River. Here, he hoped, he would still find Marija whom he had so thoughtlessly taken for granted and left behind. What would be her feelings towards him now?

He did not know; but he could hope. Nicolas made no attempt to change his friend's mind.

The long distances had been conquered and the many dangers avoided while all the time positive feelings had spurred him on. Terror had responded to the new energy he felt emanating from his master's every movement. Something kept urging him on.

Terror was now carrying Bernard along the causeway which led to their goal. The rider was sitting in the saddle happily watching the fields go slowly past. The reins were hanging loosely over the horse's neck. For days now Terror needed no human hand to guide him. He set his own pace leading him to a destination which was calling him. That destination was also calling the person on his back.

Not long now. The trees and the houses of the village were in sight. A couple of farm labourers could be seen in the distance working in one of Herr Schulte's paddocks. They stopped their work and stood and watched as the horseman rode past. They gave no sign that they recognized him.

Terror quickened his pace. He could sense that the end of this long, tiresome journey was nigh. His head was higher. The previous tension in him caused by unknown surroundings had left. The same did not apply to Bernard. His casual riding position, slouched easily in the saddle, belied the questions cluttering his mind. How will they welcome us? Yes, I know that Marija will be pleased to see me. Will she be the only one to welcome me? But I have only myself to blame. There were others who wanted to be friendly to me, but I was hesitant. She was the only one who ever showed any love towards me. Oh! And then Redbeard.

Yes, Redbeard. How will he react? Shoot me again?

But how will Marija react when she sees me in front of her? How will she welcome me? How did I repay the love and care which she had shown me? Oh, Terror, my faithful friend, are you as excited as I am? We shall soon find out.

'Now where are you going?'

The horse had turned off the main road into the village and was following a track which led down to the riverbank. He headed towards a woman sitting on an embankment gazing across the meadows. She seemed unaware that someone was approaching.

Eventually when Terror was some twenty metres from her, she slowly turned around and gazed at the horse and its rider.

'Terror?'

The horse trotted up to her and snuffled his nose into her neck. She patted his head fondly. Then she looked up at the rider. 'Bernard, it is you. My prayers have been answered.'

Bernard slid off the horse and stepped towards Marija. He looked at her longingly and said, 'Please forgive me, Marija.'

'Forgive you? What is there to forgive?'

'I went away and left you. I should have known better.'

'No, you had to go and find out. I understand that now. But you came back.'

She threw her arms around him, with her lips searching for his. Terror stood beside them, forgotten. Eventually they walked arm and arm back to the village with the horse following.

It did not take long for the whole village to be aware of what had happened. The wounded French cavalrymen had come back to Kinischken, to Marija, the one who never stopped loving him. No one could imagine that he would ever leave again.

Vadimas returned late from a distant field in which he had been working. He looked at Bernard and smiled.

'So you came back, Frenchman? Couldn't keep away from me.'

'Yes, Redbeard, I have come back home.'